Conduit: The Beginning

James Alexander

J&A PUBLISHING

Dedication

For my wife and my family who never stop in helping me to achieve my dream. I'm one lucky guy.

Contents

Prologue

Marisol clutched her baby tight as Rafael wrestled the steering wheel, keeping the rusty pickup steady over the dips and ruts of the desert plain. Dust billowed behind them, swallowed by the night. Every jolt reminded her it could fall apart at any minute. Rafael insisted it would make it. He had to believe that. She wasn't sure she did.

Marcus cried out as a bump rattled the frame of the truck. Marisol brushed the tears from the newborn's eyes with her cheek. Rafael shrugged apologetically. They both knew what stopping meant. They both knew the risks. Soon, they'd be across the border and in the United States. Maybe there they finally would be safe. His blue eyes peered up at her. They didn't match her dark brown eyes.

"I'm sorry, Marisol. I'm sorry, Marcus. Soon we can stop," Rafael said as he watched intently ahead. He never looked back. Marisol thought that best. It was easier to pretend they weren't being followed.

Ahead, the wall. Ahead, the gate. Marisol knew his plan. There was no plan. Just ram it.

"Something's wrong," Rafael said.

Marisol saw it too. The gate was unmanned. Lights blinked, casting shadows across the desert ground. A man lay lifeless next to the gate. Somehow, they knew. They always know.

Marcus cried louder. Then it appeared. Her worst fear. A shadowed figure in their path. The truck shuddered to a stop as if it had hit an invisible wall. What should have thrown them from impact instead kept them secured. They froze mid-road as the truck's rear end tilted at an unnatural angle.

Marisol clutched Marcus tighter as he wailed. The back of the truck fell, clanking. Before, the truck was barely running. The fall completely ruined it now. Rafael reached into his jacket, pulling out his pistol.

"Run, Marisol." Rafael brushed the hair from her face.

Marisol nodded. Running was the only option left—even if she knew she wouldn't make it far.

The figure stepped closer, its body illuminated by the lights of the truck. Its face was hidden beneath a shimmering robe that seemed to shift with the moonlight. Its dark eyes, devoid of any emotion, made Marisol want to vomit.

Rafael kicked open the truck door and slipped out, ducking behind it. He gave them one last look and moved out, firing at the figure. The open space of the night desert swallowed the noise.

Go now! Marisol thought and ran into the night.

She heard more shots, then a cry of pain. She focused on getting as far away as she could. To look back meant a sooner death.

A wicked shriek filled the night. Then silence.

Desert plants ripped at Marisol's ankles as she ran. Her heart beat wildly in her chest, and she felt as if she might fall over and die from overexertion, but she kept on. Waves of energy poured through her, pushing her to run farther than she ever had in her life. Marcus whimpered at her chest as she clutched him tight.

Ahead, a small church next to a dusty old road stood like a beacon. Better to die in God's house than alone in the desert.

Every step became more impossible. She gasped for air and stumbled forward, barely regaining her balance. The sense that the shadow was near—what they called it, since it had no name—pushed her forward.

"Mommy's got you, Marcus. It's OK." Her voice wavered, and even to her, it sounded incoherent. She could see her pulse in her vision, and her lungs burned like fire.

Falling into the door of the church, she fumbled with the handle. The door was locked. Of course it was locked. Normally, she would have cried. Not now.

Banging on the door, she cried for help. Marcus joined with his strong wails.

The presence announced itself. Not by sound or action. It was just there. Marisol turned to face it, her back pressed against the cold wood of the church doors.

"Get away!" she scowled. "You can't have him."

The shadowed figure closed the distance, almost gliding across the ground. The moonlight shone on its face—long and smooth. A small slit for a mouth, no nose at all. It towered above her, looking down at her holding her baby close.

"Your task is complete. You have no more use."

It did not speak to her, yet she heard it in her mind.

Then the pain.

As if her body were burning from the inside, starting with her brain and then creeping down her spine.

She shrieked in agony—the same sound she heard when she ran from the truck.

She took one last glance at her baby boy. His beautiful blue eyes brightened—glistening, then turning white. A howl erupted from the shadows. The wicked being lifted into the air, then disintegrated into dust.

Marisol slumped to the ground, holding Marcus in her arms. "Mi vida... mi dulce bebé..." Her breath had become ragged, and her vision was fading. Marcus's cries became distant. Behind her, a robed man stood.

"Angel," the man said.

***

Nefirtiri felt it. The entire hive experienced it—or what remained of it.

Her last soldier—eliminated like a bug. By what? An infant? And now, there were no more traces.

No, that path was blocked.

Now, all that remained was to take over their minds—and hope it worked this time.

Chapter 1

Jack squeezed Adrianna's hand and smiled as she smiled back at him. It always amazed him how he managed to get such a beautiful family. Adrianna's blond hair hung down over her shoulders. It had been a long time that the two of them had gotten to get out of the house since the birth of their newborn daughter, Ashley. A car moved in front of him and directed his attention back to driving. The exit for his job was approaching, and he realized he had his blinker on and he was already in the lane to leave the highway.

"Jack, where are you going?" Adrianna asked with a smile.

"I know, I went on autopilot." Jack switched the blinker on to get in the right lane and veered back on to the highway. A horn sounded behind him and he muttered under his breath.

"Seriously, can't anyone have any patience?" Adrianna turned and flipped the bird to the upset motorist behind them. The car behind honked in return. She turned to sit back in her seat and adjusted her belt. "People!"

Jack laughed. "It was my fault. I did cut him off."

"I know, but it's not like he's any later. He could have just let you back in without having a hissy fit."

The man passed by and returned the hand gesture. Jack smiled back and the car sped off.

Jack took a deep breath and rubbed his eyes. *These late hours at my stupid job are killing me.*

Adrianna glanced at him, her face creased with worry. "You can't keep working so hard. It's catching up with you. Maybe it's time to find something else?"

"Like what? No one is hiring right now. I could wind up with something worse."

"Worse than working seventy hours a week? Or driving every day to a job you despise?"

"There aren't many jobs I wouldn't despise."

Adrianna nodded, "True."

The sign for the mall exit approached. Traffic was surprisingly busy for the weekend. The news began to play on the radio, and Jack turned the volume up to catch the weather. The newscaster was stuck on a segment of the latest hot news about a grisly murder in another state. It had caught the country in shock at how a thirteen-year-old boy could murder his father.

"What the hell is wrong with the world?" Jack shook his head.

"Well, I understand the boy was being abused badly. I suppose he snapped." Adrianna replied over the noise of the radio and the fan.

The reporter began to dig into the details of the murder and Jack switched the station, shaking his head.

More news was playing. It seemed finding any music was a fruitless endeavor.

"There are some out there who really believe aliens have visited Earth many times," the radio disk jockey proceeded to mock the latest news referring to crop circles and alien sightings.

One thing is for sure, there is no shortage of nutjobs out there. He snickered to himself. *At least this is a break from murder and politics.*

The jockey continued, "So, what I want to know is, how many of you listeners have been abducted — perhaps probed and prodded. I mean, are you people for real?"

Well, better than kids murdering their parents.

"Caller, you're on the air."

"Good afternoon. What makes you think people who believe in alien visitations are any less sane than you?" the man's voice was gruff.

"Well, how about the stupid stories of abductions, crop circles, etc. Why the hell would aliens bother with that bogus stuff? I mean, c'mon! Wouldn't you just invade and make yourself emperor, and have a bunch of slave girls at your feet, rather than mess around carving circles in the fields?" the disk jockey responded.

"Consider this: Would you invade a country without first researching it to determine the likelihood of success, the costs, and the benefits? It seems to me any species intelligent enough to arrive here would invest time in various forms of research before taking a risk that would jeopardize the success of the operation."

HONK!

Jack changed lanes to avoid colliding with the woman weaving in and out of traffic as she talked on her cell and drank whatever iced coffee concoction she held in her hand. *Shit! Stupid drivers!*

Ashley stirred from her sleep in the back seat and Adrianna reached back to reassure the baby that all was fine.

"I would have hoped you would have been more open-minded," the caller responded. "Obviously you spend too much time talking and not enough thinking. How would you explain the unexplainable? How would you explain the pyramids, Stonehenge, the Mayan calendar? All things way beyond the technology of the times. Where is your curiosity?"

Good point, I guess. Still a wack job though. Jack found a parking spot at the mall parking lot.

Adrianna opened the door and glanced at the ground. "You parked a little crooked."

Jack gritted his teeth. "It's fine. I'm in the lines."

"OK, don't complain when the guy next to you hits our car with his door."

"Go ahead in, I'll straighten the car out and meet you."

"OK, I'll be in the food court. I'm starving." He watched her head towards the mall entrance with Ashley in her carriage and began to straighten the car.

A man walked in front of him as he moved the car forward slightly and he slammed on the brakes. Jack threw his hands in the air and the man flipped him off. He looked disheveled and wore a long green trench coat. It was torn in several places. He continued walking in the same direction Adrianna and Ashley had gone. The back of the man's coat had a strange emblem Jack had never seen before. There was some text under it, but it was in a language he could not recognize. The man limped and was muttering to himself. *Fucking wacko.* Jack finished parking the car and stepped out. The air was hot and sticky. Much too hot for the outfit the crazy man was wearing.

Just walking to the entrance of the mall was draining. The heat and humidity sapped all motivation for doing anything. Jack just wanted to be in air conditioning, out of the relentless heat. As he opened the door, the cool air rushed out to greet him, promising relief from the summer air. Jack spotted Adrianna moving the baby carriage forward and back as she scanned a menu on a board and walked to meet up with them.

"What are you going to get?" Jack asked, glancing at the menu.

"I was thinking about a salad. You?"

"Probably a bacon burger."

Adriana glared at him. He could feel her gaze burning him.

"What?"

"Seriously?" She patted his gut. "A bacon burger."

"I need the sustenance."

"Didn't you just say you were going to start dieting again?"

"I didn't say when. I just said I would start soon...I'm hungry."

"You need to think about your health. But do whatever you want!" Adrianna's face was tense and flushed red. Jack could tell he'd crossed into the danger zone. Adrianna, daughter of a former marine, knew very well how to hold her own and wasn't one to back down when angered. Jack was just as stubborn when the moment warranted it. This was one such occasion.

She was worried about him, and he knew it. He had been battling his weight for the past six years. All indicators pointed to him being obese and likely to die of everything because of it. He glanced at himself in the reflective wall and sucked in his belly. *Not that bad, really.* No, he would fight the power and get the burger he wanted.

"I'm heading to Burger Zone. I'll see you in a few. If you are through first, can you find a table?" This was one of the moments that his manhood depended on him putting his foot down and winning the point. In a world of ever-increasing sissies, this was where one either joined the world of men-in-pretend or really stood out as a real man unwilling to take guff from his woman. He knew she'd back down eventually.

She rolled her eyes. "Fine. Enjoy hardening your arteries!" She stormed off, disappearing into the crowd. *I wonder how long I'll be doing damage control on that one. She left without getting her salad. She must be really pissed.* Jack sighed and walked to Burger Zone.

Jack imagined the man in front of him ordering, *I'd like a number 2, extra grease, and a helping of cholesterol please.* Jack stood watching the crowd while waiting for the man to complete his order. Sitting at a nearby table was a pretty brunette gently moving a stroller containing a small baby who was sleeping peacefully. It made him think of the day he and Adrianna had first brought their baby girl home from the hospital. It was such an exciting and scary time. Both he and Adrianna had very little exposure to babies so it was all very new and magical. Now he could change a baby's diaper while blindfolded.

Jack noticed the strange man he saw earlier in the parking lot. He appeared agitated and pacing back and forth near a garbage can. He was still muttering to himself and was rubbing his forehead. Tatters of his coat ran across the floor as he paced. He glanced continually at the woman and her baby. He pointed at the lady and turned away, grabbing his head.

"Can I help you?" the kid at the burger counter asked, obviously wishing she were somewhere else.

He stepped forward, trying to recall what he wanted to order, when the sounds coming from behind him suddenly changed. A chill crept up his spine. Something was not right. Jack turned his head to see why things felt the way they did. Out of the corner of his eye, he saw the crazy man with his jacket partly open. The brunette's face seemed to lose all color. Jack followed her gaze to the man's coat. Something about the outline under the coat appeared out of place. He focused on the tall man's hip section. A black clip jutted out — he had a gun!

Everything seemed to slow down. In one fluid motion, the tall man whipped aside his coat and pulled out an AK47. The back of his coat seemed to float behind him from the speed at which he moved.

Screams erupted as the man fired a few bursts into the air. The next bursts released from the gun were not into the air, but into the crowd around him. The man, once just a creepy outcast in the crowd, now was a force of death. He didn't seem to have any reasoning for whom he targeted. He was simply firing at anything or anyone that moved. The once bustling food court was becoming a graveyard littered with the blood of the dead and dying.

The man paused and cackled, firing into the air. "The day of reckoning is coming. I am but a messenger. They are coming. Soon. All who stand against them will meet the fate they deserve." He fired at a man running for cover, and he fell to the ground, lifeless. "I don't want to do this, but you all need a lesson."

Unable to comprehend the fast change of events, Jack stood there motionless. *This can't be happening!* He watched helplessly as bodies overturned tables as they fell to the floor. Blood splattered against the walls. Screams of pain and fear echoed throughout the building.

POP! POP! POP! The janitor cleaning the lunch area took the bullets in his torso. He slumped forward, landing on his knees, pressing his hands to his chest. Blood seeped through his fingers. He shook violently as he slowly fell face-forward onto the floor.

Snap out of it! Get down, you idiot! But it was too late. The shooter saw Jack standing there – or maybe he didn't. Maybe he just happened to aim that way for the heck of it.

THUNK!

A bone-cracking sound radiated through Jack's brain, and a jolt of extreme pain sent him down to his knees, then to the floor. He rolled over onto his back. *Am I dead? No, not yet. Why did I have to insist on that damn burger? Goddammit!* The pain was coming from his left shoulder. He put his hand over it. It felt warm and sticky. *Fuck! My shoulder! He shot me!* He lay there and turned his head to the side. He saw the brunette still in her chair. Her head was tilted, blood dripping down her neck. She had taken one of the bullets in the head. The baby was still in the stroller, no longer fast asleep but shrieking out to its mother. *My God! How can anyone do this?*

POP! POP! POP!

The room was getting quieter – fewer people were screaming, yet the gunman still had rounds to go through and people to maim and murder. Jack imagined the baby as his own. He thought of Adrianna and Ashley, but thankfully they were not around. He hoped they would stay away from this carnage. Pain shooting through his side, he rolled onto his belly and used his good arm to prop himself up to get to his knees. The room seemed to fade in and out, his vision wavering. He looked up to see the baby still crying. A bullet ricocheted off the table two inches from the baby's stroller, showering it with broken bits of particle board and debris.

A large muscular man, now a short distance behind the shooter, seemed to be trying to sneak up on him. *That baby is going to be shot!* With that thought, he hoisted himself up to his feet and struggled to get to the baby's stroller. Just as he managed to release the baby from its safety straps, he and the shooter locked eyes. Jack saw nothing but emptiness. No emotion or reaction to the carnage around him. This man was pure evil. *So, this is how I go?* Jack smiled at the man who was pointing the gun at him and turned his back, protecting the baby in his arms.

POP! THUNK! POP! THUNK! POP! THUNK!

Jack fell to the floor with three bullets in his back. Landing on his side with the baby cradled in the crook of his arm, Jack gently rolled the baby to its back onto the floor. He could see the pool of blood escaping from his body, beneath his side. *God, I wish I could kiss my little girl one more time.* A tear rolled down the side of his face. The pain seemed to be fading — now there was more of a dull throbbing, much like a wound feels after the relief from a good painkiller.

Too weak to move, Jack looked into the baby's eyes, staring back at him. "You better be worth it kid," he said as his vision faded until complete darkness enveloped him.

Chapter 2

Dwight muttered something to himself. Tim turned to glance at his friend as they walked to the mall entrance. Dwight pushed his round glasses up his nose, appearing lost in his own thoughts. He saw Tim staring at him and shrugged.

"What?" Dwight asked.

Tim laughed. "You are talking to yourself again. Something about the guy that just walked in?" Tim pointed to the entrance of the mall; a door was closing behind a ragged-looking man wearing a trench coat.

"No, I just don't like people. Major germ sources. Do you think that guy washed his hands after he crapped? I don't think so based on what I saw of him."

Tim shook his head, smiling. "You need to lighten up. You must be stressed out all the time. You know, I could get you in touch with someone who could help you."

"My problem is not psychological, regardless of what you think. My problem is that I know how filthy most people are. God only knows what illnesses are brewing that we don't even know about yet. Then all these nasty, germy people go to the mall. They hack, they sneeze, they spread their lovely germs around in a closed in space."

"Fine, Dwight. You don't have to come in with me. I just need to get my phone checked out. It'll be five minutes, tops." Tim looked at his bald friend. A couple of sprigs of hair bobbed in the back between two strips of buzz-cut hair on the sides. "Maybe while you're waiting you can get a hair cut."

Dwight brushed the sprigs on the top of his head back scowling at his friend.

"No, it's too hot to be stuck waiting in the car. We only have a few minutes." Dwight glanced at his watch. "My presentation to the university is in an hour."

Tim patted his friend's back. "You'll be there with plenty of time to spare. I'm glad you let me drive you. It's nice to catch up with you again, my friend."

Dwight smiled. "Yes, it's nice to catch up again. I just hate presentations and all the stupid questions that come up. Sorry if I'm a bit short tempered. Hopefully we won't wait as long to reconnect again after this trip. Life tends to keep us both busy."

The door to the mall stood in front of them. Tim waited to see if Dwight would open the door. Dwight stopped and gave him a stare. Tim laughed and opened the door. The sound of people talking and going about their shopping filled the air. Someone coughed in the distance, and Dwight smirked at Tim before walking through the door.

Tim stopped near a table in the cafe. "You coming with me, or do you want to wait here?"

Dwight pulled out some wet wipes and began cleaning the table and the chair. "I will wait here." Tim could see Dwight staring at the man with the trench coat.

"You really don't like that guy, do you?" Tim could sense Dwight's irritation.

"He's odd. Something isn't right about him."

"No, something isn't right about him, but who is sane these days?" The man was scanning the food court, his large jacket riddled with holes. One arm of the jacket was dangling loosely. *OK, maybe he's missing an arm.*

"No, I mean, he seems agitated. Look at how he's watching everyone, and he's not able to stand still. Something is wrong."

Tim could feel his eyes rolling. "OK, Dr. Zeller. I'm going to get my phone fixed." He was moving to pat his friend on the back when we saw the man in the trench coat reveal a large gun. *Oh my god!* Sounds of gunfire stung his ears. People screamed and ducked.

Dwight reacted immediately, flipping the table down on its side and pulling Tim to the floor. Tim looked over to see the janitor who was cleaning the table next to them take a hit square in the chest. *That could have been me!* he thought as the poor man doubled over, most likely dead before he hit the floor. The janitor was a small Asian man, bald and overweight. The thought crossed Tim's mind that a moment ago he was likely being made fun of by some of the people leaving the messes for him to clean up. The janitor, like most everyone, probably had a family who loved him regardless of his station in life. Maybe even a kid or two. Blood dripped from his wounds to puddle on the floor.

The noises Tim heard were surreal. Voices cried out and he swore he could hear bullets hitting tissue. Tim loved treating the wounds of the injured who were brought to his hospital. He loved the adrenaline rush it gave him. It was exhilarating to think that he was the only link to life for many of his patients. Some people would look at that in a bad light, but Tim wouldn't feel that way if he weren't good. He wasn't just good, he was great. He was arguably the best surgeon in New England. As much as he loved to heal trauma, he hated what he was seeing today.

The man was yelling something about a day of reckoning. Tim wasn't focused on the jumble of words the crazy man was spewing, he was more concerned with the count of injured people steadily increasing. He rolled to his left so he could peer out from the edge of the table. The man in the trench coat was recklessly aiming at anything that moved, firing rounds in all directions. He saw another man run closer to the gunman and stop at a baby's stroller. He appeared to have been wounded in the shoulder. *You fool! Get down!* Tim thought, but the man appeared to be focused on the straps holding the crying baby in its carriage. The shooter noticed and aimed at the baby's rescuer. The man smiled a disdainful smile at the gunman and turned his back, taking a few hits and going down.

Off to the left, a large man was sneaking up on the shooter from behind. With a surprising burst of speed, given his size, he charged and tackled the bastard, taking him down. The two men were locked in a violent struggle on the floor. A few other people rushed to help, and together they disarmed the killer. Tim could hear the metal of the gun sliding across the floor. The sound of a baby's cry echoed through the food court.

God! What happened to the guy with the baby? Tim's doctor reflexes kicked into gear and, without thinking, he rushed to the man who had protected the infant. He called to a man standing near holding a cell-phone. "Call 911, now!" The wounded man was bleeding on the floor.

A case of the wrong place at the wrong time, but isn't it always? The baby was safe, smiling on the floor beside the man, who was staring at the child. He could tell the man was fading fast and he needed to act quickly. "Hang in there, buddy!" Tim yelled to the injured man as he crouched at his side and pressed against the worst wound in the man's back.

As he examined the injuries, it appeared that there was no damage to any major arteries or organs. However, with the trauma his body had taken, he'd likely have pain for the rest of his life. Blood pooled from his back, and Tim examined it a bit closer. The bullet appeared to have cleanly entered the man's back and exited the front, narrowly avoiding the heart but very close to his backbone. *He may actually pull through from this. This man shouldn't have to pay with his life for saving another.*

"You're going to be all right," Tim assured him, but talking was no use now. The man's eyes had closed and his breath was shallow. Tim did his best administering first aid, but he did not have any equipment.

"Jack!" A pretty woman with blond hair ran to the man Tim was kneeling over and practically knocked him off his feet. "Jack! Oh my god. Please be OK." Tears ran down her face as she knelt in the blood and cradled the man's head.

"Miss, I need you to step away." Tim put his hand on her shoulder. "He's still alive, and if help gets here in time, he has a chance. But I need you to step back and let me do what I can before the ambulance gets here. I'm a doctor. Please let me do my job."

She looked to him, her eyes pleading, her body trembling with fear. "Please!" She sobbed, shaking and crying. "Please, help him!" She kissed the dying man's cheek and let Tim move back over to help him.

She fell back to the floor, out of control, and pulled her knees up close to her face in a violent fit of tears. It wasn't long before the ambulances and police arrived. First the police rushed in to make sure everything was safe, and then the EMTs charged through the entrance.

Tim stood up and waved his arms, "Over here! This one's still alive, but won't be for long if you don't take him now!" Two men rushed over and began the process of prepping him for the ride to the hospital. The woman ran to his side, tears streaming down her lovely face.

She would not be swayed from her determination to accompany her husband to the hospital in the ambulance. She held his hand as they carried him off.

Other medics rushed in to help the injured but still breathing and to start identifying those who were not so lucky. *I did what I could. It's up to him now.* He looked at his hands, which were soaked in blood, as were his clothes. He looked across the room. Bodies littered the floor, seemingly floating in red water. His friend Dwight was being led outside by the police. He appeared to be in shock. *I don't blame him.*

Chapter 3

Dwight sat in the cushioned armchair across from Tim. Always the intellectual, he was lost in his thoughts, his tea on the table. "You should eat something, Dwight. At least try." Tim held out a bowl of grapes, but Dwight shook his head.

"I'll be fine. I can't eat anything right now. This was supposed to be my vacation and all I can think about are those poor people at the mall. I close my eyes and I see dead bodies; I hear the screams and the gunfire. It is beyond my comprehension how anyone would do such a vile thing." It had been a day since the shooting.

Tim examined his longtime friend sitting across from him. He looked worn out. Creases lined his long, skinny face and his giant round glasses enlarged the wrinkles hidden behind them. He tried to recall how long it had been since he had last seen his friend before this. *Years*.

"I don't know, Dwight. I don't think it's anything anyone could ever explain. He was just nuts, and something made him crack further."

Dwight leaned forward and rested his forehead between his hands. "I have gained understanding of things that many people would never comprehend, yet it's random events like this that I have never been able to understand," he sighed. "What snaps in someone like that? Where is the logic? What is off? Better yet, how could it be cured? That's what I need to study!"

"Just relax. These are things you can't fix. It's just life. Shit happens." Tim threw a grape at Dwight, and it bounced off his forehead. "Remember when Crazy Stew ran around the dorm buck naked? What caused him to do what he did? He was just batshit crazy. Some people just can't be explained beyond that."

Dwight couldn't be steered from his thought process. "The man mentioned something about a warning of something bad coming. He was willing to die for his belief in something that he believed deep in his soul that no one else has any idea about. Maybe he's nuts, or maybe he sees or knows something we don't. If it's the former, what causes someone to have such conviction over a random thought? I don't think anything is really random." He shook his head, but then smiled.

"What?"

"I know what I'm going to do next. I'm going back to Pennsylvania with a new project. There has to be a way to treat these people so no one has to experience the tragedy we lived through. There must be ways to diagnose and prevent this type of mental breakdown. I'm going to find them. It's all in the mind — something is broken, so it can be fixed."

Tim put his hands up, "No. Some things are unfixable. There's a place in the world for everyone — a balance that needs to be maintained. A yin and a yang. That's all there is to it. Don't try to play God – it will only bite you in the ass."

Dwight stood up. "You know not to bring up the subject of God up with me. We've had these arguments since college and you're never going to convince me that God is real. Science and logic rule the world."

"Dwight, I work in medicine. I see miracles every day."

Dwight shook his fist, "Miracles? Where was God when that poor mother was shot? When all those people at the mall lost their lives to the actions of a madman?"

"Have you ever seen a baby be born? Or a man survive wounds that by all accounts should have killed him? Or how about a man that had been dead for a few minutes returning and telling everyone about his departed loved ones hugging him a moment before? As hard as you try to abandon him, God is there." Tim reached out to his friend, but Dwight backed away.

Tim could see through his friend's thick glasses that his eyes were glazed with fatigue. *He hasn't slept at all.* Dwight turned away toward the door. Tim stepped forward. "What are you doing?" he asked, his voice filled with concern.

"I'm heading to the airport. I've plenty of work to do."

"Work? Don't bring hurt upon yourself. You cannot change people. Don't go right now, just stay and talk to me."

Dwight looked back at him with a steady gaze. "Do you know what I was doing before I came to Maine for my seminar?"

Tim shook his head.

"I have a good job as professor. I teach students and I'm good at it. I have a house; I have a nice car. One would think I'm happy. The truth is, I have nothing to aim for anymore. I've achieved everything that I wanted, but have made no lasting contribution to society at all."

"OK, so you're depressed. Lots of people are depressed. You can get past all that with help."

Dwight shook his head. "It's not like that. It's not depression. I'm fine, just bored."

"So find yourself a woman."

"I had one, until I found her screwing one of my students."

"Ouch, that's rough."

Dwight shrugged. "She annoyed me, anyway. Kind of ditzy."

"All right, what's your plan, then?" Tim asked.

"The brain is a computer. I will find a way to fix it when it's mal-functioning, and the world will be a better place. Maybe then you'll see God is nonexistent. We make our own destiny and solve our own problems."

If there was one thing that Tim knew about his friend, it was that when he got a plan, he acted on it with tenacious ferocity. *Well, work could be good for him to get over all this.* Tim smiled back at his stubborn friend, "I don't think we'll ever agree, but you're my friend and are always welcome here."

He held out his hand. Dwight grabbed it and they shook. Without a word more, he let himself out.

Chapter 4

"IT'S BEEN FIVE YEARS since the tragedy at the Portland mall took place," the local news was blaring the usual non-news crap. The news was a reminder of his limp leg. He rubbed the section of his leg that was always asleep. Pins and needles constantly bothered him - worse than the never ending ache. Leaning against the cabinet for support, he pressed on with the dishes. The doctor had told him to press through the discomfort. If he didn't, he'd be in a wheelchair sooner, rather than later. Sighing, he glanced at the clock. Adrianna wouldn't be home for another four hours. The days were long when he was the only one home.

A picture of Jack appeared on the news segment with a head line of "Local Hero". Jack shook his head. Pepper, their large black lab nudged against him, pleading for food.

"Must be a slow news day. Digging up old stuff again." Jack patted the dog and hobbled to the fridge to pull out a slice of ham. "Don't tell anyone I gave you this." He threw the meat to the floor and the dog greedily wolfed it down.

The house phone rang and Jack cringed as he hobbled to answer it. Looking at the caller ID, he rolled his eyes. Adrianna's mom.

"Hello." Jack tried to hide his annoyance.

"Hi, Jack? It's Ellie."

Jack smiled and tried to sound upbeat. "Yes, Hi. Adrianna is still at work."

"No, I wanted to talk to you. Did you see the news?"

"Yes, they were talking about old stuff again."

"Old stuff? Jack, you are a celebrity!"

Jack settled into a nearby chair, stretching his bad leg. *This won't be a quick call,* he thought and took a deep breath. "Well, not sure about celebrity. If I were, I'd be dealing with job offers through the roof. Better yet, I wouldn't have been kicked out of my old job when my medical bills were sky high."

"Well you are a hero. You know, you and Adrianna should move up this way. Lots of land and low taxes. I could use help on the farm."

Here we go again. "Adrianna has a good job, and I'd hate to put any stress on you."

"No stress at all! I've told you time and time again to get your butts up here."

Jack pictured himself answering to Ellie on a daily basis. "No thanks. I'm grateful for your offer. We are doing fine."

"Fine? Adrianna says your leg is really bothering you and you can't find work. It would be good for Ashley to have a place to play without worry. She could learn so much on the farm. It's all going to you when I die anyway. I'm not a spring chicken anymore."

Now the drama and guilt. "Stop. You'll outlive us all."

"I'm serious, Jack. Things are changing for me. I'm getting old. We need to talk about these things. Moving here would be good for everyone. Since I lost George, I can't keep up with everything."

Jack shifted in his chair to get weight off his leg. Just the thought of Adrianna's dad made him irritated – even though he's been dead for some years now. George never liked him much and the feeling was mutual. The ache in his leg was getting bad and he'd need some pain reliever soon. He could feel his temper starting to flare with the pain increasing.

"I can't talk about this right now. Anything else before I go?

"Jack, why won't you think it over?"

"I told you a hundred times, we are staying here. I'll tell Adriana you called."

"I have rooms ready for you all. Ashley can have her own pig -"

"Bye Ellie." Jack hung up the phone. *Shit. Adrianna will give me an earful when she finds out I hung up on her.*

Looking for his cane, Jack pushed himself to his feet and hobbled to where the cane leaned against the wall across the room. He wondered why whenever he needed the cane it was somewhere out of reach.

Each step he took sent jolts of pain up into his hip and back. Grabbing the cane, he leaned against it for support. A mirror hung on the opposite wall reflected his image. He could see a beaten and grumpy old man staring back at him. *What the hell have I become?* he thought. The man in the mirror was aged and tired looking; a shell of what he once was. *I've become bitter and miserable.*

Pepper, sensing a change in mood, walked over to him. Her grey muzzle and her limp gave away her age too. Her tail wagged with each step. She was stronger than him. She was happy, even while old and in pain. Jack smiled, sadly, and patted her. Leaning against the wall, he slowly slipped to the floor. Pepper, with all her weight, settled into his lap. Jack grimaced but laughed at the big old dog and scratched her neck. Pepper lapped his hand and looked up to him with her giant dark eyes, knowingly.

"You are right. I was an asshole. I AM an asshole. I need to work on that." Jack wiped a small tear from his eye. "Time to stop wallowing in my sadness, right?"

He thought about the shooting, the recovery and years of therapy after, the job he lost; everything seemed to fall apart that day. He wondered if it was worth it. He had no idea of what happened to the baby since. It never occurred to him how much he needed his work. He tried applying to countless jobs since recovering, but no one would take him when they saw him limp into interviews with a cane. Eventually he gave up trying.

"I'm done, Pepper. I'm not going to let this all keep me down any longer. Time to get past this."

Pepper put her head down on his leg. First thing, he needed to apologize to his mother in law and Adrianna. He shook his head. Maybe he could wait until later. Pepper needed to be pet first.

Chapter 5

"Boom!" Joseph shouted as he smashed his toy car into the wall near the blaring TV.

Belinda leaned forward in her chair, scowling at her son. "Joseph, quiet! This is mommy's rest time. This is my favorite show, and I'll be damned if you are going to take it away from me. You took my youth and my beauty. Now you want to take away my one enjoyment. Little rat. Five years old and still a filthy little baby!"

Joseph felt his eyes puddle, and his heart pounded in his throat. "Momma!"

"Shut up! You know to leave me alone with my shows!"

The TV played in the background. Some old man was talking with a young woman about a baby. Belinda smiled. "This will be perfect for the next sermon!" Belinda moved to jot something down on paper. She pursed her lips, muttering something about heathens.

Joseph sat in the same spot, watching her through tears. "Momma!"

"Joseph! That's enough. Take your car and get your behind out of here. I'm listening to my show right now."

Joseph cried louder. He just wanted to hug his mom. Why wouldn't she hug him? "Momma! Hug!"

Belinda stood and stomped over to where Joseph sat. She towered above him. Maybe she'd hold him now? She raised her hand into the air.

"By the mighty Lord's grace, you will stop your whining this minute!"

Joseph could feel his body shake. He knew what was coming. It happened a lot, but once the worst was over, it would get better. Closing his eyes, he whimpered. Then it came. A clap, a flash of light, and then the heat. His cheek burned and he wailed. He didn't want to, but it was all he could do. It hurt so bad.

"Look what you made me do. My poor boy." Big arms wrapped around him and picked him up. "God frowns upon little boys who disrespect their parents."

A hand brushed his hair away from his forehead. He opened his eyes and saw his mother smiling at him through blurry vision. His cheek still stung, but it felt so nice to be held.

"What do you say, my little Joe?"

"I'm sorry, Momma." His voice cracked and he tried to keep it from shaking.

"That's right, you should be sorry. I don't want to have to do that, but it's my job as your mommy to make sure you understand the sins you caused." She sat down with him in a rocking chair. "You need to understand sins. Do you know why?" she asked. Her smile faded and her face took on the look he didn't like.

"Because I'm a boy. Boys get filthy thoughts and are dirty."

Belinda nodded, her eyes narrowed. "That's right. Thank God your daddy is the reverend and is close to God. If he weren't he'd burn in the pits of hell like all the other men."

Joe nodded, proud he answered her correctly.

"Someday, you'll take his place and you'll be closer to God. Until then, you need to listen to your mommy and daddy. When we hurt you, it's because we fear for your soul."

"Yes, Momma."

She began to rock the chair and brush his hair with her large hands. Jewels glittered on her ring. "Why do you think daddy uses the belt on you every night?"

The thought of his father hitting him with the belt made his butt sore. He reached down and rubbed his backside. Belinda moved his hand and smacked it. "Answer the question!"

"To remind me of my wickedness so I can be better like daddy."

Belinda nodded, smiling. "Little boys need to be taught that so they can grow to be good men. That's why daddy instructs all the boys every week. Watch and learn from your daddy. He's doing the Lord's work."

Joe nodded and took a deep breath. It was nice to be held. *I won't ever do that again,* he told himself, but he couldn't remember what it was he'd done wrong. A tear rolled down his cheek once more. "I'm never going to be a good boy, Momma."

Belinda nodded. "But you have to try. Otherwise, it will be very painful for you." The fat jowls under her chin shook as she spoke.

Joe wiped his nose. He remembered what had happened when he'd refused to eat a bowl of mashed peas. Peas made him gag. When he refused to eat them, Belinda rushed him into his bedroom and beat him. He was locked in his bedroom for a day without food and was told that he needed to beg for forgiveness from the Lord. When she finally let him out, Belinda had told him that the Lord came to her in her dreams and told her that the Devil had influenced her son's actions and so she forgave him.

"I'm really sorry, Momma." He tried to nestle his head into her arms but she moved him to the floor.

With a heave, Belinda lifted herself out of her recliner and reached for her cane. She bent in order to look him in the eyes.

"Now you go and play with your toys quietly!" she scolded, shaking her fatty finger at him. "Momma's going to go get a snack. You be a good little boy now. The Lord has no room for troublemakers!"

She limped into the kitchen, every step an arduous task. Joseph could hear his mom fishing around in the cabinets for some more Twinkies. That was her favorite snack food. Every day around the time her favorite soap blasted on the TV, after her main lunch and before her mid-afternoon lunch, was Twinkie time. If Joseph was an extra good boy in the mornings, he'd get a Twinkie as well. Today, he spent most of the morning behaving well, but knew he had screwed up when he challenged his mom right before snack time.

At that moment, it occurred to him that Daddy would treat him better. Little Joseph made his way to the large wooden door leading down to the basement where Baxter was holding his lessons. Joseph always wondered why he was never included in the teachings. "One day, when you're older, you can participate," his father would explain to him.

Reaching into the air and standing on his tiptoes, Joseph could barely reach the door knob to open the door leading downstairs.

"CLICK!"

"JOSEPH! What do you think you are doing? Get away from that door, you rotten brat!" Belinda hobbled out of the kitchen, cane in hand and panting to catch her breath. The floorboards beneath her feet creaked in agony as she walked over them. Joseph sunk to his knees looking up at his mother's furious eyes. His jaw quivered as the woman loomed over him. Her lips pinched.

Joseph braced himself when he saw her raising the. He didn't have long to prepare before it came swooping down. Pain shot up his back as she whacked him on the butt. He screamed.

"SHUT UP!" she bellowed. "You worthless, piece of rubbish boy!" Not happy with the first strike, she brought the cane back up over her head and swung it down, striking the little boy's butt one more time. Pain, stronger this time, again shot up his spine, and he rolled to his side in a ball, whimpering.

Belinda's frown grew more hideous. "If only you were the daughter your father wanted. Things would be different. May the Lord give me the strength to raise you into a proper man!"

He lay on the floor and held back tears as well as he could, knowing tears would bring on more lashes from the cane. Belinda hobbled down the hall with her cane in one hand and a pack of Twinkies in the other. He heard her fall into her recliner, muttering under her breath. The wood frame of the recliner let out a creaking noise as her weight settled into the chair. Joey was not allowed to sit in her recliner, unless he was being held. It was her special chair. Even his dad wasn't allowed to sit in it. It was one of those expensive chairs that could adjust into many different positions. There were days when she would recline herself back, her legs propped into the air like a June bug on its back, and she would stay in that position all day long watching her shows.

Just as she finished wiggling around for the most comfortable position, the doorbell rang, and she jumped. "Lordy! Lordy!" she exhaled. She adjusted the seat so she could stand up and struggled to get to her feet again, hiding the Twinkies under the tablecloth on the stand beside her chair. The cane, resting against the recliner, fell to the floor and clacked as it skidded a few feet from where she stood. Joey hated that cane. One of these days he was going to sneak it away and bury it somewhere his mom would never be able to find it again.

Belinda grunted as she bent down to pick up the cane. She made her way to the door and stopped a moment before the mirror to primp her hair. She grabbed a shawl that was hanging on a peg from the coatrack and draped it over her shoulders, trying to hide the flabby cleavage bursting from her house dress. It wasn't very effective. The shawl didn't make it all the way around her big shoulders to cover the middle of her chest.

Having done the best she could to look presentable, she opened the door. Joseph peered around the corner to see who was there. It was Mrs. Thomas with her two boys, Ray and Tony. Ray was the older of the two and was here for lessons. Tony was about the same age as Joe. Sandra was a fairly attractive woman, but in a mousey way that was accentuated by her tiny nose. Her slight, very slim frame radiated timidity; she would never purposely treat anyone wrongly. Her voice was very quiet.

"Oh, hello, Sandra. And hello there, Tony." Belinda was wearing one of her warmest smiles. Tony looked down at his shoes at the mention of his name.

"Hello, Belinda. Ray is here for his lessons. I do appreciate what you and the reverend are doing for him. Since his daddy moved away, he's been very frustrated. If it weren't for you two, showing him the way of the Lord and all things good, I'm not sure what we'd do!" Sandra frowned when she mentioned her husband.

"Oh, that's quite alright. We do what we can to assist in our Lord's teachings. Though I can't say I approve of your situation, Sandra." Belinda put her hands on her hips. She looked like a mother hen overlooking her chicks.

Sandra looked like she was about to cry. "I know it's not the best situation for little Tony. I'm doing the best I can. The Devil had his influence on my husband. Lust took over when that young hussy caught his eyes." Her face reddened.

"True, the Devil is always working to sway us off the righteous path. But men are men. If you treat them right, they won't wander. You mustn't have been treating your man right. Forgiveness is hard, but perhaps if you forgive him, he'll forgive you. Both of you should be looking for the Lord's forgiveness. It's not right to blame the other woman, either. Your man running off is your own doing, Sandra."

Sandra looked down. "Yes, Belinda. I pray for forgiveness every night. I only hope it's not too late for me and my husband. Please help my boy. I don't want him to be caught in sin like us." She put her hand on Ray's shoulder. Both boys had tears in their eyes.

"Well, we'll do what we can. We'll also pray for the both of you." Belinda took Ray's hand and led him through the door. "Now Ray, you can go straight downstairs. The reverend has already started his lessons," Belinda told him and patted him on the back as he walked past. Ray smiled at Joseph before he went down the stairs. Belinda turned to Sandra and said, "God bless you" as she closed the door.

She hobbled back, the cane clacking as she moved along, to her favorite chair. She fell back into it, muttering about the Lord's work never being done and grabbed her Twinkies while turning up the TV. She had switched it to one of her favorite reality shows. She liked to turn the volume way up so she didn't miss any juicy conversations.

Joseph got to his feet again, the pain subsiding. He rubbed his butt and winced. It would likely be black and blue soon. He had received many marks from his mom's teachings before and was used to it. He looked up at the doorknob. It had a carved indentation, and it seemed to smile at him. *Joe. You can do it. Come on...don't be a baby, Joe. Don't you want to be a big boy?* The temptation of finding out what the big boys did was too strong. He once again got on his tiptoes and reached up for the doorknob.

"CLICK!"

His stomach turned at hearing the noise of the latch give way. He immediately looked over to where the TV was blaring, but this time his momma hadn't heard him. He turned back to the door and opened it just enough to slip through. Peering through the open crack, all he could see was blackness and the steep wooden steps leading down into the dark. He could make out faint noises from below: the sound of a kid whining and, in between, the his dad's deeper voice cutting the boy off. He knew he'd be in severe trouble if his dad found out he was sneaking up on him and spying, but the urge to know what he was missing was too great. He swallowed his fear and slipped through the opening, ever so quietly closing the door behind him.

***

The air seemed chillier than it had been upstairs with his mom. The dank basement smell wafted up the stairs, and it made him think of big spiders. He hated spiders. *Little boys are afraid of spiders. Are you a little boy?* The voice in his head taunted him, urging him to toughen up and go down the stairs. His heart pounding, he looked back at the door and jumped as his mind made shapes in the darkness. He swallowed hard when he thought he saw a giant bug run across the door. His skin hardened on his arms into goose bumps. *Go!* the voice commanded. *It will catch you and eat you!*

Joseph plopped down on his butt and started down the wooden stairs to the basement. The wood stairs were cold and dirty. He didn't care about the dirt, but if his mom saw how dirty he was, he'd be in big trouble. He moved on, afraid to look back at the door. He felt bugs all over him, crawling on his back, eating his skin. He began to itch, scratching at bites that didn't exist.

It occurred to him that he'd made a bad decision. Joe hated dark rooms, and going down into the basement felt like he was descending the steps into Hell. He would never get out again. His mom would say, "He was a little devil, and now he's where he belongs! He's not worthy of God and Heaven!" The thought of being condemned for eternity made his stomach shake, and he almost lost control of his bladder. Now he had to pee. Squeezing his legs together and sitting still a moment, he felt as though he'd regained control, though his front felt a little damp. *Ha ha ha! What a baby!* The voice came through again, and it sounded like his mother's voice. It made him angry, and with that he became more determined. He moved a step further down.

"Please don't make me do that, Mr. Baxter" a young voice echoed out.

"Quiet, son. You know what has to happen when you sin! You must repent for your actions. It's the only way you can be clean again. It's for your own good!" Joseph heard his dad's voice reply to the younger voice.

"But I have to every time I'm here! Why do I always have to do it?" the younger voice asked.

"It is what the Lord has directed me to do. Do you question God?" he asked.

"No, sir. I'm sorry," the boy replied.

"You need to understand, Ray. You are a dirty boy filled with sin. When you question the Lord's motives, you allow the Devil entrance to your soul. To absolve yourself of your sin, you need to do what I tell you. First him, then me. Understand?" The reverend's voice was stern.

"Yes, sir. I understand. Please forgive me." He was sobbing now.

Joe, anxious to see what was going on, moved down a step, then another.

"I'm cold," another voice said, this one a bit higher pitched.

"Both of you just be quiet and do what I told you to do!" The reverend's sounded more annoyed.

Just another two steps and Joe would be able to peek under the railing. The sound of his mom's cane and the sound of her footsteps shuffling along the floor caused Joe to look back at the door, half expecting to see her looking down at him with a scowl. He was relieved to see nothing but darkness and the door still closed. A clanking sound came next, which probably meant she was using the bathroom off the hallway near the door to the basement. Joe sat a moment, not wanting to risk any noise. With any luck, she'd finish her business and then go back to her show. The toilet flushed and then the noise of the cane and heavy footsteps moved back past the door to the living room. She was back to watching TV. Satisfied all was well, Joe took two more steps down.

Peering through the railing, he could see two boys standing side by side, wearing nothing but their briefs. Both were shivering from the cool of the basement. The older boy, Ray, had his arm around the younger boy and was rubbing his back in an awkward manner. Not far away, standing in front of the boys, stood Reverend Baxter. A light on a pole was aimed at the boys. Joe didn't really know what was going on, but for some reason he felt like he wanted to take a shower. To his father's side was some boxy-looking thing on three metal legs with a glass eye looking straight at the boys. Joe was cold, and thinking about the boys not wearing anything caused him to shiver. His foot slipped down to the next step, making a loud creak.

"Who's there?" he heard his father yell out.

The sound of footsteps rushing over to the staircase made Joe wish he could run up the stairs. He was going to be in so much trouble! With the thought of the next beating he would get, he completely lost control of his bladder. Burning warmth spread across his lap, leaving a huge wet spot on the front of his pants. Baxter peered up and saw his son sitting on one of the steps, eyes wide in fear.

"Son? What are you doing?" He shook his head. His dad looked over to where the two boys were standing.

"You two. Get dressed. Lessons are over for today." Baxter pointed at their clothes on the floor.

Joe could hear them rushing to get their clothes, and they were dressed in a heartbeat. Both Ray and the younger boy rushed up the stairs past Baxter and his son. Ray patted Joe on the shoulder as he passed, and Joe looked up to see concern in the boy's eyes. The door closed behind the boys as they left. The room was eerily quiet now.

His dad looked down at him, his tall, skinny shape towering above. He wore jeans and a black T-shirt with a black suit coat. "You know you should not have come down here. You are not to say *one word* about this to anyone! Not even to your mother. Do you understand?" His hands were on his hips and his face was tight. Sighing, Baxter paced the room, rubbing his forehead.

"Son, this needs to stay between you and me." The smell on his dad's breath reeked of that bottle his dad drank from—the one Joseph was always told to avoid. His voice was a bit slurred and he had to hang on to the railing to keep from swaying.

He looked down at the boy's pants and laughed when he saw the wet spot. "What did you do?" He shook his head. "My son, the baby! You must have gotten that from your mom's side." He paused a moment, looking up at the ceiling before he continued. "We all pay for our sins in different ways, son. Mine is to be bound in wedlock with that witch for the rest of my life." He reached down with his other hand and grabbed his son's arm.

"Someday, when you are older, you may understand." His father stood towering over him. "Now you get yourself on upstairs and tell your momma what you've done. Tell her Daddy already gave you a good spankin'. If you're a good boy for the rest of the day, I'll pray for you tonight."

Baxter pulled his son to his feet, turned him in the direction of the top of the stairs, and gave him a firm pat on the butt. Joseph was still sore from the last whack he had received from the cane, and he let out a slight yelp. His pants were cold now, and he was beginning to get extremely uncomfortable. Not wanting to be in any more trouble than he was already in, he took a few quick steps to the top of the stairs.

Joe hesitated a moment near the door, not sure what awaited him from his mother once she found out where he had been. He didn't need to open the door—it swung open on its own, and on the other side was Belinda, sour looking as ever. Her big frame blocked any light the open door would have normally let in.

She frowned at him. "WHERE HAVE YOU BEEN?" she yelled, spittle flying from her mouth.

"Momma! Dad—" he stammered.

She jumped in before he could finish. "What did you do to your pants? Did you pee?" She tilted her head back and laughed, the fat around her belly bouncing like Jell-O. "Dumb, dumb boy! God help me." She stopped laughing. What she considered a smile disappeared from her face and turned into a frightening scowl.

"Just get your behind up here and go straight to your bedroom!" She raised her cane into the air. "Don't make me whack you again." The cane shook in the air above her shoulder. The fat under her arms jiggled as she shook it. Joe cowered, feeling tears rushing to his eyes.

"Get your little butt moving, NOW!" Some spit landed on his forehead as she yelled. She yanked him off the top stair, and in one movement shoved him down the hallway toward his bedroom.

He toddled to his room, holding the wet section of his pants away from his skin. It felt awful and cold. He pushed the door open and slammed it behind him. Tears pooled in his eyes, and he fell to his butt, crying. He hated to make his mom so mad. Tears streamed down his cheeks. He looked down to the wet spot on his pants, which made him cry harder. They didn't have to make fun of him. *Dumb, dumb boy!* His mom's voice haunted him over and over again. He slammed his fist into the carpeted floor. A vision of his Dad and Mom standing side by side, pointing at the wet spot on his pants and laughing entered his mind. His mom was turning to his father, saying *Dumb, dumb boy!* Blood rushed to his face, and he felt his anger flare hotter. He cried louder and hit the floor repeatedly with both hands.

Rip, rip, *riiip*.

He looked up to see Puffy sharpening his claws on a scratching post. He'd found the kitten in the barn, and his dad let him keep it. His short fur was completely black aside from a white strip that ran up his nose. Joseph got to his feet and slowly walked over to where Puffy was happily using his claws. When the little cat saw Joe approaching, it meowed for attention. Joe didn't look down at the kitten. *Dumb, dumb boy!* He glanced down to the desk next to the scratching post. On the desk was a pair of scissors he used for various crafts. He would often make crosses out of craft paper and hand them out at his father's sermons.

Joe felt his jaw beginning to hurt, and he realized he had been grinding his teeth. *Why did they have to laugh at me?* Another tear rolled down his cheek, and he watched as it fell to the floor. Puffy was at his legs now, rubbing his side against him, his tail wagging back and forth. *Hah! Wet your pants like a little baby?* he heard the cat say.

He reached down and grabbed Puffy with one arm and picked up the scissors in his other hand. Puffy wiggled and tried to escape, but Joseph held tight and squeezed a little tighter. "MEOW!" He squeezed tighter. "Call me a baby again!" he said. "MEOW!!" This time the cat's cry was a bit more desperate. His arm squeezed even tighter. "MEOWWW!!!" Puffy was frantically clawing at Joseph's arm. *Dumb, dumb boy!* Joe squeezed harder.

Pain radiated through his arm as Puffy ripped into his flesh with those small, sharp claws. Red trails of open flesh covered Joe's arm. Blood oozed out from the gashes the cat created in its struggle to escape. He watched as the bright red fluid rushed out from the cut, fascinated by the flow of blood as it dripped down his arm. *Dumb, dumb boy!* His mother's voice continued to taunt him. Looking down into the cat's eyes, he could see his mother's wicked smile.

"I'm not dumb!" he shouted as he brought the tip of the scissors to the front of Puffy's eye. Puffy turned his head to the side away from the scissors,, but Joe yanked its head back and held it tight. "Let's see how you'll look without your eye and then we'll see who the dumb one is!" Slowly he pressed the tip of the scissors into the kitten's eye with more and more pressure.

Joe watched and smiled as fluid dripped from the cat's eye. Some blood and some other sort of fluid mixed together. The cat squirmed and the scissor blade gashed open a bigger slice of the kitten's eye.

Puffy let out another cry this time a shrill scream. *Dumb, dumb boy! You will always be a dumb, dumb boy!* it cried. In one quick thrust, he pushed the scissors further into the cat's eye. The cat jerked once. Twice. Then stillness.

"Don't call me dumb!" he yelled. The cat didn't move, and the voice in his head was quiet. He felt strong and collected, no longer angry.

He looked down at the kitten in his arms, blood flowing down from where the scissors protruded from the kitten's head, and he let out a giggle. The thought that the little kitten had a pair of scissors sticking out of its head was more than he could handle. He started laughing louder. Trying to think of a way to make it even funnier looking, he scanned the room for another pair of scissors. If one eye with scissors sticking out of it was funny, two would be even funnier. Joe jumped when he heard knocking on the door to his bedroom.

"Joseph, its Daddy." The door opened. His dad stood still, mouth open wide at the scene. He quickly stepped in and closed the door behind him. "What have you done?"

"I was playing with Puffy, Daddy," Joseph answered calmly. He stood still a minute, not knowing what to say or do next.

Reverend Baxter sighed deeply and seemed almost relieved with his exhalation. Joe watched his father as he stood, his finger tapping his chin. It's what he usually did when he was lost in thought. After a moment, Baxter's face lightened up and he spoke. "Son, remember what I told you about never saying anything to your mom about what you saw in the basement?"

He shook his head, "Yes, Daddy." The cat was still in his arms, limp. The blood from the cat's head was cold and sticky now, no longer dripping.

"Well, Mommy would be quite mad if she found out what you have done here." His dad's face had an ever so slight smile. "Let's make a deal, you and me."

Only the Lord was witness to the pact they made that day.

Chapter 6

RICK'S HAND WAS IN his pocket, stroking the cold steel of the blade hidden within. Reverend Baxter was up on the stage spouting something about how the Lord will arrive soon and that he's taking notice of those who are God fearing. A basket for donations was being passed around by his son, Joseph. From what Rick knew, he was two years younger than his age of six-teen. Joe was taller than him and had short brown hair. Rick considered him a handsome boy, though he preferred his dark hair color over the other boy's colored hair. Lost in his own thoughts, Rick didn't even notice when the boy offered him the basket for his contribution. His mother, who was sitting beside him, took the basket and threw in $5.00 before passing it further down the row, shaking her head and muttering when she glanced at her son. *What is she so ticked off about? If it weren't for me, she'd still be getting the shit kicked out of her by that so-called father of mine.* Images of slicing flesh with his knife ran through his mind, his thumb running carefully along the edge of the blade. Memories of the night he stabbed his father brought a smile to his face.

***

"Now, Ricky, Daddy's going to be home soon, and you know how he gets when he's been drinking. You go to your room and get to bed like a good boy." Janet, Rick's mom, was picking up clutter as she spoke. Her was voice tense and shaking. She had that tick that Rick couldn't stand. Whenever Janet was stressed, her top lip would twitch. Not wanting to go to bed yet, Rick continued playing war on the floor with his toys and made no move to get up. The knife he'd gotten from a friend at the park was safely hidden in the back pocket of his jeans. *Tonight's going to be different*, Rick thought to himself. The door burst open and David, his father, came stumbling through.

"What the Hell is he doing up, woman?" Bottle in hand, he was sending spit flying as he spoke.

Janet shook her head. "He was just getting ready for bed, honey." She spoke to the floor, her body shaking.

Dave glanced at Rick, "Get your ass to bed! Your mom and I have some things we need to catch up on!" He stumbled over to where she was picking up a few of Rick's toys and slapped her hard on the butt. She let out a screech and jumped up, turning to face David.

"David! Ricky is watching!" she whispered, embarrassed. "Ricky..."

His dad interrupted her midsentence. "I don't give a rat's ass! Get him to bed, woman!"

Her face was flushed, "David, honey, please don't swear like that."
SMACK!

His backhand knocked her to the floor. "Don't you talk to me like that!"

She was crying on the floor, her face beginning to form welts from the hit. Rick stood up. He clenched his fists. His stomach turned. *Don't hurl!* he thought, and he tried to stand tall.

"Stop it! Don't hit her!" he shouted.

"Ha! You think you're a big man, boy?" His father stepped to where the boy stood. "Stupid brat!" He raised his hand and swung it down.

Rick easily avoided the sloppily aimed sweep of his father's big hand. The alcohol had made him lose accuracy. In a heartbeat, Rick bounced back from his sidestep, knife in hand, and thrust it deep into the big man's gut. It glided in smoothly, and he could feel the tissue giving way to the sharp, pointed blade. The knife was hilt deep in his stomach. Rick looked up to see his dad's eyes filled with shock. He could see the pain radiating through his face, his mouth tightening, eyes wide, and face red with rage. Ricky liked the feeling of being Death's servant. He could hear his mom cry out, telling him to stop. Without realizing it, he twisted the blade and pulled up. Flesh ripped, blood gushed onto his hand, as did a brownish fluid that reeked of poop. His dad fell back, still standing, hands at his middle, staring down at his life was spilling to the floor in a red-brownish mess.

"You...little...shit..." He fell to his knees.

Rick stood up, holding the red-coated knife upright, and watched his father. Then he moved forward, pressing his left shoulder against his dad's. He stabbed, and stabbed, and stabbed, and stabbed, and stabbed. Each time, he felt more powerful. Like he was stealing his prey's strength. His dad's body fell backward to the floor.

Just one more! Ricky lifted the blade high above his head, and in one motion he brought the blade down as his knees landed on the man's bloody midsection. He buried the knife in his father's eye.

Janet sat on the floor, mouth open wide in shock. "LORD! Ricky, what have you done? God Save your soul!" she exclaimed.

***

Too late for that, he thought. Now the reverend's wife was up on the podium, explaining how a woman needs to support her man. Rick was tired of looking at the fat woman, and he began to scan the audience, thinking about who he wanted to kill and how. *Kill—hammer; kill—ice pick.* His eyes stopped on a pretty teenaged girl. She was quite a bit younger than him, but was quite captivating. She had thick blonde hair and a beautiful face without any imperfections aside from a lone zit. She was sitting next to her younger brother, who was close to her age and obviously irritating her. She looked up and saw that Rick was looking at her. His gaze didn't shift, and he stared into those beautiful blue eyes. Her eyes darted away and she began to twirl some of her hair with her finger. *Live—with me.* She must have realized what she was doing with her hair because she stopped when she glanced at him briefly once more and her face turned bright red.

"A woman's place is by her man's side." Belinda was still spouting bullshit. The fat under her chin was shaking as she spoke. She raised her hand, pointing to the sky. "I guarantee you, if you do right by your man, the Lord will look down upon you and shower you with love!"

A woman in the audience shouted, "Praise the Lord!"

Belinda smiled out to where the voice came from. She stepped off the podium. People were standing up to leave; the sermon was over. Belinda walked up to where Joseph and the reverend were standing and leaned in to give her husband a kiss. The reverend subtly cringed when she laid one on his cheek. When she backed away, he put on his most sincere and affectionate smile. *I know about you, Reverend. I know something you don't want me to know. I know you are more into little boys than you are to your fat wife!* Ricky stood as his mom pulled him to get up.

***

The reverend's family made their way to the exit to shake hands as people left. Rick watched as his neighbor Sandra was leaving with her son Tony; they were directly in front of him and his mother in line. Tony cast his eyes down when they approached the Baxter family.

Sandra was wiping tears from her eyes. "Good day, Reverend. Good day, Belinda."

"Good day, Sandra." Belinda let out a little smirk.

"Belinda, I pray every night for my husband, and I'm doing the best I can. Do you really feel the Lord looks down upon me with such ferocity?" Tears were flowing faster now, and her nose started running. The reverend put his hand on her shoulder and offered a handkerchief from his pocket, but Belinda shooed his hand away and he backed off. "I just don't know what I could have done to keep him around. He was cheating and abusive!" Sandra continued.

"Sandra, a man doesn't just become hateful. As I told you before, if you were more 'attentive' perhaps he would have stayed." Belinda rubbed Sandra's back and glanced at the line behind her. She smiled at the folks waiting to talk with her. *She loves this attention*, Rick thought and rolled his eyes.

Belinda continued when Sandra regained some composure. "Until you find a way to get him back under your roof, I am afraid, as is everyone in this congregation, that the Lord will see you as a sinner. You can't raise a child without his father!" She crossed her arms. "This is why my husband has agreed to spend extra time with Tony! We pray it will be enough to teach him how to be a righteous man without a father in the house."

Tony's face reddened at the sound of his name, and he stared at the floor.

"Thank you, Belinda. Please continue to pray for us." Sandra put her hand on Tony's back, and they started walking out.

The reverend watched them leave, and Rick could tell he was mostly focusing on Tony. *Oh, you dirty freak!* He and his mom made their way to the exit. As they approached, the reverend smiled at Rick, and Rick smiled back. *C'mon, dirty man; you don't know have any clue who you're messing with.* Rick's hands were in his pockets, one hand on the knife. He found that holding the weapon gave him a kind of peace.

"Wonderful sermon, Reverend!" His mom shook the reverend's hand.

Belinda smiled at her and primped her hair. "It was nice to have you attend, Miss Marnell."

Rick and his mom had just moved to Pennsylvania last month. No one really knew about what happened to Rick's father, other than that he'd died in some sort of accident.

Sandra smiled back and continued, "I understand you have a Sunday lesson for a small group of kids. Ricky needs to become acquainted here, and it might be a good way for him to make some friends."

The reverend smiled. "I'm sorry. I don't just let anyone in. I'd like to first get to know Rick a little better before letting him accompany us in the lessons." He saw the disappointment on Janet's face and continued, "However, my boy Joe would love having someone to hang out with. I know Rick is quite a bit older, but Joe knows a lot of kids and the town. And that would give me a chance to get to know Rick a little better so that he could join the lessons down the road."

Oh, it will be you joining in on lessons. The knife felt like it was crying to be let out. It wanted to be deep in this man's throat.

"That would be perfect!" His mom sounded pleased and turned to look at her son. "Wouldn't that be great, Rick?"

Rick tried to look ecstatic. "Oh, that would be great! I really would like to have a lesson with you, Reverend!" he smiled at the man.

Baxter laughed. "Well, maybe soon. A true pupil wanting to learn about his Lord and Savior is a joy to work with." He patted Rick gently on his head, then moved his hand to Rick's shoulder, where it rested. He let out a sigh before continuing, "Maybe tomorrow Joe can give you a call and the two of you could hang out for a bit?"

Joe, hearing his name, ran over. "Is this the new guy?" he asked.

"Yes, Joe, this is Rick. I told him you wouldn't mind having him over tomorrow and helping him get set up here." His dad removed his hand from the boy's shoulder, but not before giving it a slight pat.

"Sure! I can show him around town!" Joe was thoroughly excited.

"Well, that is wonderful!" Janet smiled. Belinda was smiling back.

"Why don't you stop by as well? We can have some tea and discuss the available men around. You are widowed, right?" Belinda asked.

"That would be lovely. It would be nice to meet a few gentlemen. I do have higher standards about men since I found the Lord. I could not settle for someone who is not born again and shares my values." She paused and smiled. "Obviously no liberals. Definitely no man of color, unless he'll be cleaning the house!"

"No, of course not, dear! Heavens no!" Belinda smiled back. "I can tell you follow the Lord in all things, Janet. I think we are going to be good friends."

Rick and his mom left the church. Janet wore a smile all the way out. Rick finally released his grip on the knife. His knuckles were red from gripping the handle so hard.

Chapter 7

Meagan watched the Reverend deliver his speech, trying her hardest not to fall asleep. Glancing over at her younger brother, Sam, she could tell he was having similar difficulty. Both she and Sam had curly blond hair and blue eyes, which she'd always felt odd about since both her mom and her dad had brown hair. They were, however, lucky to be tall and slender like their parents.

This was the second time they had attended Reverend Baxter's sermon. Her family was not the extreme religious type, and she knew this would likely be one of the last times they visited this church. It was interesting, though, to see such a well-known person up close. She would often see Rev. Baxter on television during the early morning hours. He would travel to different states to preach and gain new followers. Oftentimes, someone would get up on stage, and he would hold their hand and the two would raise their arms, hands locked, and pray. She thought he had a book out as well. Her mom had insisted they all attend since the church was so close to where they lived. She was a science lab professor at the local university, and she felt it was good for the kids to see alternate views so they could grow up to be more well-rounded individuals.

The reverend's son, Joseph, was collecting money. *He's cute!* She smiled at him. He was perhaps a year older than she was. Her thirteenth birthday was soon, and he appeared to be around fourteen. He was dressed neatly and had an innocent look about him. She thought she remembered seeing him a few times while walking to school.

"Hey, Stupid!" her brother hit her on the shoulder.

"Ouch!" she rubbed where he hit her.

"Look at that weirdo staring at you." He nodded to his left. "Isn't that the new guy? Rick, I think." He snickered. "I think he's got the hots for you, Sis."

She glanced over to see Rick looking at her. When she made eye contact with him, his eyes darted away. She felt her face warm a little bit at the thought of an older boy looking at her. Not realizing it, she was curling a strand of hair with her fingers. When she noticed what she was doing, she could feel heat rush to her cheeks.

"Oh my! Sis has a boyfriend," her brother taunted her. This time, his laugh was loud enough for their mother, who was sitting next to Sam, to hear it.

"Shhh! Stop being rude! If you two keep it up, there'll be no ice cream after!" She looked at them with a scowl.

For being good during the sermons, the two kids were given bribe ice cream. Sam looked down at his feet and then tilted his head sideways to look at his sister with a shit-eating grin on his face. *Immature turd!* Her face scrunched up, and she stuck her tongue out at him.

The sermon seemed to last forever, and of course the fat wife of the reverend had to get up and speak her gibberish. All Meagan could do was think about how much money her gold necklace must have cost. *She does have style, I have to admit!* The woman was always dressed nicely and obviously spent a lot of time in front of the mirror to get her hair just so. But no matter how Meagan could spin it, she seemed to be a sour pickle. *A fat sour pickle!*

As they made their way out the door, the reverend shook her dad's hand and nodded. He said thank you to all of the family, but he seemed to spend a little extra time on Sam. Meagan looked behind her but did not see Rick anywhere.

"Looking for your sweetie, Sis?" Sam mocked her.

"Shut up, turnip breath!" She was finally able to return that hit she had taken in the shoulder earlier. He cried out when she hit him. Belinda must have seen Meagan hitting her brother because she was staring at them, her face scrunched up in disapproval.

Belinda stepped forward to stand in front of Meagan. "You know, that is not how a proper lady behaves."

Meagan could smell the sickeningly sweet perfume overloaded on the woman's neck. She wanted to apologize, but could not get the words out. Instead she sneezed loudly, and a spray of spit flew out of her mouth, covering the big woman's open cleavage. Sam erupted into uncontainable laughter. Belinda stepped back, her face holding back a flood of rage. Meg could tell that if she weren't in a public setting and if her parents weren't present, she'd be scared about the punishment she'd receive. Instead, the fat woman backed away and attempted to brush the fluid off her chest, trying her hardest to smile instead of frown.

"Well." Meg breathed in deeply and let it out slowly as she composed herself.

"I'm so sorry, Mrs. Baxter." Meg's face flushed, and her brother's laughter made her even more embarrassed. She heard her mother telling Sam to stop.

"No, no, dear. The Lord has bestowed upon me forgiveness and patience." Belinda smiled, and Meg could make out the stains of lipstick on her teeth. She could tell the woman was doing all she could to hold in her anger.

When they were out the door, their father, Max, let out a deep breath and unbuttoned his caller. "OK, I know it's a 'house of the Lord' and all, but something feels off about it. I mean, really Maggie, enough is enough. I'm through with this place." He shook his head as he unlocked the car doors with the clicker. "All the mumbo jumbo about what's right, what's wrong. Let me be the judge of what's right or wrong for me. I don't need some kooky reverend and his hippo wife telling me what the Lord would want me to do." He winked at his daughter and smiled.

Go Dad! Her mom wasn't so impressed, but she let it go. They all piled into the car. Meagan was dreading the ride home sitting in the back with her brother. He was at a stage in his life where all we wanted to do was fart and make as much stink as possible, just to see everyone's reactions.

"One, two, three...ERRR...squeak." Her brother's face was red from the exertion.

"Good one, moron! You fart like a mouse." She turned her head to watch the scenery pass by.

Maggie turned to look at her daughter in the back seat. "Tell me about this new boy at your school. I saw him watching you at the church. He seems like an odd boy. Please be careful, honey."

Meagan rolled her eyes. *Blah blah blah.* "Yes, Mommy!" she said, but kept looking out the window, lost in her thoughts. *I wonder if he saw my zit!* She became mortified at that thought and whipped out her pocket mirror, staring at the zit on her chin with extreme horror.

"Oh, I totally forgot to mention," Maggie's voice was filled with excitement. "Dr. Zeller is going to be at the university tomorrow."

Maggie was quite into this doctor's work. Evidently, he'd been studying some kind of ant or some stupid thing like that. Meagan shook her head. *She's all into this science junk when I've got major issues here.* She poked the zit, sending slight pain into the skin surrounding it.

"How would you like to go with me to see what he's researching?" Maggie asked her daughter.

She is way too much into this junk. "No, that's OK, Mom. I've got more exciting things to do." Meagan was thoroughly annoyed.

"I'll go, Mom!" Sam jumped in.

Maggie shook her head, "No, Sam. You're behind in your school-work and haven't been doing your homework."

"It means you'd have an extra day to recover from your dire situation."

Meagan realized her mom was talking to her. She put the mirror down and smiled.

Well, maybe I will survive this. A zit could disappear in a day, right?

"OK!" She was relieved she wouldn't have to face all the kids at school looking like an abomination.

Her thoughts about blemishes were interrupted by the sound of the car blinker as her dad turned the car into the parking lot of the local ice cream shop.

"What's going on here?" Max asked no one in particular.

Meg looked up to see an ambulance parked next to a car. Police and the fire department had shown up as well. She could see a baby seat through the open back door of the vehicle. It was empty. A woman, who she guessed must be the mother, was frantically crying out as a policeman held her back. On a stretcher being loaded into the back of the ambulance lay a tiny shape. Even with the windows up, she could hear the mother's screams.

"My BABY! Please! Please! Let go of me!" The woman's arms were flailing at the man holding her back. It all he could do to keep her from pulling her baby away from the crew.

Meagan rolled down the window to hear more.

"Please, miss. Let us do our jobs," a medic told the mother. "Can you tell me what you were doing before the reaction?"

"Nothing!" the woman cried hysterically. "We just came from the doctor and she had her shots," she paused to catch her breath and wipe away a flood of tears. "It was her six-month checkup! Please, help her!"

Max brought the car to a stop and they sat still. Meg swallowed a lump in her throat thinking about what might have taken place. *Maybe it choked on something?*

After the baby had been loaded into the ambulance, they let the mother get in. Not a second passed and the sirens were on, the ambulance skidding out of the parking lot. Onlookers watched and shook their heads in wonder.

"The poor thing wasn't breathing," a man in the crowd said to someone else.

"She said she didn't give it anything to eat, so it wasn't choking," another voice replied.

"Poor woman," Max said before taking everyone's order.

No one mentioned anything about what they had seen, but the ice cream seemed flavorless. Meg watched as they drove past the empty vehicle. It was a nice car. The back door was wide open, and the keys were in the ignition. Its owner didn't care about what could happen to it, her world turned upside down in a matter of a few moments. *How could you recover from that?* Meg wiped away a tear forming in her eye and tried to think of something else. Anything else, it didn't matter what. Even the zit on her face was a welcome distraction.

Chapter 8

Janet rushed Rick out of bed and had him dress in a tan button-down shirt and khakis. *I look like a brown turd,* he thought as they left the house for their planned meeting with the Baxters.

The Baxters' house had a beautiful yard, neatly mowed and nicely landscaped. The church elders took great care in maintaining the property for their beloved pastor. Although the house itself was not extraordinary, it was located near the church in the nicest part of town.

"Now, you be on your best behavior, Ricky! We need to make a name for ourselves here!" His mom's tone was all business.

"Don't worry, Mom. I'll be soooo nice!" He emphasized "so" with the best sarcastic tone he could muster as they walked up to the front door. She didn't use the doorbell but instead used the large knocker decorated with a figure of Jesus on the cross.

The door opened, and Belinda stood there in a flowery dress, and a heavy gold necklace strung around her beefy neck. Joseph was standing by her side wearing khakis and a button-down shirt covered by a V-neck sweater. *Well, Mom, guess you underestimated the dress attire!* He laughed to himself.

"Come on in, you two. Joey, why don't you show Ricky around the house and the new kitten Daddy got for you!" she looked at Janet. "His last kitten disappeared quite a while ago and he hasn't returned. I can't imagine what could have happened to him! We have a hard time with kittens. I believe some wild animal must get them when they sneak out."

Rick looked at Joe, who was looking off at nothing in particular. *Ha! I know where the little kittens went!*

"C'mon Rick, I'll show you my kitten and my new stereo!" Joe grabbed Rick's shoulder and they both walked down the hall.

Rick took notice of a door halfway down the hallway that had a sturdy lock installed. The outside of the house was nothing spectacular, but the inside of the home glistened with wealth. Crown moldings with intricate patterns carved into the wood lined the upper walls, and the floors were all an exotic-looking hardwood. As they passed a bathroom, Rick peered in to see a tiled room, the tiles laid on the floor to form a cross pattern. A large tiled walk-in shower was in the back of the room, and next to it stood an ornate pedestal tub. He shook his head as he walked past when Joe wasn't looking. *They got money alright. Not bad for a pastor!*

Joe's room was cluttered with toys and electronics. There was a desk was on the far side of the room. A stain dotted the carpet near a scratching post. *Interesting,* Rick thought. His hand wrapped around the handle of the always present knife he carried hidden in his pocket. It reminded him of the stains that remained on the carpet in his home after he stabbed his dad to oblivion. Joe walked over to where the kitten was hiding in the corner. As the boy approached the cat, it arched its back and backed as far as it could, but there was nowhere left to go.

"Retarded cat!" Joe grabbed at the cat, and it swiped at his hand, letting out a hiss. The kitten's claws were still very small, so Joe didn't show any sign of pain. He grabbed the cat and it let out a slight cry.

He lifted the cat up to his chest as he stood up. "This is Mack! He's my latest kitten. The others were all dumb and ended up hurting themselves."

The cat was clawing frantically at the boy's arm, but he had the poor cat in a vice grip. Rick noticed one eye was completely shut. Upon further scrutiny, it wasn't completely shut, but slightly open and hollow inside. The cat was jet black and appeared malnourished. *Ha! This kid is screwed up as bad as me!* Rick let out a slight laugh.

"Very nice cat." Rick reached to pet Mack's head.

The cat bit Joe's arm. "OUCH!" He threw the cat down and tried to kick it, but the cat was too fast and ran under the bed, where it hissed.

"It seems to me that cat needs some discipline, Joe." He smiled at the younger boy.

"I know. He's a little shit, and I've taught him a few lessons when he's been bad." Joe looked down at the floor as he spoke.

Rick reached into his pocket and withdrew the sharp knife.

"Hey, check this out!" He held up the knife so that Joe could look at it.

The knife was small, but it was sharp and had deadly jagged grooves carved into its base. The light reflected off the clean blade.

"Shit! That's a nice blade!" Joe's eyes went wide. "Where'd you get it? My mom and dad won't let me get anything like that. They said I couldn't be trusted with anything so dangerous and that those things were the Devil's tools." His face reddened.

Putting away the knife, Rick faked a sympathetic look. "Joe, I know you've hurt your animals. It's OK. I've hurt things too. It feels good. You can trust me; I won't tell."

Joe looked up at him, surprised. "Really? My dad knows, but my mom doesn't." He looked a bit relieved.

"What's your dad like? I want to join him with one of his lessons, but he won't let me. What are the lessons like?" Rick sat down on the bed, ignoring the hissing from underneath. Joe walked over and sat down next to him.

"I saw one lesson one time, but my dad told me never to talk about it. You won't tell anyone, right?"

Rick shook his head.

"Well, my dad had a couple of the boys doing something. They didn't have any clothes on. I think he films it. He says it cleans them of their sins." Joe went on, explaining in detail some of the things he'd seen. Rick sat there and listened. Most of what he heard solidified what he believed to be happening. In the few months that he'd been at school, talking with the kids there, he'd been able to put the pieces together. Although it was not reflected in his grades at school, and no one suspected as much, Rick had become a very observant child. How else would he have gotten away with getting rid of that damned old woman he was watching at the local YMCA? A smile spread across his face as he recalled the murder he caused a couple month's prior.

***

Annoying bitch! Rick tried to smile back at an older woman, Berta, who was peddling on a nearby bike. Rick would often try to blow off steam by lifting weights at a local gym. Rick had joined a troubled youth program a the local YMCA which was just down the road from where he lived. Berta was always kind to him, but something about her made Rick want to blow up. She was always flirting with an old man who always chose a bike next to hers, and yet she wore a wedding ring. *Always giggling and flirting. What a two-bit whore!* Rick would think to himself.

Today he'd reached his boiling point. She would pay for her philandering. Rick slammed the weights down and left the gym. He knew her car by now—he'd scoped her routine out long enough to know how long she'd spend in the gym to the usual time she left the parking lot. Scanning the parking lot for any potential witnesses, he was confident no one could see him. He tried the handle with his gloved hand and was happy to hear the click that it was unlocked. *One less issue to worry about.* Smiling to himself, he lay in the back, out of view. The car was tidy and smelled of leather from the seats sitting in the sun. Rick closed his eyes and rested for a few minutes. Like clockwork, Berta opened the door to the car at the time Rick expected her. Proud of his planning, Rick could feel the excitement building within. All his hard work would be paid for in a few minutes.

Berta was humming a tune Rick wasn't familiar with and primped at her hair in the rearview mirror. Rick heard the click of her seatbelt and scanned the parking lot to see if anyone was near. Confident no one was looking, he calmly pinned her head to the headrest and in one fluid motion ran the blade across her neck. She fought a little bit, but it was easy holding back an elderly woman. In a matter of a few minutes, she stopped moving. In one slice, he cut her earlobe off and let her body fall to the side, out of view.

He withdrew a cloth towel from his backpack and wiped the blade. *No more cheating now, you hussy!* Smiling, he packed his blood-soaked gloves and the cloth into his backpack, sticking the woman's earlobe in his pocket, and left the car with its dead owner. Like a shadow, he slipped away. The next day an article was printed in the newspaper:

"Berta Cammillo was found murdered in her vehicle. People are being asked to report any suspicious activity to the authorities. No suspects

have yet been found. When asked, police declined to comment on the status of the case. It is feared that it was a random act of violence. Berta was loved by many and lost her husband last year to cancer."

Well that was a big oops! More research next time, Rick! He did feel some sadness from hearing that news, but it also felt good to use his knife again.

***

SNAP! SNAP!

Joe was snapping his fingers in front of Rick's face.

"You there?" he yelled.

Rick came to and shook his head. "Yes, sorry. I was thinking about what you said." He stood up and he felt the cat underneath the bed snag his pants. He gave it a kick, and it let go, hissing. He looked over at Joe still sitting on the bed. "Joe, your dad is pretty famous, isn't he?"

Joe nodded.

Rick continued, "And he makes you feel pretty rotten about yourself, doesn't he?"

Joe crossed his arms. "Look, stop prodding about my dad, alright?"

Rick grabbed Joe's arm, helping him to stand up, and then put his arm around Joe's shoulders, leading him to the door. "I bet I can help you, Joey. That's what friends do."

Joe seemed confused. "OK.

This is going to be too easy, Rick thought as Joe led him outside. For the rest of the day, Joe helped Rick get acquainted with the town, and Rick was happy to use the time to befriend his target's son.

Chapter 9

THE FIRST THING MEAGAN did when she got out of bed was rush over to her mirror to look at the horror on her chin. The small red blip had morphed into a giant red balloon. She wanted to scream. *Thank God I'm not going to school today!* She ran to the bathroom and hopped into the shower, trying to think of the best solution for what to do if the zit didn't disappear by tomorrow. Nothing immediately came to mind.

She got dressed, putting on a sweater with the largest turtleneck available so she could hide her chin. She'd look weird wearing a sweater considering it was late spring and the weather was quite warm, but the alternative was worse. *It will have to do.* She sighed and made her way downstairs, where her mom had breakfast ready for her. Sam was already at school, and her dad was at work.

"Well, let's be quick, Meg. We're already late." Her mom was ready, so she shoveled the food in and they were off.

The campus yard was filled with students rushing to classes. Meagan kept her turtleneck up around her chin. *Oh my God! All these cute boys, and I look like Frankenstein! This is worse than school!* She was mortified. When they entered the science building, her mom gestured for her to go through two large doors into the auditorium, and she followed behind. The room was filled with students, and the professor was up on the podium. Maggie and Meagan made their way to a couple of seats toward the back, since all the seats closer were taken.

Professor Zeller was a tall, skinny man. He wore giant glasses that Meagan thought made him look like a bug. He had no hair except for a small group of sprigs growing out of the back of his head that he combed forward. He wore a white coat with pens in the front pocket. One must have burst because there was a small blue circle in the front of the pocket. *This should be soooo fun!* Her mind drifted off to how she would dress for school tomorrow.

But some of his speech managed to get through the mental wall she put up. As nerdy as he was, he did seem to really have an understanding of and fascination for what he was researching. From the seminar, she gathered that there had been documented findings of ants in Brazil that had a form of mold that took over their brains. The ants would lose their ability to think on their own, allowing the fungus to control the ant's movements. Eventually the ant would wander to a location and set itself down where the fungus could flourish. Unfortunately, no samples were currently available for the professor to study on his own.

The professor explained the significance to the audience of young scientists. "What if we could study this fungus and see how it could be incorporated into human beings? Maybe it would offer insight into how our brains function and even open doors into mind control, following the same process as this mold. Just think of the possibilities for treating people with mental disorders. It could be just the break-through we have needed to prevent tragedies caused by a breakdown in thought processes."

Now he's off his rocker. Meagan laughed, and her mom gave her a stern look. The session went on for a bit longer before people clapped for the geek and began filing out. Maggie grabbed Meg's hand, pulled her from her seat, and began pushing her way through the crowd as people were exiting the lecture hall. Meagan let out an irritated sigh. There was no arguing with her mom in this case. She was determined to meet this guy.

Meg hated being so confined with so many people. She liked her space and was grossed out at brushing against all the strangers exiting the room. A cute older boy walked past her, and she looked down, trying to hide the zit sticking out like a giant red sun.

A group of students were gathered around the podium, and Meg didn't think they'd get any closer than where they were. The crowd was too tightly knit to break through.

To her horror, she heard her mom shout out in a loud voice, "Professor Zeller!"

The students who were gathered around the man turned to look at who was shouting. They moved aside as she pushed through, dragging Meagan behind her. *Mom! Why?* She looked down, hoping everyone would realize this was not *her* doing. She wanted no part in this.

"Professor Zeller." This time her mom's voice was quieter, and she was breathing quickly either to catch her breath or from nervousness. It was amazing to think her mom could be nervous!

"Yes?" The man looked down to her and he removed his glasses, setting them down on the podium. Meg thought he looked annoyed.

"Aren't you the least bit concerned about the ethical repercussions of your research?" Maggie asked.

A few students nearby snickered. Maggie glared out in the direction from where the laughing came and then focused back on the professor.

"Ethical repercussions? My research is only to help limit needless violence in the world by altering or *fixing* the wiring in the brain of potential criminals." He paused. "How is that unethical?"

"Your goal is admirable, but you are playing God. We are not God. Only bad things will come of this," she replied.

He hung his head down in thought. "Maggie, right? I have heard about you from some colleagues of mine. You need to accept that God is a thing made up by those who are afraid of death. Just as a computer dies, so does a brain. There is no afterlife. If we learn to accept that fact, technology will not be hindered any longer. Religion acts as handcuffs to our advancement in technology. Science will win when pitted against religion. The sooner we can move past God and religion, the better."

Maggie's face reddened, and her tone became sharp. "How can you say that? How can you possibly think the universe was born from nothing? Everything has cause and effect. Some great force put us here, Professor. We didn't come from *nothing*."

"Go home!" a voice shouted out from behind them. Meagan wanted to slip off and hide in a corner.

"Mom. Let's go." She pulled on her mother's arm and looked over at her. Meg could see her fighting back angry tears. Meagan was embarrassed, but she also felt bad for her mom.

The professor continued, ignoring the comments from the audience. "I am not here to discuss our origins, Maggie. I would suggest that if you expect the science community to accept you seriously, you need to let go of the falsity of God and the afterlife and accept the fact that we live and we die. Humans need to look after themselves, and no force is out there directing us. I have a lot of other students to talk with. If you want to talk about this some other time, I would be willing to meet with you. It is a shame such a talented woman is bound by religion."

Maggie shook her head in frustration, took Meagan's hand to leave, and they made their exit. When they were outside, Maggie took a deep breath of fresh air. She seemed to have calmed down for the moment.

"What did you think? Pretty fascinating, wasn't it?" She was talking as they weaved through students either on their way to class or leaving.

"Oh, best time ever, Mom!" Meg replied with an annoyed tone. They had finally escaped the crush of students and were able to make their way to the parking lot.

Her mom seemed upset at her daughter's negative demeanor. "You don't get it, do you? I'm trying to help you understand the world more." She wiped away a small tear.

Meagan looked around, afraid someone would see her being scolded, embarrassed at her mom's emotional outburst.

"Meagan, science is very important. People like Professor Zeller are very smart, and they think they are working on projects that they feel will ultimately be beneficial for society." They walked a little further, looking for where they had parked the car. "But what they don't understand are the ethical components of it all. Sure, modifying DNA so that the body can better withstand viruses or injecting some foreign mold that might cure Alzheimer's can be good, but what are the unknown repercussions of that?" She paused and looked up for a moment before continuing. "I see so many people throwing out their faith in the name of science. Why can't there be both? God gave us the ability to think for ourselves, so why not embrace science, but keep God in our lives? It doesn't have to be one or the other."

Meagan could tell she had pressed too many buttons and upset her mother. "Mom, I'm sorry. Can we just go home?" Maggie's eyes narrowed and her face tightened. *Uh oh! I've done it now!* She lowered her head, waiting for the hurricane to come down on her.

"Yes, Meg, we can go home. You can run upstairs, lock yourself in your room, and pretend the world is all about fashion and boys." She grabbed her daughter's arm and stormed off. Meagan felt like she was being dragged along like a two-year-old child after a tantrum. She could feel the college boys watching and laughing. She looked up, relieved to see that no one was actually paying any attention.

Chapter 10

Marcus stared at the birthday card handed to him by his foster representative the same day she dropped him off at his current home. He turned thirteen today. *I wonder how long I'll be with this fat slob!* he thought to himself as when he looked up at his present guardian, Henry, sitting in his favorite armchair. It ripped to shreds and smelled like ass—Henry's ass, to be more specific.

Most of his life, Marc had moved from foster home to foster home, never having a chance to settle down in one town. He had been adopted once when he was a baby. Shortly after his adoption, the family moved from Maine to Massachusetts. He was with his new family for about three years, until both parents passed away in a car accident, hit by a drunk driver who, of course, lived. Since then, he had been in the system, bouncing from foster parent to foster parent. Nobody wanted him. Marc figured it was because of what he read when he snuck a look at his file when no one was looking: "high needs child." He would often have "episodes," where he would suffer head pain and visions. Marc knew some of his foster families thought him insane, unbalanced, or mentally ill. He suspected their complaints and even heard the terms Asperger's or autism, though he had no idea what that meant. It didn't matter anyway.

Marc thought about all the pills he was prescribed and would try to hide. They made him feel loopy and not care about anything at all. Marc felt the pill in his pocket. His head was clearing after his missed dose. He'd been given medical and psychological support from time to time, but the support would consist of giving him stronger pills, and he'd suffer bouts of constipation or excessive drooling. The excessive drooling didn't help him at all with placement either.

Marc sighed and decided to open the card. He smiled when he saw Libby's handwriting. Libby was the only person that he'd really connected with in his short, screwed-up life. Her picture fell out of the card as he opened it. She must have known Marc was going to be leaving for a long time and wanted to give him something to remember her. Marc picked up the picture and felt a little happier looking at her bubbly and goofy grin. He remembered when she was left with his foster home. Marc didn't know the details of Libby's past other than that her mom was an ICU nurse and was killed in a late-night mugging as she left the hospital. Libby had no relatives come forth to claim her, and she was put into the foster care system.

Marc had felt protective of her the minute she'd walked through the door. Marc had often worried about the way their foster father looked at Libby every time his wife went out of the room. She was a decent woman, but her husband gave Marcus the creeps.

BURP!

Marc looked up from what he was doing to see Henry throw an empty can of beer against the wall into a small trash can overflowing with other cans. Beer stained the wall from its excessive use as a backboard. Henry was wearing his usual attire, consisting of a pair of navy pants held up by suspenders that wrapped around his bulging gut. Even with the suspenders, his pants seemed to be revolting, trying to get away from the stench of old sweat, leaving his crack visible. Marcus didn't think he bothered with any nice clothes—except for the one time social services held the meeting for his new placement.

Images of Anne, his Social Services agent, explaining his relocation ran through his mind.

"Now Marcus, Henry will be your new foster parent," Anne explained. "Let's try to be a little appreciative this time for the sacrifice he's making to provide you a good home." She looked at him, eyes burning through her big-rimmed glasses. "No more acting up, you understand?"

Marc assumed she was referring to his last foster home, where he had beat his foster dad, a sixty-year-old man, to within an inch of his life, for trying to molest the other foster child, eight-year-old Libby. Marc couldn't let him hurt her.

Fucking system, he thought as he stared at Henry with disgust. A rerun episode of *Married with Children* was on. Henry's giant pit bull was lying on the floor next to the man's chair. The dog looked up at Marc with its sad eyes. *You and me pooch, we're both stuck in this shithole with nowhere to go.* If only he had the chance to get out on his own. It was obvious Henry wasn't going to help him in any way.

Henry turned and noticed Marc staring at him. "What the fuck do you want, boy?"

He shook his head.

Henry scratched his fat belly. "You and me, we need to have a talk. But first, go grab me a beer out of the fridge."

Marc sat on the couch across from him, unmoving, and said nothing.

Henry got to his feet, grunting as he got out of his chair, "You got a hearing problem, boy?" Spit flew out of his mouth as he shouted.

Cerberus, the pit bull, stood up as his master shouted at Marc. "Go get him, boy!" he ordered and snapped his fingers once. Cerberus rushed at Marc, baring fierce-looking teeth.

Marc, startled, jumped to his feet. "OK, OK, just settle down, boy!" His voice wavered at the sight of the upset pit bull. They both stood there for a moment, Marc's legs trembling, and the big dog's growl low and deep.

"You gonna get me a beer now, boy?" Henry was amused.

"Sure, just call off your dog!" Marc's voice was a bit steadier now.

"Cerberus! Get the fuck over here!" the dog turned and walked over to Henry, tail between its legs and head lowered. "Well? Get me that goddamned beer!"

Marc made his way to the kitchen. Behind him, he could hear something that sounded like clasps on a briefcase being snapped open. The kitchen was a disaster zone. The putrid smell of old garbage stung his nose. Trash and empty wrappers littered the stained yellow linoleum. *Oh boy, Marc, this is a hell of a mess you're in now. You need to get your ass out of here.* He sighed. Afraid of what he'd find in the fridge, he slowly opened it. Fortunately, considering its surroundings, the fridge was fairly clean. No real food to speak of; the shelves' contents consisted mostly of liquor and beer. He grabbed a can of Budweiser Light. *Light beer, huh? He lives and eats like a pig, but drinks light beer.*

When he was back in the living room, he saw Henry standing with his dog by his side. He made a motion for Marc to throw him the beer. Marc chucked it at him hard, hoping it would hit him in the head, but for such a lazy slob, he had good reflexes and caught it before it did.

"Time for us to have a chat, boy! Come over here and sit down. Don't make me rile up big Cerberus again." Henry pointed at the smelly seat he had previously been sitting in.

Marc walked over to the chair and reluctantly sat down, taking note of the briefcase that lay open on the floor next to Henry. The seat cushion sank, and it felt like he was sitting on the floor. The smell of old sweat made him want to gag.

The bottom of the briefcase was filled with cash. In the top section, Marc could see a DVD case with the picture of a boy without his shirt on. He had an odd look about him, like he was sort of unsure about what was ahead for him. Under the photo, it read "*Tony: The Carnal Desires of Youth*." The room was dark and the shades were pulled down.

Henry set the beer down on the side table next to the chair and picked up a syringe that appeared to be filled with some fluid. He withdrew a stretchy band that Marc thought might be a tourniquet from his pocket.

"Now, boy, I'm not just your foster dad. Think of me more as a business partner." A smile spread across Henry's face, showing his stained teeth. "See, I sell things to people that help them to live their lives...happily. But they don't realize how good the product is and are afraid to try it. This is why I need you, boy. You are going to help me market my great product. In turn, I'm going to provide you with a *good home.*"

This guy is bad news, and I need to get the fuck out of here now! Marc stood up and Cerberus backed away a little bit. "I'm not doing shit for you. I'm leaving now, so get the fuck out of my way." He had been in bad situations before and knew he needed to come across as being in control by using a firm and authoritative voice.

Henry laughed. "Boy, I knew you wouldn't understand. See, Cerberus here is very well trained." He snapped his fingers once, and the dog, baring its teeth, rushed him again. Marc tried backing away a little bit but was up against the chair. "One more snap of my fingers and you'll be a girl, if you get my meaning. So why don't you sit back down?"

Marc fell back into the stinky chair. Henry called off his snarling dog and continued. "Speaking of girls. That little girl you are so protective of, what's her name, Libby?" Marc's eyes widened in surprise that Henry know who she was.

Henry continued, "Yes, I know where she is. If you don't do as I ask, I'll have to finish what that old man started, and you won't be able to do shit about it."

Marc's face reddened with anger and his fists clenched. "You can't get away with this. I'm going to report all this to Anne!"

Henry started laughing, his belly jiggling with every chuckle. His suspenders were having all they could do to not snap, already at their limits. "Anne's my stepsister." He leaned in, his face in front of Marc's. His breath smelled of rot.

"You think you're the first? I've had many kids before. All the ones no one cared about or wanted. All the waste. Waste like you." He snickered and stood up. "No one's going to help you. If you do what you're told, you'll get along just fine." He stepped closer and reached for Marc's arm. One greasy hand clasped his wrist and yanked it straight. With little work, a stretchy band was wrapped around his bicep. In a quick motion, the needle was in his arm. Cold fluid rushed into his vein, quickly followed by a rush of good feelings.

Euphoria set in. Marc's head was heavy, and he sank into the chair. His vision wavered and he thought he saw Henry laugh. "Enjoy your trip!" The words seemed come from a mile away. All his fears dissipated, and the world was a good place. No more foster parents, no more fear of where he would be next. Only peace.

***

A white bolt flashed in Marc's eyes. Pain radiated through his mind. Some faint, incoherent noise echoed and grew louder and louder. Voices or noises, he couldn't piece any of it together. The sounds did not make any sense. *What's going on? What's happening to me?* He tried to sort it out, but everything was jumbled. He remembered from his past visions the sounds, thoughts, words, whatever, would often end before he could find where they were coming from. It felt like he had hit a wall that he could not get past. Yet this time the noises were so loud he had to cover his ears. It was no help. The noises felt like someone stabbing a knife through his mind. There was no wall— the sounds and thoughts grew louder and came faster.

Although his body remained there, his being was somewhere out of Henry's dank living room. He was somewhere else, very different from anywhere he had ever been. He could hear the rumble of some kind of engine, and the air was very cool. A strong metal door stood in front of him. The noises seemed to be emanating from behind it. He took a step closer. Then the noises and thoughts seemed to change—they were no longer incoherent. He could begin to make out some meaning.

Piecing it all together, in a way that made little sense to him, he felt two different beings, and the communication between them.

"Yes, we have reports that our experiment did work, but we lost track of the subject." The thoughts came through in one mass of images and sensations.

"We need to find it. Time is running out. The invasion needs to commence," the other being responded.

"Wait, something is different...a presence unknown to me," the first replied.

Pain, unlike any pain he had ever known, shot into Marc. His whole body convulsed. It felt like something or someone else was seeing through his eyes. He yelled. His head, under someone else's control, turned to take in his surroundings. He retreated to one of the hiding places he'd discovered in his mind when he could no longer bear the sadness of his life. It was a relief to find an escape from whatever was tormenting him in his own head.

From somewhere, the thought of the wall resurfaced in his brain. He forced the pain out his mind and focused on rebuilding the wall. Piece by piece, block by block, he rebuilt the wall. As he worked, pieces kept being torn away, almost as if it were a dam holding back the force of water. Faster and faster he added pieces to the wall. With each block, a little pain subsided. Finally, the last block was in place, and Marc could still feel the presence behind it, trying to bring the wall down. But it was secure.

An hour passed. He was paralyzed and exhausted from the exertion of abilities he had not known existed within him. The presence behind the wall faded, and he spent the rest of the afternoon in a deep sleep.

When he awoke, the front of his head throbbed. He brought his hand up to his forehead. Somehow he had fallen out of the chair and was lying on the floor. Cerberus was lying next to him, and he felt the dog lick his cheek. His vision was blurry. With a few blinks, he could make out the fat, round shape of Henry standing over him. The stink of the big man's perspiration made him feel like he was going to vomit.

"Almost thought I lost you, boy." Henry put his hand on Marc's left shoulder and slapped him with his free hand. "Snap the hell out of it already!"

Marc barely felt the sting of the slap. Slowly he raised himself up to a sitting position, trying to ignore the pain in his head. His vision started getting clearer. "What happened?"

Henry stood over him, shaking his head. "You went into some kind of shaking fit. Those drugs I gave you were some good shit, I guess!"

"No, they weren't. My head feels like someone hit me with a concrete block." Marc massaged his temple.

Henry put a glass of water in his hand. "Drink up, you've been out awhile. I've never seen anyone have as big a fit as you did and snap out of it in one piece." He laughed, his belly shaking. "Now that you know the product, you'll be making some profit for me. You need to earn your keep."

I'm going to kill you at some point, you son of a bitch, Marc thought as he smiled back at his new "dad."

Henry pulled Marc to his feet. "Go rest your head and leave me the fuck alone."

Marc stumbled to his small room, which more like a large closet, and fell to his bed. His head was still in a spiral. He glanced at the wall, where the only personal effect he had from his past hung in the corner of a small mirror. She was a beautiful woman, a happy-looking woman. Marc compared his features to hers. Like her he was tall, had jet-black hair that he kept parted on the side, a slender nose, and a dimple on his chin. She had a pleasant smile, and his matched hers. His eyes were of a different color, not the dark brown of his mom's eyes, but a deep blue. It must have been from his dad's side of the family. He didn't know who his dad was or what he looked like.

Marc would often take the photo out when he was trying to get to sleep. He'd stare at it and drift off to a world where she was there and she loved him and wanted him around. They would play games, he would tell jokes, and she would laugh. In this other world, he had a normal life. Then morning would come and he was back to facing the day and its realities. Marc closed his eyes and drifted away.

Chapter 11

"WHAT THE HELL, KID?" Henry towered above Marc as he huddled in the corner. Henry raised his hand and brought it down at him in full swing. Closing his eyes, Marc waited for the flash of light and the dull pain from Henry's powerful slap—and there it was. His head twisted to the side from the force of the blow. Marc smiled and tasted blood drip into his mouth from the side of his lip. It felt good to feel something, even for a moment. It took away his craving for the drug that was the center of his world now.

He opened his eyes to see Henry's large belly bursting from the stained T-shirt he wore. "What you laughing at, boy?"

Marc shook his head and rubbed his burning face. Cerberus sat in the corner, his large eyes sympathetic. *How long has it been since I've been with this bastard?* Marc tried to remember how long he had been dealing for Henry, but it all was a blur. This latest beating was the result of a trip to the school principal's office over the latest fight he'd started.

"Tell me, how the fuck do you let some shits steal your supply?" Henry kicked him in the side. Marc fell to the floor, laughing as he spat out the blood that collected in his mouth.

"Fuck you, Henry." Marc braced himself for the next hit, but surprisingly it didn't happen.

"Kid, I know I put a lot on you. Who was it? Donny's kids?" Henry pulled Marc to sit upright. He reeked of beer. "It was, wasn't it?"

Marc nodded, panting for air.

"I'll take care of that son of bitch. They won't bother you again."

Just do what he wants so you can get a fix. Marc smiled. His lip throbbed and he could feel it swelling.

"You making friends yet? You should have friends to help you out. Who the hell you dealing to?" Henry pulled a rickety chair and sat down in front of him. The chair creaked from the pressure bearing down upon it.

Marc shook his head. "No one talks to me. They know what I'm up to."

"Bullshit. You start making some friends to sell to or I shut you down. No more candy for you. Got it? You better make some sales tonight on the street."

Marc trembled at the thought of losing his supply and nodded his head yes. He couldn't deal with the visions without being medicated. The last of his experiences had involved pain he had never experienced before. His skin felt like it was on fire. The heroin kept the pain away at least. Marc wiped his face with his sleeve. The smell of his dirty shirt reminded him of a dumpster in the alley.

"I think we need to go a little younger on our distribution." Henry patted Marc's head. Marc needed a shower, but now he wanted one so much more, but the tub was filled with junk and needed a cleaning worse than he did. "I want you to start talking to the younger shits."

Even half-stoned, Marc didn't want any part of this. *But Libby...he said he'd hurt her.* He nodded his agreement. *Just shut up and give me some more, you fuck.*

It seemed Henry understood Marc's reservations about the idea and backed it up by handing Marc a syringe. "On the house today. More of that when you make a make a customer of some the younger kids. I've got some *candy* we can hook them on."

Marc took it from him and was soon drifting away. No more problems.

***

Shaking off his drowsiness the next morning, Marc stumbled down the street on his way to school with a bag of heroin. Cerberus and Marc had become good friends. Henry gave in to the idea that if the dog were with him, people would think twice about roughing him up. Cerberus would sit outside the fence of the schoolyard until Marcus was out. Instead of going straight to the high school, he took a turn down a different street and made his way to the elementary school, where the kids were still at morning recess. He spotted a group of kids playing basketball and walked up to the edge of the fence. *I can't do this. This is wrong.* The voice in his head nagged him. *But Henry...Fuck Henry!* He looked down at Cerberus. "C'mon boy, let's go."

The dog hesitated and let out a whine, almost saying, "But I don't want to bite your balls off."

Marc reached down to pet the dog on his head. "Don't worry, boy, I'll deal with Henry."

"Hey! You!" a voice bellowed out.

Marc turned to see a cop approaching him.

"You're that guy hanging out on 32nd Ave every night." He was unbuckling his nightstick as he got closer.

Cerberus growled at the approaching figure.

"What are you doing here, son?" Marc didn't wait to chat but instead bolted, Cerberus close behind. "You run, kid! I know what you're about! I'll find you and take you in, mark my words!" the cop shouted as the distance between them widened.

Shit! I won't be able to sell anything now! Henry's going to kill me and Libby! With the cop far behind him, he slowed to a walking pace, trying to catch his breath, but still keeping on the move. When he got back to Henry's one-story home—really not much better than a shack in dire need of repair—he stopped. He didn't know why Henry lived in such a dump, considering the amount of money he had stashed away in his suitcase. *Maybe he has some elaborate plan to spend it?*

Cerberus was looking up at him, and it seemed to Marc that he knew nothing good was going to happen in the next few minutes. He patted the dog on his head and then made his way inside the house. He saw Henry jump out of his chair and pull his boxers up past his fat ass. He had been sitting in the chair naked, his boxers at his ankles. On the TV, Marc could see two young, nude boys kissing each other. He looked back to Henry, his fat belly hanging over his boxers, the middle open revealing his erect penis underneath. Marc felt like he was going to vomit. He knew Henry was sick, but this was over the top. Rage burned through him. He had known freaks like Henry before, and luckily he had never been hurt, but he felt for the poor boys in the movie. His hands tightened into fists. He could feel his face burning hot.

Henry stood staring at Marc, confused. "What the fuck you doing here, boy? You should be out dealing."

"You sick fucking freak!" Marc replied.

"Sick? Watch your fuckin' mouth or you'll be in the next movie! Get your ass back out on the street and make us some money. I'll give you some of the special batch." Henry's belly shook as he yelled.

Marc swallowed hard. Resisting the drugs was turning out to be a hard feat. "Henry, the cops are onto me. They know what I'm doing each night. And I'm not going to sell this shit to kids."

"You fucking little shit! I ask you to do your share of work and you do this. You ungrateful bastard!" he shouted.

Henry came at Marc with full speed and brought his fist up to hit him.

Marc sidestepped, and the blow went to the door behind him. He could smell the stink from Henry's armpits. Not allowing a second to be lost, Marc pounded him once with his right fist and then again with his left. Henry fell to the floor on his back with a loud thud. He held his nose as blood gushed between his fingers and ran down his face to pool up on the floor.

"You fucking turd! Cerberus, get over here!" The dog hesitated. "CERBERUS!"

Cerberus walked over slowly to his master, his head hung. The dog's owner snapped his finger once. The dog turned on Marc, growling, spit falling to the floor. Marc backed away. But this time he didn't fear him. Something was different. He almost felt like he was the dog. The command brought anger into the dog's mind, but also a regret. Marc took a step toward the fat man on the floor. Cerberus stood, growling at Marc. He knelt down and grabbed Henry by the shirt.

"How many lives have you ruined? You will never hurt me or Cerberus again." The thought of Libby entered his mind. She was just a little girl, and pigs like Henry craved their innocence. He punched the old man as hard as he could. He felt a crack as Henry's jaw broke, and he fell back to the floor on his butt. Rolling to his side to try to stand, Henry looked like a fat beetle struggling to right itself. Panting, Henry rubbed his jaw and pulled out a tooth. He threw it to the floor.

"I WILL KILL YOU!" The vulgar man spit a stream of blood from his mouth and snapped his fingers again.

A rage engulfed Marc, but it wasn't his own. He could feel the need to attack and the hair on his back stand on edge. He rubbed his neck for the crazy feeling that he had grown fur. Cerberus growled, staring at Henry. Spit glistened on the dog's sharp teeth. *I'm feeling what Cerberus is feeling.* The thought chilled him. *What the hell is going on with me?*

Marc could feel the swell of power as the dog lunged. But it wasn't at Marc. It was at his former master. Both front feet landed on Henry's chest. Henry let out a grunt from the weight of the large dog standing on him. A look of surprise followed by panic was visible on the man's face. Hatred filled Marc's mind. The dog was on complete autopilot now, attacking a foe. Its jaws clamped on Henry's throat and ripped flesh away, tearing his windpipe. Marc recognized the taste of blood. The dog backed away, and Marc could feel its shame.

Henry gasped for breath and covered his throat with both hands. He reached for Marc, his hand soaked with fresh blood. He said something Marc could not make out, but Marc assumed he was asking for help. He stepped over his former tormentor's body. Henry grabbed at his leg but he shook his off hand and walked back to the TV. The movie still playing. He didn't focus on what was on the screen, but the sounds made him sick. He pulled the power cable from the wall.

Marc rubbed his head. *What now?* Blood was soaking into the carpet. *I'll go to prison.* Marc had to get away from the sight of the mangled man. He rushed to the bedroom and slammed the door shut. He paced the room, trying to get an even breath. The world felt like it was closing around him.

His vision wavering, Marc fell to the floor. Henry was making gurgling noises, and the sound of his arms flailing ceased. Cerberus whimpered from the other room. *The dog did it. Not me.* He tried a deep breath but couldn't inhale fully. His skin itched. Some heroin would take this all away—at least for a little while. Marc shivered as he sat huddled on the floor. Under the bed, he could see the briefcase in which Henry kept his earnings. *Take the money and run*, Marc told himself. He knew the cops wouldn't do anything for him. They would see the dog bite marks and assume it was Cerberus. He'd leave the door open, and the cops wouldn't care about a troubled and missing orphan. They never did.

Marc picked up the suitcase. It was heavy. He opened it to examine its contents. Stacks of one hundred dollar bills covered the bottom of the case. Before closing the briefcase, he noticed one of Henry's kid-love movies in one of the inner pockets. *Pig.* Nearby, a siren wailed. Marc's heart pounded and he felt an oncoming headache.

He slammed the briefcase shut and ran to his makeshift room. He grabbed the photo of his mother from the mirror and the card he's received from Libby. Looking down at his flea-ridden bed, he couldn't help but scream and kick it. He searched the house for Henry's heroin stash, but he was running out of time. A siren in the distance made his heart race harder. *God, I have to get out of here. Get it together,* he told himself as he ran out of the house. He'd have to collect himself more elsewhere. Cerberus ran after him, trailing behind, his head low, cowering. Suitcase in hand and with nothing else but the clothes on his back, he left the hovel and its dead inhabitant behind. He and Cerberus were finally free.

Chapter 12

MARC'S LEGS SHOOK AS he walked and he tried to catch his breath. The sight of all the blood soaking into the carpet repeated in his mind. *I'm going to go to prison*, he thought, and tried to push that thought aside.

Cerberus kept pace next to him. Marc glanced at the dog and remembered what he'd felt back at the house before Cerberus attacked his owner. He had never experienced such a thing. He had seen through Cerberus's eyes and felt what the dog was feeling. Cerberus looked up at him as they walked, like he knew Marc was thinking about him. A bus stop bench was just ahead, and Marc sat down to rest his feet. He put his head in his hands. It felt good to rest for a minute.

Marc took a deep breath to steady his nerves. *OK, I need to figure out where to go next. I'll need a safe place to sleep, and I'll need some H to get me by. Shit, I can already feel the need. OK, score some H, and then find a place to crash.* His skin itched, and he could feel his muscles twitching. Glancing around, his leg bouncing, he spotted a man across the street in a large trench coat making a transaction with a woman.

Marc crossed the street without another thought. As he approached, the man eyed Marc and his marked arms. A grin spread across his face, showing a gold-plated tooth. A large silver chain hung from his neck. He took a look at the big pit bull walking next to Marc and the smile faded. Marc waved him over. He cautiously approached Marc and the dog. Cerberus let out a low growl, but Marc calmed him with a rub on the neck. The dog sat down calmly.

"Hey kid. You look like you could use a little *help*." The dealer opened his trench coat to reveal syringes and bags of powder along with other various forms of poison.

"Cut the bullshit and just give me some of your best H," Marc replied.

"I got some real good shit here kid, but in my business there are risks for selling to people I don't know. It's goin' to cost ya."

Marc snapped his fingers once, and Cerberus immediately rose to his feet, growling. The dealer stepped back. "Don't fuck with me. I need some H. I would have bought it, but you pissed me off. So now I'll take it."

The dealer's face turned pale, "OK, just settle down now. No need for that."

Just as Marc thought he was going to hand him the drugs, the man turned around and bolted. Marcus was starting to feel ill and wasn't thinking straight. His head pounded. *I don't have time for this!* He snapped his fingers again and Cerberus was off. It didn't take long. The dog was much faster than the dealer. He ripped at his legs, his giant jaws clamping down on the man's right calf. The skinny dealer fell face-forward to the sidewalk. Marc made his way over to the man, who at this point was crying like a baby. *Such a tough shit until you add a little flesh wound. Then he caves in faster than anyone.*

"Give me what I need, now! You don't want to know what happens with the third snap of my fingers."

The dealer took off his jacket and threw it to Marc. He rummaged through the coat and took out a few syringes filled with heroin.

Just to get me by. Damn! I need to be done with this stuff. He threw the coat down and walked a few steps away before calling to Cerberus. "C'mon boy, let's go." The dog released the man's leg and ran after his new friend and master.

And now for the next priority: a place to crash. Marc's goal was to find a hotel that would accept an underage customer, which really wasn't the hard part when the right amount of bribery cash was offered. The daylight was starting to fade, and his legs ached. He contemplated finding a place to shoot up and then crashing on the street. At this point, it didn't matter to him if it was under a bunch of garbage or in a soft bed. All he wanted was to rid himself of his need for a high.

Just as he was about to give up his search, he came across a seedy motel along the road. The half-broken sign illuminated the ground underneath. Trailer trucks took up most of the parking space, and half-naked women paced the lot. One woman stumbled and struggled to get back to her feet before one of her friends helped her to stand. Together, they walked to one of the rooms and knocked on the door. Mark could see a large man standing the room when the door swung open, and he motioned them in. The man peered out at him before slamming the door shut.

Mark felt the syringes in his pocket and felt like vomiting. *What am I becoming?* It occurred to him to thrown the drugs away, but he couldn't gain the strength to do it. It had gotten to the point that he didn't care about food or sleep. The only thing that mattered to him was his fix.

The motel offered free internet at the lobby, which was the selling point that sealed the deal for Marc. He paid the clerk an upfront monthly rate of $600. Then he slipped him another $600 for not noticing when Marc entered a false date of birth. The front desk clerk also charged him an additional $100 for allowing the dog to stay.

Now he again had to choose from a list of priorities:

1) sleep;

2) find something to eat and drink for him and Cerberus;

3) shoot up and crash.

Obviously, number three won. He made his way to the room. It was a simple place to stay, with one queen-size bed and a TV. The place looked like it hadn't been redecorated since 1980, and the bed made his skin crawl. *It will have to do. Hopefully I won't be here long.*

He sat down on the bed, withdrew a syringe from his pocket, prepared his arm, and stuck the needle in, releasing the fluid within. He hated the whole needle part, but the effect after was worth it. The nausea he was beginning to feel that evening subsided, and so did that constant panicky feeling. He fell back onto the bed and drifted away, not caring about the chill of the room or the bugs lying in wait for his meaty flesh.

***

He awoke the next afternoon, his stomach rumbling, crying out for food. He slowly raised himself off the bed. Cerberus ran over to him from where he'd been lying nearby. In his haste to stab himself with the needle, he had forgotten to close the shades. The sun shone in through the windows. It was blinding, until his eyes adjusted.

"We need to find some food," he said as he patted the dog's head. The air was stale in the room and smelled of mildew. He scratched at his arm where he had been bitten by the bed's other occupants.

"I'll go see what I can dig up. You keep guard of our castle. I'll get you out to take care of your business as soon as I get back." He walked outside and made his way to the office.

In the same décor as his room, the office was stuck in the '80s. Marc took it all in, surprised he hadn't noticed the night before what a dive this place this really was. He'd been so worried about his fix, nothing else seemed to have mattered. He glanced at his arm where he had stuck himself the night before. *I need to get off the heroin.* Another voice interrupted his first thought: *You got about ten shots, and you used one last night. That leaves only nine. Might as well use those up. No harm in that, right?*

Marc let out a small chuckle. "I'm so screwed up!" he said faintly, under his breath. "Thanks, Henry. You messed me up more than I've ever been messed up before." He heard the clerk in the next room over taking care of the continental breakfast that was offered to all the guests. A computer for guest use was set up in a corner of the room. Marc scowled as he sat in the old computer chair. He tried not to think about how many nasty people had sat there before him.

Now, let's find my favorite representative from Social Services. Where are you, Anne? It only took a few minutes to track her down using Google. He recorded her home address on a pad of paper lying next to the monitor. He also took a few minutes to research what he knew about the shooting that had taken his mother's life, thirteen years ago in Maine, hoping he might find some information on his past. He scanned a half-dozen old newspaper articles, each similarly focusing on the gunman and why he acted as he did. Each article seemed to come to the same conclusion—that the reasons were unexplainable. *Typical news. No answers to questions. They just lead you to more questions.* But there was one article dated a few weeks after the shooting that stood out to him.

"Jack Connor, who saved an unnamed baby from the shooting, has been moved out of the critical care ward. Had it not been for the doctor, Tim Eddins, who witnessed the shooting and was first to Jack's aid, he most likely would not have survived. The baby's identity is still unknown, but according to local authorities, it appears that the mother was lacking proper identification and could have possibly been an illegal immigrant. When asked about what will happen to the infant next, Detective Matt Hart explained that unless someone steps forward, the baby will likely be put up for adoption. His concern was that if the mother was in fact here illegally, no one will step forward due to fear of being deported."

Well, Mr. Connor, maybe I'll pay you a visit as well. But he'd first need to say goodbye to Anne. He grabbed the paper with Anne's address and closed the web browser on the computer. Since he had shot up the night before and his stomach was rumbling much louder now, food became the highest priority on his list. He made his way into the room where the breakfast items were being served. The clerk was a different person from the night before. Marc normally would have been skeeved by the fact that the clerk was handling the food without any gloves, but at this level of hunger, that didn't bother him at all. The breakfast was pitiful. He had a choice of Jimmy Dean breakfast sandwiches or mini-muffins. The only healthy item available was the mini milk cartons. Hastily, he grabbed a handful of mini-muffins, milk for himself, and two Jimmy Dean sandwiches from the cooler for Cerberus. He exited the room before the clerk had a chance to look up and notice him.

He had eaten three of the muffins by the time he made it back to the room. Cerberus was growling at the sound of the door opening, but once he saw Marc, he settled down.

"Well, I'm sure you'll like this boy. Anything has to be better than the dry food you got from Henry." Opening a sandwich, he threw it down for the dog.

Cerberus swallowed the sandwich in two bites. He then sat drooling, watching Marc eat the rest of the muffins. Marc downed the milks he had taken before throwing the other sandwich down. Cerberus began to whine. It was obvious they needed to get him outside. They walked down the street to an alley where it seemed Cerberus wanted to urinate on every piece of trash or blade of grass he could find. The rest of the morning was put aside for taking a shower.

He lifted his arm and took a quick whiff from his armpit. The odor almost knocked him out. *I don't remember the last time I was able to take a shower.*

He walked over to the TV, and it took him a minute to figure out how to turn it on. Like the rest of the room, the TV appeared to be from older times. The knob had to be pulled out to power it up; there no remote provided. Marc messed around with the dial until he got the news, which was covering something about crop circles and other junk about aliens. That wasn't something that interested Marc, but the clip after that caught his attention. He loved reading books about zombies, so naturally, the next clip about some professor who was studying a type of fungus that caused ants to turn into zombie ants made him sit on the foot of the bed, listening to the latest find.

"Professor Dwight Zeller has been studying a certain fungi which releases spores that attach to their ant host's brain and take control of the ant's nervous system. It then forces the ant to latch down on a twig, where it then kills its host, forming a twig like growth on the host's head. The mold grows and the cycle continues. This is an interesting find in the field of mind-control."

He was so into the whole zombie news that he was depressed when the bit was over. He stood up and took off his clothes, throwing them on the floor, and then made his way to the bathroom.

The curtain to the shower was stained yellow. When he moved it aside to peer into the tub, he could see the vinyl was not in much better shape. The ceiling above was stained, and hair was stuck to it. *How the hell do people get hair on the ceiling?* His stomach turned thinking about how dirty everything was. With some effort, he turned the dial to start the water. The pipes groaned, and brown water shot out from the shower head.

"Now that is luxury!" he sighed.

After a minute, the water seemed to clear, and he stepped into the bathtub. The water, as nasty as the sight was at first, felt great. It almost felt as though all the bad things in his life were being washed away. There were some complimentary bottles of soap on the tray. He squeezed the shampoo bottle until he could get the two drops of soap within onto his palm.

FLASH! THUNK!

Marc lay in the tub, facing the ceiling, water hitting his chest. He was staring out, unblinking. A figure loomed above him. Marc tried to focus but he could not. Mist from the water blurred his vision. An angular and misshapen face peered down at him.

"You are part of us, yet you do not know us. Who are you?"

A skinny arm reached toward him, and Marc could feel its hand brush his face.

Images raced through his mind. He felt like he was on a rollercoaster, traveling down a steep slope. He was in the dark and lights were flying by him at immense speed. Images of a place like Earth—but not Earth—came to him. Beings that looked human—but not human—were building structures. The land became more populous.

The beings changed. They began looking less human and more similar to each other. Their hair disappeared, their features morphed, their noses turned to two black holes; their fingers lengthened and become skinnier, and their muscles shrank.

The hand retracted, and Marc realized he was staring into the eyes of such a being. His head throbbed, yet he still was unable to move.

The being's black eyes widened. "This can't be! Get out of my head, human." The figure wrapped its bony hands around its head and closed its eyes. "Stop searching."

The images increased in speed, as did the pain Marc felt in his mind. He saw images of what he thought were the men of the race dying. Their scientists raced to find a cure to save what remained of the male gene, but they were unsuccessful. The women became the last of the species, as pollution had destroyed the male sex. The race became divided, split into what he perceived to be two factions. One had a leader in robes and symbolic jewelry. Creatures knelt with her in what appeared to be prayer. The other was a group much different from the first. They built machinery that spewed filth into the sky. There was a leader for that side as well. She sat upon a throne, surrounded by electronic panels, yet she did not use them. Her followers did her bidding, yet she did not speak to them. Somehow she communicated with them and they just reacted.

Marc focused on the figure towering above him, garbed in a silvery suit, still holding its head. It was her. It was the leader he saw in his vision. Marc realized he was in too deep, but he couldn't pull away or shut his mind down. It was as if he were being pulled into a dark abyss.

The group he decided to think of as the scientists overcame those who were believers in religion. Members of the religious faction who would not accept the scientific leader were killed. Their leader, in her robes and symbolic jewelry, was brought to kneel in front of the head of the science division, who still sat at the blinking panels. She did not move or look at the alien kneeling before her. She stared into space, unblinking. Something was odd about her eyes; they began to turn black. The alien kneeling before her began spewing light from her eyes, nose, and mouth, her body braced with extreme pain.

A moment passed. What had once been a strong being, full of life, strength, and faith was now only ash. It fell slowly to the ground. The followers of the slain ruler who chose to change sides lined up at various facilities, where they were injected with some sort of fluid. Some died, some became comatose, and the rest survived but were different in a way Marc could not decipher.

The images came faster and faster. The being in front of him hollered and vanished. He could not keep up with the information flowing through him. His head hurt. Blood ran from his nose and his body was shaking. Blackness followed.

Chapter 13

When Marc awoke, Cerberus was sitting by the tub, staring at him with his big, sad eyes. The big dog let out a whimper. His tail wagged when he saw his master open his eyes.

"It's OK, boy. I'm OK." The water running onto him was cool. *Shit, how long have I been out?* He got to his feet, his head ringing with pain. He turned off the water and stepped out to dry off, nearly falling when exiting the tub. The room spun, and Marc had to close his eyes a moment longer as spots dotted his vision. "What the hell was that all about?" Marc tried to recall if he had taken any heroin. Perhaps he forgot about it.

When he walked to the bedroom, the clock read 7:00 PM. When he had last checked the time, he was watching the 5:00 news. "Damn! Two hours!" Glancing at the bed, he saw Henry's briefcase strewn open. Memories of Anne dropping him off with Henry surfaced and his hands clenched. Nails dug into his palms. She was the beginning of all his drug use. She needed to be stopped from ever harming a child again. *I may be a messed-up kid, but I can stop her from hurting anyone else.*

Marc grabbed his clothes, got dressed, and phoned for a taxi. "Cerberus, let's go visit our friend Anne." He had no idea what would play out, but she needed to be dealt with.

The taxi came pretty quickly. In a few minutes, it was out front, the driver honking the horn. Marc grabbed a few syringes of heroin and some cash. Before he closed the suitcase, he saw the DVD labeled "***Tony***" under a strap running across the top section of the brief case. *I guess I might be able to use this,* he thought. Marc hurried to get outside before the taxi driver changed his mind about waiting for a fare in this part of town.

He and the dog hopped into the cab. Marc told the driver to drop him off at the mall near Anne's address. There was little chatting. Marc was not in a mood for talking. His head still throbbed. He stopped his leg from bouncing and tried to calm his jitters.

After paying the driver and tipping well, Marc and Cerberus stepped out of the taxi. He looked down at Cerberus standing next to him. "OK, boy. I need to go in and get a few things, but you have to stay here. Sit! Stay!"

Cerberus looked up at him with the depressed look he put on whenever Marc left the dog alone. Marc sighed and entered the mall. It was a fairly small shopping center. He needed to get some new clothes—his stunk beyond cleaning—as well as some other things.

At a small clothing store, he picked up a new set of clothes and found a restroom to change. His old clothes went straight into the trash can. It felt so good to have something clean and new. He hadn't had any new clothes for a long time.

The food court was fairly quiet. He bought a sandwich for him and one for Cerberus. When Marc got outside, the dog stood up, wagging his tail. Marc hailed another taxi, and they were on their way to see Anne, cramming the fast food down on the way.

The taxi drove down several neighborhood streets. Marc noted a bus station a few blocks from where they had the cabbie stop. He and the dog stepped out, and the driver pointed to the house across the street. Marc paid the driver and crossed the road. The lights to the house were on, and Anne was out on the porch smoking a cigarette. She had on her typical attire: a black skirt and top with a white crocheted shawl across her shoulders. She had a bob cut hairdo and large, round pink-rimmed glasses. She held the cigarette up near her shoulder with her right hand, her left hand supporting her elbow. She blew smoke into the air and looked surprised when she saw Marc approaching.

"What are you doing here? What's your name again? Matt?" She looked a little concerned.

"Oh, I'm here to see you, Anne. And no, my name is Marc. You know, the Marc who asked for your help time and time again? The Marc who you never helped?" His face was turning red. *This is the bitch who messed me up. More so than Henry. I trusted her, and she used me!* He was at the foot of the steps to her porch now.

"Oh, I'm sorry, Marc," she said with her typical smile. Her tiny lips were coated in red lipstick. He could see lipstick stains on the cigarette. "Where is Henry? Why are you here?"

Marc waved his hand in the air, pushing away the smoke and coughing. "Drop the bullshit, Anne. I know you and Henry are related. I know you were sending kids to him so you and he could make a little profit on the side." He snapped his fingers, and the dog moved toward her, growling. Anne jumped at the dog's growl.

"Cerberus has a new owner now, Anne. Henry was in no position to keep him any longer," he said.

Anne was visibly scared now. She threw the cigarette down and scrambled for the door. Marc jumped up the two steps and slammed the door shut with his right arm.

Anne backed away. "Marc, I never meant to hurt you. I swear, I didn't know." Her voice shook as she spoke. She glanced down to see a needle in Marc's hand. "What are you doing?" she stammered.

"Just thought I'd give you some of your own product." He smiled and pushed her to the wall.

She struggled, but she was a petite woman with little strength to match his own. The scent of strong flowery perfume mixed with the smell of stale cigarette smoke made Marc cringe.

"See, Henry introduced me to this wonderful product, and I think you should have a little, too. Especially considering how good you've been to me over the years." He grabbed her arm. She tried to pull away, but he gripped tighter and she cried out. She managed to dig her nails into Marc's arm. Marc gritted his teeth but ignored the pain as blood began to drip from where she dug in.

"Marc. I have money. You can have it. Please, just leave me alone." She was crying now.

"Oh, I already have money. Henry helped out in that department," he replied.

"What did you do to Henry?" she asked as she stopped struggling

"I didn't do anything to Henry. Now, Cerberus here," he nodded to the dog, who growling at her, drool dripping to the wood of the deck, "he did all the work."

"Marc, please. It was all Henry. He made me do everything!" She looked up at him as he held her, and she wrapped her free arm around his shoulders. "You are young, but you are a strong young man." Her arm slid down his back to rest on his butt as she pressed him against her hips. "Let me make all this up to you." Her breath warm against his neck.

Shit, her breath stinks! Marc shook his head in disgust. "You're one crazy bitch, Anne!" He pushed her back into the wall and she lost her breath.

Being an addict meant finding a vein wasn't complicated for him. He jabbed her with a needle and released the fluid into her vein. He watched her for a moment as she stood there, dazed. As much as he hated to admit it, he envied what she was feeling. She sank to the floor of the porch, relaxed.

"Enjoy it. Think of me when you wake up in a cell, bitch!" He took out the DVD and threw at her feet along with two other syringes filled with heroin.

Cerberus, now calm, sat down, but kept close watch on Anne. He looked to Marc as if to say "Good job!"

Marc stepped inside the house. It was very neat and orderly. If he didn't know Anne, he'd be able to derive that an older prude lived here. The air was stale, like she never opened a window to let some fresh air in. A telephone sat on a side table near a plastic-wrapped couch. He picked up the receiver and dialed 9-1-1.

"9-1-1. Please state your emergency," a woman's voice answered.

"Hi, I'm at 21 Esterbury Way. I think the woman here has had an overdose. Please send help!" he replied and then slammed the phone down.

Marc left Anne slouched on the porch and made his way to the bus stop with Cerberus. He heard sirens in the background and smiled to himself. *That should be hard to explain. The porn was a nice touch. After all, all us addicts are sex freaks, right?* The bus soon arrived. With one growl from the dog, the driver let them both on, with no questions or argument.

Chapter 14

On the way back to the motel, Marc had the taxi wait for him while he grabbed some groceries. He stocked up on bottled water and easy-to-prepare foods that would stay fresh for a while. His arm throbbed, and he kept it hidden from nosy eyes. He also picked up some dry food for the dog. Cerberus was going to bankrupt him if kept feeding him real food. It was about 11:00 in the evening when he finally rolled into the parking lot. He had accidentally left the window open a crack, and the room was cold from the brisk night air.

"Yikes! It's frigid in here, isn't it, boy?" Cerberus shook his spiked collar.

Marc slammed the window down and turned up the heater. It came on with a rumble and a bang. Dust blew out from the grill in the front, and the air being pushed out was cool.

Wow, I sure chose a classy place. He peered into the fan opening and could see crumbs and dust from where the housekeepers routinely skimped on cleaning. He waited a moment to make sure the heater would start to work, and finally the air began to feel a little warmer.

He didn't even turn on a light, he was so exhausted. *Well, great going. Only six shots left. How could I let that bitch have so much of my stash?* The urge to shoot up was haunting him. Without realizing he was doing it, he opened the drawer to where the remaining needles were stored. He grabbed one and sat up. The needle was aimed at his vein but he hesitated, the voice of his subconscious arguing. *I'm better than this. I don't have to do this.* He was surprised to see he was shaking. He wanted the fade from reality with the tide of pleasure the drug brought him. *I'll just use what I've got and call it good.* Shaking his head, he screamed out, throwing the needle down on the ground. His heart raced.

"ENOUGH!" He grabbed the remaining syringes and threw them onto the ground next to the one he had already discarded. "No more!" he shouted and slammed his foot down on the needles.

Glass cracked under his feet, and tears streamed down his cheeks. He knew what was ahead of him, but he didn't care. It was time for him to move on from this dark stage of his life. Cerberus was on the bed watching him. He fell into the bed fearing what was to follow. He lay with his arm was around the dog, his only friend. Cerberus rolled over, putting his warm, comforting back against Marc's body. The presence of the sturdy animal gave him a sense of security and a small amount of reassurance. He drifted off to a restless sleep.

***

Dark dreams attacked him. He dreamed of Henry hurting him. The man was yelling at Marc and abusing him, while wearing nothing but his dirty boxers. With his mean words and powerful blows, Henry was well fit to be the demon in a nightmare.

Dreams of the past came next. In one, Libby was cornered by that horny, disgusting pig who was supposed to care for her, the man who Marc had beaten to a pulp. Yet this time Marc could do nothing to stop him from hurting Libby—his hands were tied. Then the man's flesh started melting. He took on the shape of one of the beings Marc had seen in his visions. It turned around and looked at him.

"We need you. Don't fear us. Let us in. We are you. You are us. Together, we are one. I am Nefertiry." The creature took a few steps closer and reached out to Marc.

Then suddenly Marc's hands were free and he was running. Walls appeared in front of him, but he sidestepped, never losing stride. He ran in his sleep for most of that night. Henry was chasing him with his throat ripped open. Marc ran past Anne, who was smoking a cigarette and smiling at him, her lips coated with red lipstick. The old horny man laughed at him in the distance. His mind felt like it was closing in on him. No matter what direction he ran, something was there to scare him. He was shaking in his sleep—the panic was overwhelming.

Then he felt a warm, slobbery tongue hit his cheek, followed by a bark. He ran to the sound. He could see Cerberus in the distance, standing in an open doorway, lit by the glow of soft light. Guided by the light, Marc finally caught up to his friend.

His eyes opened as he came awake with a jolt. His body and clothes were drenched with sweat. Cerberus was standing on the bed watching him. His stomach revolted, and he rolled over and puked onto the floor. He curled into a ball on his side and he laid there for a while. The room was spinning all around him.

HONK! HONK!

Fear raced through him. Was it the police? Or maybe Anne? How did she know where he was? He relaxed a little; no, it was just traffic. *Relax. I'm OK. I'm just getting off the drugs.* He breathed in deeply, *I'm OK . . . I'm OK . . . I'm OK,* he kept repeating to himself. The nightmare of a day seemed to go on forever. It was a mix of panic attacks, throwing up, dry heaves, and paranoia. He lay there, unmoving except for the occasional shakes, until evening, when he finally felt well enough to drink some water.

He fed Cerberus and somehow got him outside long enough for the dog to take care of his needs. The light outside blinded him, and his head pounded in pain. The effort of such simple tasks took a terrible toll on him. However, he knew how much the dog depended on him and what he owed the animal for his role in helping him escape life with Henry. Back inside the room, the stench of vomit was overwhelming. He could not clean it up. He tried, and that just resulted in a larger wet mess of vomit. He rolled back onto the bed and continued with what seemed like a never-ending cycle.

The next morning he felt slightly better. He managed to get some food down and have a shower. He was up for about an hour— long enough to take care of the dog and check the news. After that, he was bedridden for the remainder of the day. The room smelled like a pigsty. He was able to sleep for a while without the nightmares recurring.

By the next morning, he felt like he had a bad cold. Regardless of what he did, he could not get warm. But at least he was able to stay up for most of the day.

He left the room only long enough to take the dog out and stock up on some of the cartons of milk from the breakfast room. Before going to bed in the evening, he checked the news, worried about what the police might have discovered at either Henry's or Anne's homes. He was exhausted from these small tasks. But at least the fatigue was so overpowering that it meant he was able to get some deep sleep without nightmares or visions. Two more days passed in much the same manner before he felt well enough to open the windows and let some light in. He did his best to clean the room.

Poor maid, he thought. Marc was feeling stronger and was able to stay up most of the day. It was his best day yet. The next morning, to his relief, his stomach felt good. *Looks like I might survive!* A new day was beginning.

Chapter 15

MARC AND CERBERUS STEPPED outside, and Marc glanced at the card he'd kept from Libby. Her address was on the envelope, and he made sure he could remember the details. Packing had been easy: the few clothes he had and the suitcase full of money. He left all the food remaining from his foray to the grocery store, as well as a hundred-dollar tip, for the maids.

His stomach was still a little off, but overall he felt a lot better. He only took one bottle of water and some snacks for the road. The sun was shining brightly. The spring breeze was warm against his face. Cerberus sat by his side. A few minutes passed before their taxi pulled up. *One more thing to do,* he thought as he ruffled the dog around his neck and they both got into the car. He told the driver the address of where he wished to go, and the cabbie nodded. The radio was on and Marc caught some of the news playing.

"Social Service agent Anne Seawall was found unconscious on her porch after an unidentified caller reported a possible overdose and requested help at her address. Police and paramedics arrived at the scene to administer aid and uncovered a stash of child pornography. Anne was given treatment for a large dose of heroin and was later taken into custody."

"What the hell is wrong with people?" The taxi driver shook his head as he pulled the car out of the motel parking lot. He turned up the dial a little a louder.

"Ms. Seawall was responsible for many needy children in her role at Social Services. Records indicate many of her clients did not receive adequate supervision and dropped out of the system. Police have confirmed that she had ties to a drug operation and hope that her arrest will provide leads to more notorious criminals in drug trafficking in our metro area. The body of her stepbrother, Henry Seawall, was found in his home nearby. He also had ties to a drug operation. His death is being ruled as suspicious. He was caring for a foster child, a male Caucasian, aged 13. Police are searching for him and ask anyone who has information regarding his whereabouts to please call."

"Poor kid. Must've gone through hell." The driver peered into the rearview mirror, and Marc turned to look out the window, hoping he wouldn't start prying into his situation.

They left the outskirts of the city. Houses seemed to lose the layer of smog on their exteriors and appeared in better repair. Before long, they were in a quaint neighborhood. All of the homes were Colonial style, and lawns were well manicured. Marc paid and tipped the driver before both he and dog were out of the car. The house in front of him was fairly new, with white paint and black shutters.

He didn't want to draw attention to himself, so he found a secluded spot under a maple tree where he could still see the house. No one was home. This was where Libby lived now, and she was likely in school. Her new family—a mom and a dad—were good, hardworking people, and they were probably still at work. He sat down against the trunk of the tree and dozed off, the sun shining through the leaves and warming his face. He felt happier than he could remember being in a long while.

The sound of the school bus stopping nearby woke him up. He saw Libby step off the bus and talk with some friends. She looked happy. *I could go talk to her. What am I waiting for?* He thought about how creepy he must look now. His hair had gotten pretty messy. He couldn't remember the last time he had a haircut. He was still pale from his nasty recovery. *No, best if she doesn't know I'm here. She is safe and happy; that's all that matters.* He watched her go inside and sat there under the tree, his arms wrapped around his knees, and waited until dark.

The air had become cold, and he was shivering in the darkness. "Stay here, boy" he told his friend as he got up and ran to the garage of Libby's house. The garage door wasn't locked, and he lifted it just enough that he could roll under it, letting it close quietly. The garage was very orderly. It was all finished, and tools hung neatly on the walls. A minivan and a sedan were parked inside. *Everyone must be home now. I hope so.* At least the garage was warmer than it was outside.

He could hear talking and laughing coming from the house. *If I'm going to get in there, I've got to do it before they lock the doors for the night. Wealthy people lock their doors, right?* He walked to the entry door and quietly turned the handle, cracking the door open. The garage led straight into the kitchen. He could hear the clinking of silverware on glass coming from another room. He figured they must be eating dinner.

Feeling a bit more confident that no one was in the kitchen, he opened the door further and snuck through, closing it behind him. The floor was covered with tile, and the counters were granite. *These people are doing pretty well.* Everything was clean and neat. The smell of dinner was almost more than his empty stomach could take.

The noises of talking and laughing came from the hallway leading away from the kitchen. It made him think of not having a family of his own, but he was happy for Libby. Off to the left was what appeared to be the family room. The floor was hardwood and there was a fireplace was in the middle of the outside wall. There were stairs in the far corner of the room. Sounds of plates being stacked and silverware clanging together made Marc concerned.

"Are you all through?" a woman's voice asked.

They must be finishing up. I have to hide! He rushed into the family room and quietly made his way up the stairs. At the top of the landing, there was a bathroom directly in front of him, two rooms to the left, and a large room to the right. He figured the large room was the parents' room. Of the two rooms to the left, the further one appeared to be a spare room since the room on the right had pink curtains. Libby loved pink. *That must be Libby's room!*

He could hear more noises coming from downstairs. He hurriedly slid into the pink room, where he saw two large sliding doors on a wall near the foot of the bed. He guessed that was the closet. He slid one side open and ducked down into a corner, hiding under various stuffed animals.

Please, Libby, just go to bed. An hour passed. The pressure in his bladder meant he could not stay there much longer. Then he heard the door shut, the light being turned on, and feet shuffling toward the bed. He peeked through the crack of the door. It was Libby. She was dialing a phone.

Must be chatting with a friend, he thought.

"My Dad – I can't believe I have someone I can call "Dad" – is going to get me a puppy!" Libby sounded ecstatic and happy to be where she was. It made Mark smile to know she was doing well.

Marc shifted his weight, trying not to make any noise. He sat in a cramped position in the closet for what seemed like forever until she got off the phone and turned the lights out. Marc got to his knees, feeling the blood rush to his feet from where his legs had fallen asleep. It felt good to be out of the crouched position he had been forced to maintain. As silently he could, he slid the door open, just enough to peer out into the room. He could hear Libby's steady breathing, signaling she was sound asleep. His bladder's capacity was just about to its max.

Ever so quietly, he opened the door further and stepped out from the closet. The room was dark, except for the soft glow of a streetlight coming through the window from across the front lawn. He saw a desk with a chair at the far side of the room and started making his way over to it.

CREAK! A loose floorboard shifted.

Shit! Marc stood in place, watching the lump of blankets covering Libby. She didn't move. Letting out a deep breath, he moved even more cautiously now. He made it to the desk without any more loud creaks. A computer chair on wheels sat in front of the desk and he cautiously moved it out, setting the briefcase down in the seat. He had removed about $10,000 before he'd left the hotel. There was likely a good $80,000 remaining. He had also written a note, which he now attached to the briefcase.

Libby, please use this for your college education, or whatever else you may need. I hope this will help you get on your feet once you are on your own. I'm sorry I couldn't talk with you. I'm not the Marc you once knew.

Love Always,

Marc

Before heading out, Marc looked at the girl, sleeping safe and secure in a home with a family. There was a picture on the nightstand next to her, Marc's face staring back at him. The picture had been taken when they were living with the same foster parents—before the dirty old man made his move on her. Libby was the only friend he'd ever really had. Pushing away the urge to run over to her and hug her, he quietly made his way out of the bedroom, avoiding the loose floorboard. His heart was pounding at the thought of being caught. Luckily, everyone was fast asleep, and no one heard him make his way out of the house. On his way out, he couldn't resist the temptation of grabbing a little leftover dinner from the fridge for both himself and Cerberus. Wiping away a tear, knowing he'd likely never see Libby again, he stepped out into the cool night air.

Cerberus was lying under the tree where Marc had left him. The dog sat up and wagged his tail at the sight of his master. He gave the hungry animal the remaining scraps from the food he had taken from the fridge. About ready to burst, he relieved himself on the tree. Together, they made their way to a convenience store where he was able to call a Taxi. It felt liberating to be free of the past. He was on his own now.

Chapter 16

Marc had the taxi drop him and Cerberus off at a Greyhound bus station, where he paid the clerk much more than the price of a standard ticket so he could board the bus without an ID and with a dog—especially this dog, a prime specimen of a breed feared by many. After a few hours, sleeping most of the way, he arrived at the station in Maine.

The air was a little cooler there, being much further north than where they'd come from. Spring was taking a little longer to make its foothold here, but the air felt cleaner. He entered the station, found a bench in the corner of the building, and napped with Cerberus next to him on the floor. He slept for a few hours before getting up and stretching.

"OUCH!" he blurted out in the middle of his stretch. The bench was not a good place to rest for an extended period of time. He hobbled over to the payphone hanging on a wall across from where he stood and dialed a taxi. When his ride arrived, he gave the driver the address of where he wanted to go.

The neighborhood consisted of a mix of homes: higher-end houses all the way down to mobile homes. *People just doing the best they can with what they have,* he thought as the car pulled into the driveway of a well-cared-for ranch-style home. He paid the driver, and he and the dog got out and walked up to the front door. "OK, here goes nothing," he muttered. Hesitating for a moment, he rang the doorbell.

The sound of someone approaching the door made him even more nervous. With each step, there was the sound of something else making a clicking noise. When the steps stopped at the door, the latch turned and the door swung open. A man, probably in his forties, stood looking at him, grimacing. His graying hair—or what was left of his hair—was styled in a buzz cut. Marc could tell the man was in pain, noticing that his weight rested heavily on the cane in his right hand. He was slightly hunched forward and was wearing a striped robe with a T-shirt underneath. Even with the visible signs of pain weighing on him, the man had a friendly appearance.

"Hello. Fundraiser or something? You do realize it's only 8:00 AM? If I don't get my sleep, I turn into a cranky turd." The man cracked a slight smile.

Marc wasn't sure what to say. His heart started beating a little faster. *I came all this way and I've got nothing to say?* His face reddened a little.

"Seriously, I will turn into a cranky turd if you just rang the doorbell for the heck of it at 8:00 in the morning. I'm making pancakes and they're probably blacker than shit now. If you got something to say, c'mon in and have one of the burnt pancakes while I make some more." He started turning to go back to the kitchen.

"Sir!" Marc managed to get out. The man, looking a bit annoyed, turned back to face the boy. "Is your name Jack Connor?"

Jack looked at him. "Yes, why? Oh, you're that new guy my daughter just started dating? Did she dump you already? She's probably having one of her mood swings again. She might change her mind at some point. You never know." He shook his head.

"No. My name is Marc. I think you saved my life when I was a baby." His voice was shaky at first, but grew steadier toward the end.

Jack stood silent for a moment, and then his eyes narrowed in on him. "Oh my God! You must be kidding! How did you get here? How did you know about me? I can't believe it!" He was staring in disbelief. "Well, you definitely need to come in for pancakes now. No burnt ones for you. I'll get another batch going." He put his left hand on the boy's shoulder and started pulling him in.

Cerberus got to his feet and started growling, and the man released his grip.

"Dog stays out here though! He can have the burnt ones." He scowled at the dog.

Marc shushed Cerberus and told him to stay. He took a deep breath and stepped inside, closing the door behind him.

As soon as Marc was inside, he could feel the warmth of the space. He felt something he hadn't felt in a long time, or maybe ever. He felt safe. *Good people live here*, he thought.

He followed Jack into the kitchen. Every step the man took seemed like it must be painful for him. The smell of burnt food radiated out from the kitchen, and Jack made it just in time before the fire alarm started beeping. He scooped up the burnt pancakes and set them on a plate to cool off before he started making some new batter.

"Go ahead, have a seat." He gestured to for Marc to sit in the nearest chair. "Tell me your story, son."

Marc sat down. "I was hoping you might be able to help me figure out some of my history."

Jack poured some fresh batter into circles on the griddle. "Well, I'm not really sure about much, Marc. The shooting happened, which you already know. And your mom, well, she was shot." He paused and looked at Marc a bit awkwardly, not sure how to explain everything before continuing.

"She was a very pretty lady. That's all I know of her. I'm sorry. Anyway, you were alone and I was sure you'd be hurt, so I picked you up and took a spray of bullets in the back—which hurt worse than sitting on a bed of hot coals with hemorrhoids—not that I've ever done that." He flipped the pancakes over once.

"I was lucky. There was a doctor watching the whole incident. He saw your mom get hit, and he saw me trying to get you out of that damned stroller. It took me so long. It gave the shooter a slow target. That doc's quick response is the reason I made it. I was in the hospital for a good long time. I had to go through a lot of physical therapy, but I can walk, which is good. All I heard was that you were put into foster care. I know it's not much, and I wish I could help you more, but that's all I know." He looked at Marc apologetically.

Jack scooped up the pancakes into a pile on a plate and placed them in the center of the table, which was already set up with syrup and butter. Marc noticed additional plates around the table. He started feeling anxious about meeting more people.

"I really should go. I'm sorry to have bothered you." He started to stand up, but Jack put his hand on his shoulder and pushed him gently back into his seat.

"No, no, no. You made me burn a batch of pancakes, so the least you could do is have a seat and eat some breakfast with us." He smiled at the boy and limped to the chair at the head of the table. "They'll both be up in a few minutes. So, tell me about yourself, Marc. Do you have parents or foster parents? Aren't they worried about you?"

Marc shook his head. "No sir. I'm on my own." His stomach grumbled as the smell of pancakes reached his nose.

Jack must have heard it because he reached over and moved the stack of pancakes next to the plate in front of Marc. His eyes showed concern as he spoke. "You go ahead and eat, Marc. You must be hungry."

He was right about that. Marc ate the whole stack of pancakes while Jack made some more. When the next batch was done, Jack sat back down at the table. He watched the boy for a minute. The silence was a bit awkward for Marc. *Don't tell him anything. They'll lock me up in juvie if I do.* He squirmed in his seat.

Jack's gaze felt like he was able to read Marc's mind. "Are you in trouble?"

There it was, all out on the table. A tear streamed down Marc's cheek.

He couldn't hold it back, no matter how hard he tried. "Yes sir. Please don't call anyone. I'll leave. I don't want to go back into foster care. They hurt me—they always do."

***

Jack sat quietly and listened to Marc's story. He told Jack everything from the mean old pervert trying to molest Libby to Anne setting him up with Henry and the disaster that turned into. Marc didn't know why he was telling him all of this, but it felt good to tell someone. He instinctively knew he could trust Jack.

When he was through, the air seemed lighter, and he felt like a balloon floating after its string was untied from a brick.

Half expecting Jack to leap out of his chair to call the police, Marc was surprised when he just shook his head. "That's a hell of a story, kid. You've been through a lot. It's more than someone your age should have to handle. I'm not going to report you. I'm going to try and help you. But you must realize people are probably looking for you. I'm sure they've found that lowlife son of a bitch Henry's stinking body by now, and that scumbag stepsister of his will have made up a bunch of crap about you."

Jack was interrupted by the sound of footsteps in a nearby room, which meant someone would be in for breakfast in a minute.

"You can stay in the house today. I don't want you to be seen until I can think of what I'm going to do. You need to trust me, though. I'm not like those other people, Marc." Jack's voice was calm and collected.

"Mmm . . . I smell pancakes!"

Marc looked up to see a pretty girl, roughly the same age as him, standing in the doorway.

"Oh! Who . . ." She looked down and realized she was in her nightgown. Her face flushed with embarrassment. She turned around and rushed back to her room. Marc could hear her slam the door.

"Not exactly the best introduction, but that was my daughter." Jack didn't seem the least bit surprised at the situation.

They heard more footsteps, and this time it was a pretty woman about the same age as Jack. Her features were very similar to those of the younger girl. The woman stopped when she saw the boy sitting at the table. *At least this one is in more than a nightgown.* Marc squirmed in his chair, unable to think of how to introduce himself. He noticed her looking at the marks healing on his arm, and he moved it to the side to try and hide the bruises. Luckily, Jack spoke up before he had to.

"Hi, honey. This is Marc." He gestured towards Marc. "Marc, this is my wife, Adrianna." He nodded at the woman, who looked confused about why some kid was in her house so early in the morning.

It's time to leave. This is getting to be too much. But before Marc could stand up and make his escape, Jack stirred the air more than he could have ever imagined.

"Marc was the baby I helped at the mall, and he has no parents. He's been through a lot and has escaped some pretty bad stuff. I told him he could stay with us."

Chapter 17

Adrianna's jaw dropped at the news Jack had just unloaded on her. "Jack, are you serious? Is this a joke?" She smiled uncomfortably, expecting it all was some kind of prank.

Jack took a deep breath and shook his head no.

"You can't just make that kind of decision without first talking it over with me and our daughter! We need to talk about this in private." She looked furious.

Oh, she's mad. No way I'll ever recover from this one. Jack stood still and quiet while she vented some more.

"Unbelievable! Have you ever thought someone might be looking for him?" She clenched her fist and tried to regain her composure.

Jack looked over at Marc, pleading for him to speak up on his own behalf.

Marc looked away when he saw Jack drawing attention to him. *I dug this hole by myself,* Jack thought and took a little step toward his wife. "Honey, Marc doesn't have anyone. He's been in foster care for a long time and has been hurt a lot. It's been rough for him for a long time. Let's go talk about it in the other room."

Adrianna looked at Marc, who was still sitting at the table and looking down at the floor, his face red with embarrassment. She shook her head and walked off in a fury.

"Marc, please stay put. She'll be fine." Jack turned and walked out of the room, dreading the hurricane he was about to face.

When he entered their bedroom, his wife's back was turned toward him. He cautiously stepped closer. *Careful now. Not too fast, but not too slow. It's all an art!* He reached out and put a hand on her shoulder. She shrugged it off. He cleared his throat before speaking.

"I'm sorry, honey. I should have talked with you first. But I can't just turn him away when he's obviously desperately reaching out for help," he spoke to her back. It is always hard to speak to someone's back, even the pretty ones. She was crying now. *Oh damn. Tears! I'm never good at this crying stuff.*

She turned around to face him. "I don't know if I can have that boy in my house. If he and his mom hadn't been there that day at the mall, you'd still be fine. You would have hidden, and you wouldn't have been shot. You wouldn't be in the pain you are in. I'd never have had to go to the hospital in the ambulance, afraid that you might die. How can you expect me to forgive him for almost taking away the man I love?" Her tears were flowing faster now.

He felt his eyes starting to well up a bit with tears as well. *Why does she have to cry? I can deal with a lot, but not her crying.* He reached out to hug her, but she backed away.

Jack kept his voice quiet and soothing. "You can't know that. Maybe it would have been worse. Maybe he would have killed me instead. But it really doesn't matter anyway. All it comes down to is that there is a boy in our house who needs our help. Just give it a little time, and when he's able to he can move on. Just give him a chance. He seems like a good kid who's had a rough time and is just trying to get by. If he turns out to be a bad apple, he's on his own." He sighed, "I took those bullets so that kid could live. Let's not waste that by turning our backs on him now."

"What if people are looking for him? What about school? How can we explain his being here?" She shook her head.

"I know. I was thinking about that, too. But I don't think anyone is looking for him. And if they do, we'll just say he needed a place to stay. I can try and teach him things. I'm bored anyway. Plus, he can do some things around here that need to be done." He could tell she still wasn't close to being happy with the situation.

"I don't like it at all, Jack. I'm afraid I won't be nice around him. He may be a good kid, but this whole thing has caused you so much pain. It has haunted us all these years. You're back hurts all the time. With him here, I am afraid we will constantly relive that terrible day when our lives were turned upside down and we almost lost you. I know the boy did not do this to you, but I can't help this terrible anger I feel. Plus, did you even notice the marks on his arms?"

Jack looked confused. "What marks?"

"His arms are bruised—and they aren't just bruises, Jack. They're from needles—he must be using drugs." Her face showed the worry she was feeling.

Jack sighed. "OK. If we find anything like that, we'll deal with it. Then he'll have to go."

"What about Ashley? I don't want her exposed to an addict. I don't want her to think we condone that behavior by letting a druggie live under our roof. What about the danger a drug addict could put us all in?" she asked.

"I'll watch him. Ashley is a smart girl. She takes after her mom." He reached out and pulled her close in an embrace.

***

They spent an hour going back and forth about what to do before they finally went back to the kitchen, where Marc was playing with the syrup on his plate. Holding Adrianna's hand tightly, Jack was relieved he didn't have to deal with the "ignore" mode she would get in when she got really upset. She'd sulk for quite some time, totally ignoring him.

"OK, Marc. Here's the deal. You are free to stay with us, but you won't be able to do much that might bring attention to yourself. We're risking a lot by letting you stay here. Once you're sixteen, you can apply to be legally on your own. But if you do anything that causes us to lose trust in you, we're going to have to kick you out. We know you've had some drug issues. We will not put up with any drug behavior. Period." He let go of his wife's hand, walked over to an empty chair, and fell into it with a grimace.

Jack continued, "You can sleep in the guestroom. Your dog can stay in the garage." He reached to the plate of cold pancakes, throwing one onto the plate in front of him and then proceeding to load it with butter and syrup.

"Sir, I promise I won't do anything stupid. I'll only stay until I can figure out what I'm going to do next. I'm clean now. It's been a struggle, but I won't use. I never wanted that to begin with," His face brightened at the thought that he didn't need to search for a place to stay—at least for the immediate future.

"Psst! Mom!" A whisper came from behind the doorway where Adrianna was standing. She turned her head. "Is he still there? What's going on?"

Her mom shook her head. "Come on, just get over here and introduce yourself!" She turned back to look at Marc and rolled her eyes.

"Mom! What's going on?" The whisper was a bit louder now. Adrianna turned and left the kitchen.

"NO, stop!" The younger girl was back, this time dressed and being pushed through the doorway by her mom.

"This is our daughter, Ashley," Jack told Marc.

"Hi! Ah, what are you doing here, anyway?" She waved at Marc, sitting at the table.

Not knowing what to say or think at this point, all Marc could do was respond with a wave and a small smile.

"Marc is going to be staying here for a bit. He's your unofficially adopted brother." Jack grinned.

She was speechless.

Chapter 18

Breakfast was awkward, and Marc felt bad for intruding. Jack was going out of his way once again for him, and Marc could sense the unease he was causing Adrianna. *This is it. I need to stay clean. This is my chance to do better for myself,* he thought as he gave Cerberus the old, burned pancakes and walked him into the garage. Jack was adamant on Cerberus staying out of the house. Marc opened the door and immediately noticed all the tools arranged neatly against the walls. There a four-wheeler parked inside. Marc led Cerberus inside and looked over the ATV. The fuel tank was full, and the vehicle was spotless.

"This is your room, Cerb. Promise me you'll be good." He patted the dog on its head, and the dog lapped his arm.

Jack showed Marc around the house, pointing out where everything was located. Ashley was in her room, still coping with the fact that some strange boy was going to be living with them. Marc could tell he wasn't that welcomed by Adrianna either. *One excuse and she'll have me out on my own again. I can't screw this up!* They stopped at the end of the hallway, and Jack opened the door in front of them. The room was small but neat and pleasant.

"Here is your room, Marc. I know it's all a lot to take in for you. Please understand, it's a lot to take in for us as well. Ashley will be fine. Just make sure you don't use the bathroom when she intends to take a shower. You'll never live that one down." He crossed his arms. "Now, Adrianna means the best, Marc, but it's going to take her some time to adjust to all of this. She can be the best friend you can have, so give her some time and space. Eventually, she'll come around, if you treat everyone well. She's very protective of her family." He sighed.

Jack continued, "As far as the dog goes, I'm sure he's a good dog, but he's a dangerous breed. I don't want to see him in the house. He can stay out in the garage, and I don't want to see him loose unless you are with him. Adrianna would have my balls in a vice if she ever caught wind that he was in her house. OK?"

Marc nodded his head yes. "Thank you, sir. I'm exhausted. I'd like to rest for a bit."

Jack patted him on the back. "Sure. The bed is all made up. If you get hungry, you know where everything is."

Marc stepped into the room, and Jack closed the door behind him. *Finally. I can relax a little.* He could feel how tense he was. He never was good at dealing with people, or at least nice people. He didn't think he'd ever really known any nice people other than Libby. He reached into his pocket and took out her card. Safely inside was the picture of his mom. He walked over to the bed and collapsed onto it, immediately drifting off to sleep.

***

His dreams were filled with the strange images he had come to expect. A bolt of pain shot through his head, starting in the front and then slicing through to the back. It felt like an arrow pierced his brain. Sounds flowed through the fog, and he followed them. As the sounds grew stronger, the fog would clear a bit. The air was permeated with the familiar humming noise he had heard before. The images, filled with music, textures, and aromas, attacked all his senses; yet the pain he felt earlier was decreasing. He began deciphering things he had not understood before through the incredible amount of information flowing to him. He felt like he was becoming a hub of information—almost as though he were a central connector where multiple points were communicating. The feeling of being part of a large community filled him. He was not simply Marc, but instead one of many.

"Track this subject. It is dangerous and is a threat to us. It senses us and sees what we see. It can know what we know. It must be disabled, and it must be studied. While it exists, the invasion could be impeded. It has left traces in our memory. It cannot happen again." Nefertiry's familiar voice played in his mind.

"This node has located the subject," another voice responded as an image of himself appeared in his mind, followed by those of Jack with his family as well as various landmarks.

"JACK!" Rage grew within Marc, and he felt a surge of energy ripple out through whatever this connection was.

"It's here! It needs to be stopped! Send some scouts to analyze the area and then bring it in. Functioning or not, we need to be sure it is eliminated," Nefertiry commanded.

He could feel the vibrations of something ferocious heading his way from all directions. Powerful energy, enough to turn his head to a pile of Jell-O was en route to him, and he did not know what to do. He felt like a stranded ship surrounded by giant waves at their peak, ready to crash down on the disabled vessel. At that moment, he imagined a whirlpool with the promise of safety at its base. The waves were falling now, just above him, but the whirlpool's current was strong, and he spun down, faster and faster, until finally the waves above were out of sight.

He woke the next day, late in the morning. His pillow was soaked with sweat, and his top lip tasted of blood.

Chapter 19

Marc shook his head as he sat up on the edge of the bed. *OK, I'm officially insane now. These visions are happening more and more often, and they seem so real. I need to get some help.* He slowly got to his feet.

"Yup, I do need to get some help," he muttered under his breath as he stepped to the nearest window. The shade was drawn, and light was spilling through either side. He grabbed the pull string and pulled the shade up. It was a beautiful spring day with big, puffy clouds. He figured from where the sun was positioned it had to be close to noon. He saw the flicker of a small shadow move at the tree line of the backyard. When he focused in on where he thought he saw the movement, he was pretty sure he could make out a human shape. He or she just seemed to be standing there, staring at his window, but just far enough in the cover of the trees that Marc was not sure if that truly was what he was seeing. *Must be that insanity thing I was thinking about a minute ago. Well, if I'm nuts, what does it really matter?* Still feeling a bit uncomfortable at the thought that either someone really was staring at him, or that he really was losing his mind, he decided some breakfast would be a good idea.

He opened the door and the house was quiet save for the TV on low in the other room. Not really wanting to talk to anyone at the moment, his head still hurting, he tried his best to make as little noise as possible as he made his way down the hallway to the kitchen. *Nice job! Now just grab some food and go back to my room. Simple.* He opened the door to the fridge and cringed as a small bowl that was sitting on the refrigerator door shelf slipped and crashed on the floor. Next he heard a grunt and the clicking noise of Jack's cane. "Great," he sighed.

"Well, catch up on your beauty sleep?" Jack stood in the doorway and smiled at Marc. Jack looked down at the broken bowl and leftover soup at Marc's feet. "No worries. We can clean that up easy enough. Towels are in the cabinet over there. Just be careful of the glass. What's that under your nose? Blood?"

Marc nodded. "Just a bloody nose is all, sir."

Jack seemed a bit curious, but let it drop, "OK, well clean up the spill there and come on in the other room after you've eaten. I have some things that we need to talk about, when you're ready."

Marc started to reply, but Jack had already started limping into the other room. *Great job. Really making a good impression, Marc.* He found a towel and wiped up his mess. Before heading into the living room, he grabbed some milk and cereal and ate two bowls. Still hungry, but not wanting to be a leach, he decided that was enough until lunch. He also grabbed a couple of hotdogs for Cerberus for when he got a chance to get him outside.

Jack was sitting in a recliner with his legs up and his cane at the side of his chair. He was flipping through the channels and stopped at some religion channel. Marc found a spot on the couch next to the chair.

"Ha! Can you believe this crap?" Jack pointed at the TV. A relatively handsome man was on a podium preaching about being good to one another before he casually threw in a pitch for how to donate to his cause.

Jack turned to Marc. "This guy, Baxter, drives me up the wall. He acts like he's just a simpleton like everyone else, but he preys on the poor people that believe his line, digging into their pockets and taking whatever money they have. All this done in the name of God." He seemed really aggravated. "And he's up there spouting about being good to one another, yet he also believes gays are evil, women can't think or make decisions for themselves, and so long as you believe in *his* God and donate to *his* cause, you are a good person. Ah, and how nice—there's his brainwashed family. What a frigging cult!"

A boy roughly Marc's age and a large woman were up on the stage now as well. Jack turned the TV off in disgust and set the remote down on the side table.

I see we have a temper. Marc nodded at Jack, showing that he fully agreed with him, which was actually true.

"Marc, we need to talk about how all this is going to work. We can't have you go to school, since you are not our child legally and we want to keep you safe from whoever may be looking for you. After the incident at the mall, I was unable to go back to work because the pain was too difficult to cope with. I started working from home with my own computer consultation business. It's been good for me. I hated my job, and I love what I am doing now. I'm my own boss. When I hurt, I can take a break. I can teach you what I know about computers." He rubbed his bad leg before continuing.

"I'm going to try to get some educational materials, and we'll do our best to teach you here. We'll set aside times during the day when we will go through the books and lessons and I'll teach you what I know from my work. I'm pretty good with the computer, and I bet you are going to catch on to the technological stuff quickly. I told myself being able to quit my job was the silver lining from the terrible time at the mall. Maybe you can find a silver lining from your troubles because they led you here. I hope so. I expect you to help keep things looking good around the house. With my bad leg, I haven't been able to keep everything in as great condition as I'd like, and I'm sure Adrianna would appreciate whatever help you could provide."

Marc nodded. "Sir, I really appreciate everyt—"

Jack cut him off. "Marc, stop calling me sir. It makes me feel like some old fart. You can call me Jack."

Marc nodded. "Yes, Jack."

Jack grimaced as he stood up. "Now, follow me. I think you'll like this."

Marc followed Jack to the garage. Cerberus barked as the gruff man pushed open the door. As soon as the dog saw it was Jack and Marc, he began to wag his tail. Jack patted the big dog on the head, and Cerberus lapped at him. Marc let out a sigh of relief.

"Cerb doesn't like strangers much, but he seems to like you." Marc smiled and threw the hot dogs to the floor. Cerberus devoured both in an instant.

"Us grumpy ones stick together." Jack pressed a button to open the garage door. "Ever ride one of these?" he asked as he struggled to get his bad leg over the four-wheeler's seat.

Marc shook his head. "No. It looks like fun, though."

Jack nodded. "It is. Hop on. I'll take you for spin around the area."

Grinning, Marc took a seat behind Jack, who started the ATV. The machine rumbled as Jack drove out of the garage.

Jack drove through backyard to a path cutting through the woods. Marc gripped the back grab bars to avoid hugging Jack. It was a bit awkward, but Marc smiled as they sped past trees and ran over roots, sending them into the air for a second. For the first time in a long time, Marc forgot about his problems and enjoyed the moment.

Jack pulled the ATV to stop at a hill overlooking a river below. A small speedboat with space for about five people was docked, rising and falling with the current. Jack killed the engine.

"That boat there is my pride and joy." Jack pointed down the hill.

"That's yours?" Marc couldn't hide his surprise.

"Yes. We take it out during the weekends. This river goes right out to the ocean. Do you like to fish?"

Marc shook his head. "I've never been. But I'd like to!"

"I'll tell you what: you settle yourself in, help me with some chores I'm too slow to do, and we can take a spin soon. If you keep helping out and staying clean, I'll teach you all about fishing and even let you drive her." Jack turned to look back at him.

Marc smiled. "That would be awesome!"

Jack nodded. "Now, I need to get this thing back before it's discovered I'm not busy painting the garage doors."

A twig snapped in the forest, and Marc thought he caught a glimpse of a shadow moving in the darkness of the trees behind them. He wished Cerberus were with him.

Jack must have heard it too because he was looking in the same direction. "Damned squirrels are out in force this year. Seems like it may be a bitch of a winter this year." He started the engine, and the four-wheeler began to roll again.

Maybe it was just squirrels, Marc thought, but the sound was too loud. Being a city kid, all nature sounds were different to him. It had to be just some wildlife. In any event, he was glad to be going back to the house.

Chapter 20

TIME SEEMED TO FLY by to Marc. It didn't take him long to settle into his new home. His days consisted of helping around the house with chores, working on whatever lessons Jack came up with, and tending to Cerberus. He didn't realize how much upkeep the house really needed until he started working on all the projects Jack had outlined for him. Marc found that he really enjoyed the physical labor of the manual jobs Jack needed done.

Some days he'd have to mow the lawn, and as much as it would cause him sneezing fits, the smell of fresh-cut grass made the allergies a minor annoyance. The simple satisfaction of seeing the lawn freshly mowed and neatly trimmed gave him a feeling of well-being. His major focus for the spring and summer was to paint the house. He would paint most of the morning, then have lunch with Jack. He had never done any painting in his life. He was sure he was doing a terrible job, but Jack would come out and take a look at the work he'd done and nod his approval.

Marc liked being outdoors in the fresh air. Growing up in the city, he never knew what it was like to be surrounded by trees like Jack's house was. After his morning tasks were done, Jack would teach him about the computer and how to use spreadsheets. Jack also began teaching him small bits of programming, which he absorbed easily. He was always good at math, and the programming seemed to come naturally to him.

Other days, Jack would teach him about ancient history. Marc thought Jack seemed a bit weirded out about how much he knew already. Marc would read the pages in the textbook Jack had bought at a used book store and would then raise questions or make comments about how something didn't line up. Jack would look at him, his brow furrowed in thought, unable to come up with an answer or comment. Marc didn't understand where he had gained this knowledge; it was simply there. He had no other way to explain it. As he read the text, he could see the events taking place in his mind. It scared him that it all seemed real and fresh in his brain, almost like had been there. When the studies were finished for the day, if Jack had any errands to do, Marc would tag along.

On the weekends, when Adrianna was home from work, they often took the boat out fishing. Maintaining the boat was a job Jack enjoyed doing, but he was finding it more and more difficult, so he began teaching Marc about that as well. The smells from the forest path down to the river filled Marc with a joy that words could not adequately describe. It gave him a rush of pure happiness.

Ashley mostly kept to herself, except for the weekend excursions on the boat, which she looked forward to like the rest of the family. She often caught the biggest fish of the day. Most of the time she was busy with her schoolwork and different activities, but she seemed to be adapting to Marc being around.

When Adrianna would come home from her job, she always seemed surprised at how much work had been done and how much Jack and Marc seemed to be helping each other both physically and emotionally. Jack obviously enjoyed helping Marc, and Marc, in turn, loved learning everything he could from Jack. Marc could tell Adrianna still didn't trust him, but he did everything he could to ease her worries. He kept Cerberus in the garage away from the family, and would always be around when the dog was outside. Marc made sure he did not make much of a mess and kept his room tidy. So long as Adrianna was content, he felt he was safe.

Each day, though, he felt more fatigued. His dreams continued to be filled with the strange images and seemed to last longer. He'd wake in the morning feeling more tired than the night before. Jack seemed to notice as well, because he stopped waking him up in the mornings and would let him sleep in.

The happiest year of his young life came and went. Marc was close to his fifteenth birthday when he collapsed one night while watching TV with Jack.

"Marc!" Jack's put his hands on both of Marc's shoulders and he shook him as he yelled to the boy. Marc opened his eyes, dazed. A rush of blood poured from his nose and covered his lips.

"The visions...my head...I can't deal with it anymore!" Marc was holding back tears with little success. Unable to cope with the pain and fear, he could not help crying.

Jack propped him up so that he was sitting and put his arms around him while he sobbed. "What's going on, Marc? I've seen you dealing with something that you aren't telling me. What visions?"

Marc didn't know how to explain any of it, other than saying he was having hallucinations and extreme headaches. Jack sat on the floor and listened to Marc explain what was happening.

"I have a friend who helped me recover from my injuries. He's a very good doctor. He might be able to take a look and see if there is anything he could do to help without getting us both in trouble. I'll give him a call tomorrow." Jack tried to stand up but was having trouble. Marc wiped away his tears and got to his feet to help the older man get up. *Marc, you stupid crybaby!* he thought to himself ashamedly.

Jack put his hand on the boy's shoulder. "You go on and get some sleep. I'm sure he'll be able to help you."

Marc nodded and turned to go to his room, not noticing through the window that the shadow was out in the yard—watching.

Chapter 21

WHAT THE HELL IS going on here? Tim sat at his desk, slumped forward with his head between his hands. He had been dealing with a stressful day and had lost a patient undergoing open-heart surgery. He had just come back from a walk around the nursery. Whenever he lost a patient, he liked to walk by the viewing area where he could see all the babies. It didn't matter to him if they were crying or happily asleep. Either way, it would bring a sense of peace to him—seeing life entering the world when most of the time he'd see life at its end.

Only this time it was troubling. There had been several cases of infant mortalities that should not have occurred. It was being researched, but as of right now, there were no leads as to how these deaths could have happened. From the nurses' accounts, the babies had been born healthy but had died of what appeared to be cardiac arrest shortly after a routine vaccine was administered. Even more troubling was the fact that a significant number of babies who were functioning normally before they were vaccinated became lethargic. They did not cry, nor did they react as they should to sounds and light. A nurse friend of his expressed her concern to him discreetly, explaining that not even when the mothers held their infants did their expressions change.

Tim sighed and saw a message from Dwight appear on his monitor. He hadn't heard from his friend for some time. Curious, Tim read his message:

Tim,

You are not going to believe this. For the past thirteen years, I have been researching brain disorders and how one might be able to heal those that are classified as "insane." As you might have heard, a specimen of a certain type of mold has been recovered. This mold infects ants' brains in order to control their movements. I have used this as a springboard into the realm of potentially tapping into the human mind to help control the thought centers. It was my hope to use this in mentally unstable patients who have tendencies toward violent acts. Can you imagine how much senseless violence could be stopped with that kind of a breakthrough?

Anyway, the local police department down here in PA had some interesting cases where people had done some bizarre things before committing suicide. During the autopsies, strange growths were discovered in their brains. My studies into brain disorders have become well publicized, so they contacted me to take a look. Every one of the corpses—five in all—had the same type of growth. Has someone already beat me in my research? And if so, who was controlling these people, and why did they have them kill themselves? Well, even if someone did get there first, it's still amazing stuff, isn't it?

I attached a picture of the growth, as I thought you might have some insight into what is happening to these people.

Take care,

Dwight

Tim looked at the photo. It looked like a pile of mush inside someone's head. *Probably some sort of tumor. It must be a coincidence that they all had it, right?* He didn't believe that, but it was all he could come up with. He jumped when the telephone rang, bringing him back from his thoughts. Reaching over, still lost in thought, he picked up the phone.

"This is Tim," he answered.

"Hi, Tim, it's Jack. Can you talk for a minute?"

"Jack. It's been a while. What can I do for you?" Tim felt himself tense. There were too many strange occurrences happening today. *Please let this be good news.*

Jack explained the situation to his friend, leaving out bits about harboring a runaway. "Tim, I know it's not your expertise, but if there is anything you might be able to do, I'd appreciate it."

Tim let out a deep breath. "Jack, you know, if someone finds out I'm running tests on a patient without insurance and for free, my ass will be glued to the wall. I do have a friend down in radiology, though." He rubbed his forehead, just thinking about all the trouble he could get himself into. "OK, bring the boy by at lunch time. I'll see if I can swing this."

Jack thanked him and told him he'd be there at noon before hanging up. That meant he had only an hour to set everything up with the radiology tech. *Well, I guess I'll have to take her out on a date after all.* Samantha, the tech, was a young, recent college graduate who seemed to melt around the older doctors. Tim, now in his midforties, found her to be too ditzy and, to his amazement, found her to be too immature. He picked up the phone and dialed her number.

"Radiology. This is Sam." Her voice was squeaky and high pitched. He cringed at the sound of it.

Thank God she's pretty! He cleared his throat, "Hi, Sam. It's Tim. I need a favor from my *favorite* girl."

"Only if you take me out on the date you keep promising me." She laughed. Even her laugh was unbearable. Tim held the phone away from his ear until her cackling stopped.

Putting into practice what he read in a random article that smiling helps hide negative feelings on a phone call, he put on the best smile he could manage before he spoke. "It's going to be the best night of my life!"

Chapter 22

JACK WENT INTO MARC'S room to wake the boy up. He was tossing and turning in his sleep. There was a sheen of sweat on his forehead, and there was blood on the pillowcase.

"Marc, wake up!" Jack gently shook the Marc. His eyes opened, but he seemed distant, like he was somewhere else. "Marc!" Jack shook him harder, and Marc stirred, moaning.

"What's going on? Where am I?" He looked confused.

"It's me, Jack. We have to get you to the hospital." He threw some clothes on the bed for Marc to wear. "Get dressed. I'll meet you out front, in the car." He made his way out of the room and closed the door behind him. *He's worse off than I thought*, Jack thought.

The car was already in the driveway, ready to go. Jack had moved it out of the garage before he called his friend. Grabbing his coat, he opened the door to go outside. *What the hell?* Across the street from the house were three people, standing side by side, staring blankly in his direction. He stepped out of the house, closing the door behind him, and limped to the car, watching the people across the street as he made his way closer to the vehicle. He put his hand on the roof of the car to take some weight off his bad leg.

"Can I help you?" he called over to the people, who continued to stare at the house.

On the far left was an elderly woman. In the middle of the group was a middle-aged man who wore only a pair of briefs and a sleeveless undershirt. *It's freezing out here. He's out of his mind!* The third person was a younger boy, around fourteen, dressed in school football attire and holding a football in his arm. None of them replied or even showed any interest in responding to him. He heard some movement behind him and turned to see Marc closing the door.

Concerned, Jack beckoned to Marc. "Make sure the door is locked."

Marc nodded and checked the door. He turned around and saw the three people. The boy in the group raised his hand, pointing at Marc, ignoring the football as it fell to the ground.

"Marc, get in the car!" Jack turned back to the three people. "I don't know what you all want, but move on or I'll call the police. Don't try anything stupid. I may seem old and weak, but my leg will be so far up your asses you'll never sit right again!" He opened the car door and fell into the seat. Marc jumped in, slammed the door shut, and locked it.

"Who the hell are those nuts?" He fumbled with the keys and started the car. His heart was pounding, and he could feel his muscles tightening. Out of the side mirror, he could see they were walking toward the car. He locked the car doors and then slammed the gear into reverse. The tires squealed as he backed out of the driveway, swerving around the people standing in the middle of the road. All three strangers peered into the passenger seat. The old lady closest to the door put her hand on the glass. Jack could see her face, gaunt and pale. Her eyes seemed vacant, void of thought. He didn't wait any longer before shifting the car into drive, generously applying pressure on the gas pedal, and speeding off. He watched the three people fade in his rearview mirror, walking to form a line and watching the car speed away. He took a deep breath.

He looked over at Marc sitting quietly, lost in his own thoughts. "Marc, you OK?"

The boy nodded his head yes.

"That was some weird shit. Any idea what they wanted?" He stopped the car at a red light and watched the cars pass by as he waited for Marc to answer. A man with a child in the passenger seat drove by across the intersection in front of him. The boy, probably about five, looked at them, pointing. *OK, you're just making things up in your head now, old man,* Jack told himself. He turned on the radio. Marc was clearly as confused about the situation as he was, and he hoped some music might lighten the situation. Instead of music, the latest news byte was on.

There have been some reports of reactions to this year's flu shots. No deaths have been recorded. The reactions have been changes in mood and loss of appetite. Health officials have pointed out that, although there have been some slight reactions, the flu shot is still highly recommended and that it is the best defense against the flu. This year's flu risks are extremely high.

Jack turned the radio off. *OK, more to fret about.* Worried he'd make things even worse, he just kept his mouth shut for the rest of the ride.

Chapter 23

MEAGAN WAS EATING LUNCH with her friends in the high school cafeteria before her afternoon set of classes began. Her boyfriend, Rob, was staring at the new girl who was leaning forward on a table, talking to her friends, and practically falling out of her low-cut top. *What a tramp! She's so ugly.* She rolled her eyes, aware that she was telling herself a lie. She reached over and put her hand on Rob's to get his attention. He turned to face her, annoyed at being diverted from whatever fantasy was racing through his one-track mind.

"Want to see a movie this weekend?" she asked as she smiled at him.

"Nah, I have my track meet next week and I need to get some running in. Plus, I need to work." He gave her hand a squeeze. "Maybe I can sneak over after work though?" He winked at her and snuck his hand down to pat her butt.

She looked around to make sure no one saw and faked a laugh. *My God! Is that all he cares about?*

Adam, his best friend, was sitting next to him and punched him on the shoulder. "Let's go light one up before class."

They both stood up and Rob leaned over to kiss her on the cheek. "Talk to you later."

She rolled her eyes, facing away from him. He walked off with no idea that she was upset—or if he did know, he didn't care. The new girl, Amanda, followed shortly after. *Slut!* She stood up to throw away her trash and saw Rick watching her. He was sitting at a table off to the corner of the cafeteria. No one ever sat with him, probably because he was so much older than everyone else, That, and the fact that he seemed so creepy. He wore only black clothing, which usually consisted of black boots, black T-shirt, and black jeans with a chain. He also had a black leather jacket. His hair was curly, shoulder length, and dark brown. But she loved his eyes.

If he weren't so quiet, she might even talk to him. She found him incredibly cute, and she wanted to get to know him better. *But what would all my friends think? I couldn't possibly. I'd never live that down.* She turned and walked away, aware that his eyes were following her. She felt a shiver in her spine.

"Hey Meg!" A boy's voice called from behind her, and she turned to see Ted, a nerdy guy, with whom she shared several classes, run to catch up with her. He was wearing his trademark thick-rimmed glasses and always seemed to stutter when he was nervous.

"D-d-id y-you finish the r-r-eport for English?" His face was red.

"Yes, I did. How about you?" She looked around to see who would see her talking to him. Some prissy cheerleaders were gathered in a circle in the hallway, chatting about what to wear for the upcoming dance. *Great! Now I've got this geek following me around.* She felt bad at the thought. Ted seemed sweet and was always kind, but she knew she'd be picked on by the bitches staring at her. *I need to get away from this popularity drainer!* She stopped so that she was in view of the group of girls and faced Ted. He stopped with her, looking down at his feet. "Ted, stop bugging me! Why don't you go read your comics or something! God!"

Ted looked devastated. "I-I'm s-s-s-orry." His stuttering seemed to get worse when he was upset.

Meagan felt a pang of sadness course through her for hurting him. She didn't want to, but she'd never live it down if the girls started spreading it around that she was into geeks. She stormed off, leaving Ted standing alone, and passed the group of girls snickering.

"What a freak!" she overheard one of those prisses saying about Ted. She didn't say anything but instead made her way to class.

The rest of the day was the same as any other. All Meagan could think about was what it would be like once she was finally out of high school. This was her senior year, and it just seemed to keep dragging on. She was tired of all the politics at school and all the phoniness. True, she was in one of the popular groups, but it didn't mean that she liked it. She thought about her actions and how she'd treated Ted. It occurred to her that Ted would treat her better than her own boyfriend did. *Why not just dump that turd boyfriend of mine? All he's after is ass. He doesn't care about me!* Daydreaming and watching the science teacher scratching something on the board, she decided she'd dump Rob when she saw him again. *Enough is enough. Time to grow up, Meg. Like any of this will matter when you're out of this place.* She felt some tears starting to build up, and she quickly wiped them away.

***

The bell signaling the end of this round of torture had come. She packed up her books, thinking to herself she did not remember anything the teacher had been talking about. *Science is useless anyway! God knows it hasn't done all that much for Mom.* The volume of noise around her was picking up as students were making their way out of their classrooms, anxious to be off doing the things they wanted to be doing. She packed her book and her notepad and made her way into the throng of students. She let the flow of the crowd push her out of the building.

Rob gave her a ride home each day—not for wanting to spend time with her, or at least, spend time talking. He'd gladly spend time in other ways. A sleek black Corvette was parked out front. She could see Joe Baxter through the window. He honked as she passed by and waved. She smiled, waving back, before glancing away and blushing. *Well, I guess once I dump my jackass boyfriend, I might try for him.*

Rob was waiting by the car. Leaning against his truck, his arms and legs were crossed. He didn't look happy at all. "I see you're melting for that pretty boy and his fancy car." He stepped over to her, and his clothes smelled of a foreign perfume.

She looked shocked. "Rob, I just waved to him. I've known him for a long time."

He shook his head and spat on the ground next to him. "Bullshit. I know you've been messing around with him."

She shook her head in disbelief. "You stupid idiot. You're accusing me of hanging out with the preacher's kid—which I never have—and you reek of that new girl's perfume!"

He laughed. "We'll talk about this later. Just get in the truck."

She didn't move. "No. You can have that new girl all you want. We're through."

She started to turn away, but he grabbed her by the arm. "I told you to get in the truck. Now, get in the fucking truck!"

Not thinking fully, she slapped him. Not hard, but enough to make a point, and enough that her fingers stung. His cheek was red from where she hit him. His grip on her arm tightened, and he whipped her body around like a rag doll. Rob was an idiot, but he was strong. She felt the wind whoosh out of her chest as she smacked against the door of the truck, and then he pressed against her body with his. His breath smelled of lunch and old mints, happily rotting with each other. Other kids were passing by, but they were lost in their own thoughts. They likely looked like just another amorous couple having a public display of affection. She jerked her knee up, but it missed the most sensitive area and instead landed on his thigh.

"Listen, bitch! You are my girlfriend, and you will be until I say you're not. You can walk yourself home to think it over." He moved her aside and got into the truck, slamming the door.

She could hear the radio blaring inside. Her arm ached and her back was sore. *Asshole!* She stepped away as he backed out of the parking space and squealed his tires, barreling out of the parking lot. She started walking back to the school to see if someone could give her a ride, tears flowing down her face. Her chest still hurt. She just wanted to be home and alone. She wasn't just angry—she was scared. He had never been that rough with her before. She saw Ted drive off in his beat-up Chevy. *Well, if you weren't such a bitch to him, he might have given you a ride.*

Chapter 24

RICK WAS SITTING UNDER a tree, in the shade, watching all the kids rushing to get out of school. He was snuck a cigarette as he sat and watched Rob impatiently waiting for his girlfriend. *What a prick. Thinks he's hot shit, but he's only hot shit because I let him live.* He could hear the knife singing to him, begging to be let loose again. Not just on anyone—specifically on Rob.

The thought of Meagan being pushed around by him played Rick's his mind. He hated seeing Meagan treated the way that shithead treated her. *Why do I care about that girl anyway?* He couldn't think of an answer, but he did know she needed a real man who *handled* things the way he did. Rob was slamming his hand against his truck in frustration. Rick brought his knife to his arm and began making small slices into his skin. The warmth of his blood trickling out brought him some calm, and he smiled slightly imagining it was Rob's blood, not his own.

His latest failed paper blew away from where it had lain next to where he sat. He watched it fly off into the parking lot below. It didn't matter. School was all bullshit anyway. His teachers all agreed he was a waste of effort. The principal—that fucking tool—insisted that Rick should join the military.

"They'll teach you respect—something you are severely lacking, young man." Principal Hayes shook his fist to emphasize the importance of his words.

Rick felt a deep, satisfying shock ripple up his arm, and he glanced down to see he'd stuck himself deeper than he meant to. He withdrew the knife and watched the blood bubble out of his open wound. *Not deep enough to end this miserable life yet*, he thought and tilted his head back against the tree, enjoying the feeling of feeling something. Rick recalled hearing that there is a fine line between pleasure and pain. He could attest to that. If he'd learned anything of value to his life in school, it was in anatomy class. He loved learning about human anatomy.

His test scores were terrible, and he'd been held back twice. First in junior high, where it was pointed out that his social skills were in drastically bad shape. The only reason he'd made it out of eighth grade at all was due to his extreme fascination with human anatomy. He had been studying material well beyond his peers' abilities in that subject. His mother made an effort to point this out, but the school had no reason not to continue retaining him, especially since they felt he was a lost cause anyway. As a compromise, he was placed in the special education division, which in his mind was the black hole where all the kids who the schools can't deal with went.

His next experience with being held back was his senior year of high school. One night he simply decided that he was tired of even trying to fit in. He became more of an outcast than he already had been. The school took notice of that and his terrible grades and decided another year of hell would be good for him.

Being twenty years old and still in high school was not exactly an ideal situation. So he took to just sitting back and watching all the little twerps going about their meaningless lives. The only person he ever had anything to do with was Joe. Joe was the only person he could possibly relate to. As twisted— if not more twisted—than himself, Joe knew that Rick knew what was going on with his dad, so he was forced to be nice to him. Though their contact was limited, they understood each other, which no one else did.

Meagan was standing by Rob's truck now, and Rick could tell the couple was having some sort of tiff. Rob was being a jerk, as usual, acting like the macho fool he was. Rick saw Rob pull her aside, and his temper started boiling. He gripped the knife at his side. *Soon, Rob, soon.* When the idiot sped off, he got to his feet, put the knife away, and proceeded to walk home.

Chapter 25

THE MORNING AIR WAS chilly, and Rick's clothes were damp from lying in the wet brush. He had spent many days determining what spot would be best. Ever since his hasty error in killing the elderly woman at the Y due to lack of research, he found that he had become much more careful. It was a good thing, too, considering that with every mission accomplished, the police seemed to be narrowing in. Their presence on his block was definitely increasing. He didn't think they knew about him, but they knew someone in that area was the reason for the unexplained deaths and missing appendages.

His collection was getting quite interesting. Earlobes, fingers, toes, a penis, and for some weird reason a cat's tongue. *Not quite sure about that one,* he thought to himself as he watched a fish jump from the river down the hill.

A soft thumping noise approached on the path to his right. The shape of a figure approaching through the morning fog was just coming into his line of sight. Anticipating what was going to happen next sent an adrenaline rush throughout his body. His heart quickened and his fingers twitched. *Finally, that little bastard will learn he isn't as tough as he thinks he is!* He smiled at the thought.

Rob, moving at a steady pace, was now a couple of steps away from being directly in front of where Rick lay in wait. Rick could see the steam escaping from the runner' mouth as he panted from his jog. To Rick's amazement, Rob slowed to a stop directly in front of him, turned away from where he was hiding, and bent down to catch his breath. *Must be all those dope breaks you take. Could this be any easier? I hate it when it's too easy!* He reached into his pocket for his knife, but something wasn't right. Rob was taking too long to catch his breath. His panting was louder than before, and instead of just hunching over he fell to his knees, gasping for air and clutching at his chest. *No! No! No! I've been planning this for months! God damn it!*

Rob fell to one arm with the other still clutching his chest. He finally collapsed, thrashing on the cold ground, and then went still. Rick sat there for a few minutes, unable to comprehend what had just happened.

Emotions flooded through him, and he started to sob without even noticing the sound of another runner approaching.

"Are you OK?" the runner asked the younger man.

Rick looked up to see a man roughly in his forties standing over Rob's body. He knelt down over the boy and turned him over. When he saw the pale color of his face, he put his ear to his chest.

"Oh my God!" the man stood, obviously in shock. He hadn't noticed Rick in the shrubs behind him. The man reached into his pocket and pulled out a cell phone. He fumbled around with the keys.

"Shit!" He paced back and forth. "Stupid cell phone!" He put his head between his hands and stood still for a moment before taking a deep breath. Rick could smell the sweat from him, he was standing so close.

The urge to kill was too strong; his knife's thirst for blood was overpowering. Rick sprung from his hiding spot, knife in hand. The man didn't even have a chance to register what was happening before Rick's shoulder rammed into the middle of his back. The force knocked him forward onto the edge of the hill. His ankle twisted at an odd angle, and Rick could hear a pop. The man yelled as he lost his balance, reaching in the air to grab at nothing.

Rick couldn't help but laugh at the sight of the man's surprised face as he fell backward. He watched as the unfortunate jogger rolled down the hill, trampling small trees and hitting scattered rocks. *Ouch. No time, Rick. Get moving!* He carefully made his way down the hill. He could see the man had rolled to a stop at the bottom of the embankment, very near the river's edge. His face was a bloody mess but he was still moving. He was also making enough noise to cause some real issues.

"Why? Why did you do that?" He was holding his ankle as he looked up at the young man approaching him. His foot was at a disgusting angle, and bone was protruding from the break.

Rick smiled at him. "No worries, you won't hurt much longer."

The man looked down at the knife in Rick's right hand. Panic registered in the man's eyes, as if he knew what was going to happen next. He was on his butt, pushing himself backward, trying his best to get away from the unknown attacker. Tears were filling his eyes, and a sheen of sweat covered his now pale face.

"Please, I won't tell anyone about this. Just let me go." He was crying now.

Not the way I planned, but I can still use my knife after all. As they say, when life hands you lemons, you make lemonade.

The knife helped him in all things. It had reminded him to come prepared. He took out a hand towel and three small ropes from his shoulder bag. Meanwhile, the injured man had somehow managed to stand up on his good foot.

"HELP!" He hopped, but the pain was too great and he collapsed on the rocky shore, scraping open some more wounds. Rick put his knee on the man's back and grabbed the hair on the back of his head to lift it up, exposing the neck. The man let out a grunt and tried screaming some more, but Rick's weight on his back prevented much sound from escaping. He quickly crammed the towel in the man's mouth with his other hand and then tied the rope to keep it in place. The man let out some muffled sounds, but it wasn't any use.

He then moved down and tied the man's wrists and ankles with the remaining rope. Rick could hear some people at the top of the hill. He looked up and saw them standing in place. They must have been focused on the dead body and hadn't yet noticed the scuffle below. The rushing of the river over the rocks created enough noise to muffle any sound the injured man could make through the gag. He pulled the man's body out of view from the people above. It surprised Rick how much of a fight the man was putting up. He made the most interesting moves. It was amazing the fool could think there was any chance he could escape his destiny with the knife. A jutting rock form the river bank snagged the man's ankle and ripped away some of the skin, causing more bleeding.

Rick shook his head. "Why are you being so difficult?" he muttered under his breath.

The anatomy books he had so diligently studied turned out to be of great help with his interest in collecting human parts. It was amazing how difficult it could be cutting pieces away from bodies. He examined the man's foot within his running shoe. The shoe appeared to be brand new. *How cool would it be to have a foot with a shoe?*

He looked at the man's eyes, still showing panic. He grinned, pointing at the mangled foot.

"Now really, how useful is that? It's already half off." He picked up a medium-size rock from next to where he was standing.

Slugs and some other creepy-looking bugs were sitting on the bottom. He knelt in front of the man's broken foot, and with a quick stab, jammed the knife in the section where skin was still attached, between the ankle and the foot. It struck with a thud as it hit bone. The man reacted with a muffled scream.

"Shut up! They'll hear us!" Rick punched him hard enough to quiet him but not hard enough to knock him out. The knife was still sticking out of the jogger's ankle, and blood was coloring the sand.

"Now, I want you to see this." Rick, still holding the rock, brought it up into the air. A dark-looking bug with pincers fell onto the jogger's leg below. Then, in a quick motion, Rick swung the rock down on top of the hilt of the knife, driving it deep into bone, slicing through. The man moaned in pain before fainting.

Rick sighed, "Too bad. You could have held it when I'm through."

He spent the next few minutes removing the foot. He held it up to examine it. Though blood covered the shoe, it was still a cool token. In a quick, final slice, he cut the man's throat from ear to ear, careful not to let the blood get on his clothes. He put the shoe, ropes, and towel into his bag and put the knife in its sheath before carefully tucking it back into his jacket pocket. He casually walked away, supremely satisfied with the day's unexpected turn of events. He painstakingly scrubbed his hands in the cold, flowing water to get rid of any evidence of his victim's blood. He then followed the riverbank for some distance before climbing back up to the trail.

He paused, looking back at where Rob's body had lain. *I should go, but damn, I want to see what happened!* Letting out a sigh, and checking to be sure he had no visible signs of the crime he had committed, he walked back in the body's direction. Police were there now, as was the medical crew. Rob's body had been covered and was being loaded onto a stretcher. Runners and hikers were gathered around watching. He walked up to a policeman who was making sure no one interfered with the ambulance attendants.

"Officer, what happened?" Rick put on his best concerned look.

The man looked up at him. "Some poor boy's heart stopped. Keep moving, son." He motioned for him to keep moving along.

Rick nodded and walked away. When he was sure no one was around, he smiled.

Chapter 26

Joe glanced around the room before lowering his head. The podium held notecards with his speech written on them, which he really didn't need since he'd memorized it the night before. He did exactly as his dad had instructed; he even was able to conjure up a tear.

Last evening's news had announced the tragic death of one of the high school's star athletes. The principal had called Joe to ask him to speak at an assembly of his peers. Being the son of a famous preacher carried with it the burden of helping others through tough times. He naturally loved playing the part. *I'm sure I can find a way to use this to my advantage*, he thought. He simply smiled and explained how honored he would be to speak and how sad he was for the poor boy's family.

He stood at the podium and looked around at his classmates gathered in the stands of the gymnasium. He spotted Rick, sitting alone high in the bleachers, and could almost make out a smile directed at him. Joe cleared his throat and began by explaining how hard it is to accept the death of a fellow student. He went on to explain how everyone has a purpose and how exceptional Rob was in life. He was even able to muster some tears toward the end of his address. He was definitely his father's son and had learned his lessons well. When he was through, many in the audience were wiping away tears, and all appeared moved. *Damn, I'm good!*

Slowly, the students filed out of the gym. Mrs. Fruel tapped him on the shoulder. "Beautifully done, Joe." Her eyes had welled up with tears. "You are such a smart and decent young man. I know you will carry on your father's work and do great things." She smiled at him.

"Thank you, Mrs. Fruele. No need to thank me. I only work to help spread the word of Jesus Christ." He smiled back and turned to exit with the other students.

He saw Tony not too far ahead and rushed to meet up with him. He put his hand on the other boy's shoulder and said, "Hey there, Tony!"

The other boy turned to see who it was. When he saw it was Joe, he immediately put his head down and continued walking.

"Why so bashful? There's nothing going on that I don't know about, Tony." He snickered before continuing. "I'll need you to do a little favor for me. See, our friend Rob, God rest his soul, has left his girlfriend all alone, and I need to make my move." He pulled Tony off to the side in order for students to pass by.

Tony tried to keep walking, but Joe had a solid grip on his shoulder. He whispered at him, "No, no, no. You know I could ruin you with the juicy gossip I have about you."

Tony looked around to make sure no one heard and turned back to Joe. "OK. What do you want, Joe? Whatever you want—I'll do it. Just don't say anything." His face had turned red.

"I want you to start being an ass to Meagan. Harass her a bit, or whatever. Then I'll come over and save the day." Joe was grinning as he finished talking.

Tony rolled his eyes, "OK, I'll be a jerk to her. Easy enough."

Joe laughed, "I didn't finish about how I'd save the day. I'm going to beat you up."

The other boy shook his head, "No, you won't do tha—"

Joe stepped closer and cut him off. "Yes, I will. I could always talk to my dad, you know. Get him to maybe spend a little extra time cleansing you of sin." He smirked, "Oh, you mull it over some. I have to get to class. I'm never tardy, you know!" Joe turned and mixed in with the other students, leaving Tony behind, lost in his thoughts.

Chapter 27

THAT DAY AT SCHOOL was not the standard crap as everyone came to grips with Rob's death. Many of Joe's fellow students found it hard to cope, which led to the classes being a complete waste of time. Hardly anyone in the school had experienced the death of someone close. When teachers were in sight, Joe would console his peers with passages remembered from his father's sermons. Otherwise, he'd simply watch everyone, carefully making note of how differently each person was coping.

During the last period in the afternoon, he shared a class with Meagan. She seemed to be a complete wreck. He did not have much opportunity to talk with her as she surrounded herself with her prissy friends, who each took turns sniffling with her. He'd roll his eyes whenever he'd see her crying with her circle of girlfriends. *That guy she was dating was such a prick! Why waste the tears?*

It wasn't until school was out that he and Tony could run through their plan. As the two walked out of the school, Meagan was on her way to her bus.

"This is it, Tony! Go do your magic." He gave the other boy a shove forward, and Tony ran to catch up with her.

Joe watched as Tony pulled her aside and then listened as he walked closer to them. Tony had his hand on her arm, and Meagan was trying to free herself, but he wouldn't let go.

"Rob told me you're a little slut. Why not be my little slut now?" he asked.

She broke free from Tony's grip. Tony looked over to Joe, nodding towards Meagan, who was walking away now. Tony shook his head and went after her again, grabbing her arm once more. This time he was more forceful and pulled her to him. Once she was facing him, she raised her arm to slap him. He caught her hand and brought it to his side.

"Tony! Why are you doing this? I thought you were better than this," she cried.

Joe could see Tony stammer a moment, then regain his courage.

"Shut the fuck up!" Tony yelled, still clenching Meagan's arms.

Seeing this as a good moment to act the rescuer, Joe grabbed Tony's shoulders and yanked him away from Meagan, spinning him around to face him.

"What is your problem, Tony? Leave her alone!" Joe tilted his head to hint for the other boy to continue.

Understanding the gesture, Tony motioned to Meagan. "She's a little whore. My little whore, now." Tony's voice cracked a little.

Joe slugged him hard across his cheek, and he fell to the ground. He tried to stand, but Joe kicked him in his side and he fell back down to the pavement.

"Tough guy, aren't you?" Joe grabbed him under his arms and hoisted him up to his feet. "Tell Meagan you are very sorry."

Tony appeared confused and looked at Joe, searching his face for some kind of guidance. He recognized a very slight nod not to give up yet. Tony spit into Joe's face. In retaliation, Tony got a knee to his gut and Joe threw him back to the ground. Now on all fours, Tony wretched from the pain in his stomach. Joe watched as the other boy raised his hand for him to stop, and Joe's final move consisted of cramming Tony's face into the fresh vomit.

Meagan pulled Joe aside. "Please, Joe, stop. He got the message."

He nodded. "Let me give you a ride home, Meagan. You must need someone to talk to. A lot has happened. I'm a good listener."

Meagan looked at the kids boarding the bus and sighed. "Thanks, Joe, I really don't want to ride the bus."

Success! Joe couldn't believe how well the plan had come together.

Chapter 28

REVEREND BAXTER STARED AT the photo on his desk of a young man. He had just finished his compilation of one of his favorite subjects, Tony. He let out a deep sigh. *I always hate to end such a good run. All that training since he was a little boy, over. In the end, they all grow up.*

He dabbed a tear away from the corner of his eye. Endings always affected him emotionally. Sad to think after all this time, he'd have to find some other boy to take his star's place. The thought of it made him scan the room. It was decked out with all the latest video equipment, mostly purchased from the proceeds Tony's films had brought in for him. He was like a cash cow that wouldn't stop—until now. Baxter couldn't see continuing with him; after all, Tony was old now. Who wants to watch a young man? *No, they want children. Just face it, it's over. There's plenty of younger meat I can use.* He felt excited just thinking about a new star. Lost in his thoughts, he barely noticed a shape move in the far corner of the basement. His heart skipped.

"Who's there? What are you doing down here?" No answer.

"Joe? Who's there?" Then the figure stepped from the shadows, and he could make out the face of Joe's friend, Rick. He let out some air. "Rick! You scared me!"

Rick smiled that crooked smile Baxter loved.

"You know you shouldn't be here, Ricky. If my fat wife ever learned about us, she'd have me crucified."

Rick eyed the older man from head to toe and licked his black, lipstick-coated lips. Baxter took note of the young man's goth style. He loved it when he dressed that way. Rick slowly took a step closer, and Baxter could see he was wearing a black leather vest with no shirt. Though Rick was average in terms of height, he had an impressive build.

"Ah, to hell with that bitch! I don't care!" Hastily, the reverend stripped down to his boxers. Rick withdrew a pair of handcuffs from his back pocket.

Baxter laughed as the younger man cuffed his hands around one of the cement supporting beams in the basement. Rick winked at the older man as he threw an assortment of items down on the floor. Baxter could make out some duct tape and a plastic ball but couldn't see the other items hidden in the shadows. His heart fluttered and his temples thumped.

"My. What are you planning for us, Ricky?" Baxter giggled and couldn't help but rock his hips. "You are driving me mad with all those fun things you brought."

Rick picked up the ball and tape and jammed the ball into the man's mouth. Baxter moaned as he bit down on the object in his mouth, and Rick then taped it in place. He was used to being in control all the time, and relinquishing it to the young man in front of him was intoxicating. Any pain from the tightly wrapped tape was washed away with the thought of what was to follow.

Rick stepped away and returned with a chair. He set it down in front of his captive. Baxter groaned with disappointment. *I can't take anymore! Please, Rick!* he thought.

Rick stared at him for some time before speaking. "You stupid fuck! You are the face of evil."

Squinting, Baxter shook his head, trying to express his confusion.

"I have waited for this moment. I've let you have your way with me and even enjoyed it some—especially when I thought of what I was eventually going to do with you."

Baxter tried letting out a yell, but it was of no use. He had sound-proofed the basement a while ago and, with the sounds escaping him muffled already, no one would ever hear him. His thoughts raced: *He has to be kidding, right? This is just some macabre new thing for us. This can't be real.*

Rick stood up and walked over to Baxter. He had a knife in his hand now. Rick licked the blade.

"You thought I loved you and admired you? This blade is the only thing I love," he said as he ran the edge of the blade down the man's cheek. Baxter could feel the knife cutting his skin.

The pain was sharp and sudden, followed by warmth trickling down his jaw. *Oh my God! Please God! Let me wake up!* This was no dream. He thrashed violently, but it just caused intense pain in his arms. He started to cry.

Rick watched him and laughed. "Go ahead and pray, Reverend. I don't think God will care to hear your thoughts. You are not going to hurt any more boys." He stepped to the man's left side, grabbed the tip of his ear, and in one quick slice, cut the ear off.

Baxter squealed. His ear throbbed. *He cut my ear off. God, what is happening?* Trying to see through the tears in his eyes, he pleaded with Rick to let him go. The ball in his mouth was making him drool everywhere. He squealed again, louder.

Rick held the flesh that was once an ear up in front of him as he spoke. "I don't think you'll need this now. You never listened to all those cries from the boys you hurt." He threw it down on the ground and stepped on it, grinding it into the cement. When he stepped away, Baxter could see chunks of flesh scattered where his ear had once lain on the floor.

Why? I didn't hurt them. They liked it! They needed it. It was for their salvation, he thought. Rick had Baxter's remaining ear in a strong grip. Instead of cutting it, he pulled. Baxter felt the skin tugging and stretching.

"I read somewhere that seven pounds of pressure is all you need to rip off an ear. That's really not much, is it?" Rick added more force and tore the ear from Baxter's head, throwing it to the floor.

Rick sat back in the chair. Blood covered the floor. "How many lives have you screwed up?" he asked and then spat on the floor. "It's your son's birthday today, isn't it?"

Baxter cried noiselessly and nodded his head yes.

"Well, Baxter, I've been planning this for a long time, and I thought, what could be a better present?" Baxter squinted in confusion and pain.

"Many years ago, I told your son I'd help deal with his terrible father. I do like to keep my promises. I think he hates you as much as I do." Rick looked at the man standing in his own blood and laughed. "You are one pretty man now, with no ears. I'm almost done—and I want you to see this last part. You'll love it!" Rick bent from his chair to pick up a small pair of pruning clippers.

No! What now? Please, enough! Baxter pleaded in his mind. Rick stood in front of him and pulled Baxter's pants down. He opened the clippers, positioning them against his testicles. Baxter tried to pull back, but he could feel his skin snag the blade, causing him to stand very still. He felt his balls retract, trying to escape the horror. *Please! God no!* The metal was cold.

"See, I like to keep something special from all my friends. I thought I'd keep something from you that you hold dearest." Rick's voice sounded like he was on the edge of laughter.

SNIP.

Pain ran down Baxter's leg. He could feel the jolt from his feet to his stomach. Rick looked up to smile at him. Baxter's vision was wavering, and he started to feel weak as his knees buckled and he fell to the floor. He cried as he sat in his own puddle of fluids, growing larger by the second. He was beginning to feel cold. His body was a mangled mess—he could only imagine how awful he must look. How would they find him? Who would be the first to find him? He squealed.

"Stupid, weak fool." Rick's voice was full of pity.

Baxter looked up to see Rick holding a fleshy ball before placing it in his shoulder bag, smiling. Baxter realized it was a testicle—his testicle. Vomit rushed up his throat into his mouth before being blocked by the ball gag. He gasped for air, trying to clear his throat. His head began to feel like he was spinning before it slumped onto his chest and his eyes began to shut for the final time. The last thing he could see was his other ball of flesh, still enclosed in what used to be his scrotum, sitting free of his body in a pool of red.

Chapter 29

Joe sat watching the news on television covering his father's death. He and his mother had been given a police escort to a local hotel, where they were now checked in. The officials were reviewing the crime scene. It was only a few hours since his mother had found his father's body hanging on one of the posts in the basement. She had gone down the forbidden stairs after he hadn't responded to her demands that he come up and celebrate their son's birthday with her.

He looked over to see her disgustingly obese form lying on the bed, a bottle of pills open on the nightstand. She still wore all of her clothes and, of course, her gold jewelry. The therapist she had been required to see finally did her some real service by getting her a prescription for a sedative to help her cope with the shock of her husband's demise. She had been in a state of hysteria and was hyperventilating from the shock of what she had seen when the authorities arrived at the home. Joe wasn't sure if it was the fact that her husband was dead and dismembered or if it was all the perverted filth the police had uncovered in her home.

Joe wasn't the least bit disturbed by the sight of his dead father. *The bastard deserved what he got. Best birthday present ever.* Things seemed to be coming together for him. The girl he was after was falling for him, and now he could take over his father's congregation. Life was going to be good.

Though the curtains were shut and it was night, the outside light was creeping through the thin, cheap fabric. The local media was being joined with reporters from larger outlets, and they were swarming outside in the hotel parking lot. He stood up and walked over to the window, moving the curtain just enough to peer out. He could see a CNN van parked just outside the police barrier.

He had already spoken to the authorities, telling them he had been abused by his father all his life and didn't know how to tell anyone. *Oh how the masses will feel so sorry for me.*

His father would never have hurt him in that way. The reality was that he'd hardly had anything to do with him, except to share their dirty little secrets. On some level, Baxter was ashamed of his son. He knew the boy was sadistic, but he let Joe do as he wanted so long as he kept his mouth shut about what his father was doing. Joseph did, however, present well in public, and members of the congregation thought he was a wonderful model for what a child should be. If for this only, Baxter knew better than to ruin a good thing.

Having spoken to his mother's therapist and deemed to be stable and competent to speak for what remained of his family, his first course of action would be to address the media. He'd explain the suffering he had endured all his life and how this had tempered him to be a better soldier for the people of his church. His forgiveness for his misguided father would be his first step in showing others how faith can heal the deepest of hurts. Hi plan was to lay blame on the media for tainting his father's soul. His message would begin with: **"The devil is delivered through the media and eats away the purities of one's soul."**

My time to shine is now. His thoughts were filled with hope for the wonderful future his father's death had laid before him.

A snore erupted from the bed behind him. He looked over to see his mother, her mouth open wide and drool trickling down her cheek. *I'll have to find a way to deal with my lovely mom at some point. Stupid bitch.* He couldn't take looking at her or hearing her anymore. He turned off the TV and went to the bathroom to take a shower. The water was hot, and it felt good to get cleaned up. When he stepped out, he dressed in the suit he'd had the foresight to pack. *To hell with the police. I need to act.* He combed his hair and smiled in the mirror. Satisfied with the way he looked, he walked past the sleeping walrus that was his mother and opened the door to the outside.

The policeman who was standing guard put his arm out to stop him and coax him back inside the room. Joe smiled, recognizing him as the husband of one of his mother's women's prayer group before slipping past him.

"Son, get back in your room!" he heard the man behind yell to him, but he ignored it.

The camera crew rushed forward to meet him. Excitement rushed through him as he inhaled the cold night air and released a cloud of steam from his mouth. This is what he needed. He thrived on attention. Lights flashed as pictures were taken. He put on his best solemn face, slowly walked to the camera crews at the edge of the police line, and brushed aside the yellow tape. Reporters rushed forward, yelling out questions. *Time to shine!*

The woman nearest to him shoved a mic in his face. "Can you tell us how many children were hurt by your father, and how did you not know of anything that was taking place in your own home?"

Joe nodded and looked to the night sky above before answering. "It's shameful what Reverend Baxter did. His actions were those of the devil. It proves that no man is beyond temptation, and we are all fallible to the manipulation of the dark one. While my father had ultimately succumbed to carnal desires and great sin, I was shielded and raised by my dear mother to be a free of my father's need for flesh. It is times like these that we must come together as a community to shun Satan's wicked ways, acknowledge we are all sinners, and seek the Lord's forgiveness."

A man burst through the lines, pushing the first reporter back. "What will you do now? What will become of your father's legacy?"

"First and foremost, I will establish a fund for the students affected by my father's spiral into sin. I personally know one of the students and will always be here for him. I cannot erase what my father has done, but I can be here to help with any emotional needs of those affected. I seek our Lord's advice and hope to channel his goodwill to all who are suffering from these atrocities."

The reporter pressed on. "Just recently, a case was opened regarding the murder of a hiker that is still unresolved. Is it possible your father's murder is connected?"

Joe shook his head. "I have no knowledge of any connection whatsoever. Please be assured that we will work with the authorities on whatever questions they may have. Whoever the murderer is, they need to be brought into custody, and I pray for their soul."

The thought of Rick entered Joe's mind. Rick was a twisted young man and was certainly capable of both crimes. He had known of Rick's demons since they'd first met years ago. Joe prided himself on being a master manipulator. He knew he could use the knowledge of Rick's twisted nature against him. He wasn't worried that Rick might have thoughts about killing him. Joe knew he'd never follow through with it. Rick needed a confidante, and Joe was the only one his blade trusted.

The first reporter moved forward once again. "Mr. Baxter, we have some news that just broke. The boy whom your father molested has been found dead from an apparent suicide. Do you have any words for his family?"

The words Joe just heard made him want to burst out laughing, and he fought to contain himself. *Can it get any better? Another loose end eliminated.*

Joe hung his head and took a deep breath before shaking his head solemnly. "I'm so sorry for Tony and his family." Joe paused and wiped his eyes. "I'm sorry, I'm a bit shaken by this information. Please excuse me." He turned and walked away, keeping his head down as he moved back to his hotel room. Once the door was shut behind him, he smiled wide. His mom still lay asleep on the bed. He liked his new role—one his dad would never have relinquished.

Chapter 30

Meagan had read the news reports on the internet about the Reverend Baxter when she was working on a paper for her English class. She couldn't believe it at first. It had been a horrible few weeks. First Rob's death, then this about Joe and his father. It did offer some consolation, though, knowing there is always someone else who has it worse than you do. *Poor Joe. How could he cope with such a horrible father?* Joe must have really suffered. He had to be strong to have put up with such awful abuse and still be so concerned about others.

She was scared that there was a serial killer in the area, but she had always distrusted the Reverend. She'd thought he was a phony, and now she knew he was an evil man. She was glad he got what he deserved in the end. Maybe it didn't justify murder but, at least for once, someone who wasn't innocent became a victim.

She tried calling Jo, but only got his voice mailbox. "Joe, its Meg. I'm so sorry to hear the news. I feel so bad for you. If there is anything you need, or someone to talk to, I'm here. I can't believe the news. I'm so sorry. Give me a call."

She paused before hanging up. She took a deep breath and stared at nothing through the window. A knock at her door startled her, followed by her mom's voice. "Meg, I heard the news about Joe and his dad. Can we talk?" She could hear her mom standing quietly outside her door.

Meg clenched her hands. *Oh my God. I can't deal with this right now!* she thought.

"Go away! Why do you have to bother me all the time! Just leave me alone!" She was even madder at herself now for lashing out like that, but it was too late to take it back.

"OK, fine! I just wanted to help!" Her mom stomped away.

Great! Way to go, Meg! Tears ran down her cheeks. She didn't know why she was mad. It made her even more mad that she was mad for no reason. *I'm not coping well with all of this, that's all. Mom knows and will forgive me—she always does.* Meg fell into her bed and pulled her pillow close. In what seemed like an instant, she began drifting to sleep. She dreamed of her ex-boyfriend, Rob. He was berating her, and then he faded into dust. Meagan reached out but he was gone. She was happy, but at the same time incredibly sad. Joe came to her and smiled. *If only I knew what he was going through. How can he still smile?*

The loud sound of a pot falling brought her back awake. She glanced at the clock, which showed it was almost dinner time. She got to her feet and took a look at herself in her dresser mirror. *I'm a mess. Get it together.* Her eyes were red from crying. She took a tissue from the box sitting on the dresser and tried her best to wipe away runny mascara before leaving her room to have some dinner. The family was already seated. A bowl of homemade macaroni and cheese sat in the middle of the table. *My favorite!*

Maggie didn't look up but instead focused on her dinner. Her dad smiled at her as she sat down in her seat. Sam rolled his eyes when he saw she'd been crying again. Max reached over and gave her shoulder a squeeze. "Glad you joined us." Meagan nodded but didn't say anything.

Maggie finally acknowledged her. "I was thinking, Meg, we should get out of the house this weekend. Maybe we should go to the beach?" She smiled, and Meagan could tell it was forced.

Meagan shook her head. "No thanks. I don't feel like doing anything right now." *Just leave me alone. Please!* Meagan could feel herself getting angry again. She hated to be pushed into doing things when she was set on being left alone.

Max gave a slight shake of his head to warn Maggie not to push it, but Maggie ignored him. "Meg. You need to get past this and get out of your room. I'm worried about you."

No one moved. Sam looked at his dad, but Max didn't say anything. Both knew not to interfere. When the two women got into an impasse, getting involved in the situation meant a catastrophic event. It was like being in the middle of two sides firing off nuclear missiles at each other and then suffering the fallout. Max shifted in his chair uncomfortably.

Meagan pushed her chair away from the table with enough force to knock her glass of water over. Water spread across the table and dripped to the floor. Her face was red with rage. "Just leave me alone!"

Now Maggie was on her feet. "Meg. Just calm down. You're going through a lot, and I just want to help."

Meg threw her hands up in the air and then let them drop to her sides, her fists clenched. "Don't! I don't need your help! Why can't you just bug off? I don't need you!" She spun around and stormed off. She paused at her door. Her heart raced in her chest. It seemed like everything was falling apart. She could hear her father talking to her mom, trying to help as he always did.

Meagan could hear her mom's voice. "I just don't know what to do. Meg's so lost right now," she said in between sobs.

"I know, honey. She's just dealing with so much right now. She'll come around. Leave her be tonight. We'll talk with her tomorrow.

Let's go have some fun this weekend, and if she wants to join us, she'll come."

Maggie jumped in. "If not? What then?"

Max shrugged, "Then she won't. She needs to get over this. We're there if she needs us, and she's made it clear she doesn't. This will pass."

Meagan shook her head and went to her bedroom, gently closing the door. She turned on her radio as high as it could go. She wanted to drown out any thoughts of the day with music so she wouldn't have to face them anymore.

Chapter 31

Jack and Marc met Tim at the radiology office, which was empty. The room seemed devoid of any personality, and the florescent lights flickered above. *Must be on his lunch break.* Marc thought to himself as his knees bobbed up and down. It was a bad habit of his. Jack gave him a look that meant stop. Marc smiled and stopped shaking. The door opened, and a tall man with an athletic build walked over to shake Jack's hand and then Marc's.

Tim smiled at Marc. "Hi, Marc. I'm Tim Eddins, a surgeon here at the hospital and a friend of Jack's. We go back a ways. I hear you are having some bad headaches and some hallucinations that aren't drug induced."

Marc shook his head. "Yes, sir. I don't use anymore."

Tim nodded and turned when the door opened once again. A pretty woman walked in and smiled at the waiting group. She appeared to be in her twenties as far as Marc could tell. He was immediately taken with her—at least until she spoke. Her voice reminded Marc of a cat in heat: high and shrill.

"Sorry I'm a bit late. I'm Samantha—you can call me Sam. Today's flu shot day for the hospital staff." She gazed for a minute at Tim and smiled. "Speaking of which, you ought to get yours. I don't want you to get sick and miss our appointment!" Tim feigned a smile back at her. The "appointment" reference was obvious to Marc. She likely thought he was too young to connect the dots.

Sam led Marc to the room where the imaging machine was, and she had him go into the bathroom to put on a johnny. He had to strip down to nothing and then tie the strings in the back. *How the hell do you tie the strings when you can't even reach the damn things?* He did his best but he could feel the draft where his crack was showing through the back. *Really, who the hell came up with these stupid things?* Self-conscious of his bare bottom showing through the gown, he made his way back out to the room where Sam had him get up on a table and lay back. She then began searching for a good vein.

"You've got a lot of old bruising, Marc. Are you still using?" Marc shook his head. He felt a sting and then a slight tingle in his arm. He shivered and thought about the feeling of heroin coursing through his veins. Closing his eyes, he tried to focus on something else. *Fucking drug,* he thought, and then replaced that thought with a daydream about riding Jack's four-wheeler at home. She applied a Band-Aid to where she'd stuck the needle.

"I just injected some ink; it will help us to better analyze your brain activity. Now the table is going to move forward, and you need to keep your head as still as you can. You will hear a slight hum." Her breath smelled of mint, and he picked up a floral aroma of some perfume. It helped him take his mind off getting high. She walked away and closed the door. The process took only a few minutes before she was back and helping him to his feet.

"You go ahead and get dressed now. You did great."

Marc looked closely at her. Something about her was different; she seemed much paler then when he'd first met her a short while ago. He scuttled back to the bathroom, keeping his crack out of view from the pretty lady and closed the door behind him. *Smooth, Marc.* The johnny strings were tied tight in a knot, so he put his flexibility to the test and freed himself of the robe. Jack was busy talking with Tim when Marc came back out of the bathroom. Sam wasn't looking good at all. Her color was completely gone and her nose was running.

"Tim, I'm not feeling very well. The images should be ready shortly. Can you take care of it for me? I had the images shipped straight to your message box." Her hand was on her stomach.

"Absolutely. Thank you for doing this for us. Go home and rest," he said, smiling at her. When she left, Tim turned back to Jack. "We can review the results in my office."

Marc took a deep breath. *And now I find out I'm going to keel over and die with only a few hours left.*

Tim's office was very neat and orderly. His desk only had a few papers on it, which he stacked and then covered over with a folder. His computer was set on one corner. "Please have a seat." He motioned for them to sit in front of his desk. Jack let out a sigh as he fell into the seat. "Leg still bothers you a lot, huh?" Tim asked Jack as he pulled his own chair out and sat down.

Jack shook his head. "Nah, its fine. I just like to make it seem worse than it is."

Tim typed something on the keyboard and then reviewed something on the screen. He had a look of shock for a moment, then he started reviewing something else and his face lost some of its color. He cleared his throat. "Marc, do you mind stepping outside for a moment?"

Marc hesitated. Jack leaned forward and patted his shoulder. "Go ahead, it'll be fine."

He stood up and walked out into the hallway, closing the door behind him. He put his ear to the door, but he could barely hear enough to make sense of the conversation.

"Jack, I don't know what's going on here, but I want you to look at this brain image." He heard a chair move.

"All I see is some sort of circle of a different color." He could tell it was Jack, with his gruff voice.

"Right, it appears to be some sort of tumor. Now look at this image, Jack."

Jack's gruff voice again: "It looks similar but much smaller."

Tim jumped in: "Exactly. The first image was of the boy's brain. The second was an image my friend, Dwight Zeller, sent me."

Jack cleared his throat before speaking. "Tim, just get to the point. Is he OK or not?"

Tim's voice took on a serious tone. "Jack, you need to get him out of your house. There were five people who had similar growths, and they all went violently insane before killing themselves. I don't know what it is, but something is going on. The growth in that boy is twice the size of the growths in the other people."

Jack's chair shifted, its feet scraping on the tile floor. "Tim, thank you for your time, but Marc is a good boy. We've been watching him closely for over a year. This tumor must have been there for a while, and we've seen no changes in behavior except for the headaches. If he was going to do something dangerous, we'd have seen it by now. If you can think of anything you might be able to do to help him, please, give me a call." He was about to walk out the door before Tim called to him.

"Jack, take these. They should at least help with his headaches."

Marc moved away from the door before he was caught. The door clicked open, and he saw that Jack's face was tight with stress. After they left the office, Jack treated him to an ice cream, and they rode in silence the rest of the way home.

Chapter 32

AN HOUR HAD PASSED since Jack and the boy had left his office, and Tim had spent that time trying to piece together all the events that had taken place. It could not be a coincidence that all these strange growths—in the subjects Dwight had examined, and now in this boy—had all occurred at the same time. *But why? What is happening here?* He couldn't answer that. He took a deep breath and stretched back in his chair. *And what about the strange situations with the newborn babies? Something is not right.* He was staring at the pictures of Marc's tumor as he mulled everything over. *I'm losing it. It's just a series of strange events, that's all.* He stood up to stretch. His muscles had grown stiff from sitting too long. A memo lay next to the pictures. He picked it up and read a line out loud.

"Today is flu shot day. All hospital staff are <u>required</u> to receive a flu shot."

He shook his head. "To hell with that. I've got too much on my plate to do that right now."

He looked up at the door when he heard a knock. "Yes, come in." The door opened to reveal Sam. "I thought you were going home."

She had a vacant and pale look about her that sent Tim's alarm bells ringing. She stepped into his office. She had a syringe in her hand.

Tim smiled at her. "Sam, are you feeling OK?" She didn't respond, just kept walking closer. "Sam?" No response. She stepped a little closer, her head tilted slightly to the side. Her bloodshot eyes seemed to stare off past him in the distance. She was now an arm's length away from him. "Sam? What's going on?" He thought this must be some sort of joke.

Her focused shifted to him. "Arm." Her voice was not the high-pitched sound he was used to. Now it was flat and devoid of any emotion.

What the hell? He took a step back. Nothing registered on her face at all. It hadn't really occurred to him before how silent the hospital was. There were no conversations in the distance, nor were there staff members walking past his door as they often would on their way to the next task. His heart started beating a little faster. He could feel his stomach get a bit queasy, the adrenaline starting to work. *No, this is no joke. Something is wrong!*

Sam stepped closer, needle in her right hand. He backed away again, except now, he was back against the window. He felt the cold of the glass and he turned to glance outside, hoping for a way out. He saw a man being forced down on the ground below and one of the nurses administering a shot into his arm. The poor man was fighting, but there were three other people holding him down. *What in God's name is going on?* was the only thought he could muster.

She smiled at him, though without feeling, as she spoke. "It's flu shot day, Tim. Everyone must get a flu shot."

He heard footsteps outside the doorway and turned to see an elderly patient walking, out of breath and panic stricken. The man turned to look behind him, pleading with his eyes for help. Immediately following him was a nurse with the same vacant look Sam was displaying.

Shit! Sam was in front of him now, grabbing his left arm.

"NO!" He pulled away, but Sam would not let go.

She raised the needle, ready to stab him with it, but he thrashed his arm again and threw her back against the desk. Having been slow before, she now moved with speed. She dashed at him, but Tim met her—this time with the swing of his right hand. He could feel the bone beneath her cheek as he slammed his fist into her face. She fell back to the floor, the needle flying out of her hand.

Not wasting any time, he ran from the room into the hallway. Three doctors at the end of the hallway to his right saw him and started rushing for him. *God, no!* He turned and bolted to his left when two nurses emerged from the other end of the hall. He stopped midstride and didn't need to look back. He could hear the doctors' footsteps as they ran closer to him. *SHIT!* He made the choice to run toward the nurses. He gathered as much speed as he could and charged them. They both stood waiting to try to tackle him and catch him. He crashed into the nurse on the right—she looked to be the smaller of the two.

THUD!

His shoulder plowed into the nurse's chest, and they both slammed into the door before falling into the stairway landing. He used his momentum to roll back to his feet, but she grabbed his leg, and he fell down the first set of stairs, dragging the nurse with him. He felt his arm crash against one of the cement steps and then saw her body roll over his arm. This was followed by a sickening *pop*. He knew there should be pain but it had not registered yet. When they both came to a stop at the landing below, blood stained the floor. He panicked and got to his feet. *It's not mine. It's not mine.* The nurse had hit her head and was staring up at him, mouth open wide. He stood in shock for a moment, until he heard the noises of those following him from above. He turned to see the three doctors and the nurse running down the stairs. He was holding his left arm, as it dangled uselessly. *Still no pain? Shouldn't it hurt?* He started sprinting down the next flight of stairs. As he got ready to exit to the next floor, a group of people bolted through. *How do they all know I'm here?*

He ran down the stairs, all the way to the basement of the hospital. No one was there to meet him, and he ran through the doorway to the hall. He could hear the sound of steps running behind him. There was no escape that he could immediately see, so he charged into the first room that he could find that seemed to have sturdy doors. He did not realize it was the morgue. It didn't matter, it would have to work. He scanned the room, then grabbed a metal stand that would normally hold a sign, ramming it through the two handles on the door. It was the only entry he knew of into the morgue.

He could see at least ten people outside the room as he peered through the small shatterproof window in the door. He fell, exhausted, and tried to catch his breath. The doors shook as they worked to open them, but it was no use—for now.

He sat on the floor for a few minutes, dazed. It was then that the pain hit like a load of bricks. Waves of nausea swept over him as his body reacted to this latest assault on his senses. *What am I going to do?* He searched his pockets and pulled out his cell phone. He called the only person he knew to call. He called his friend Dwight to warn him and to tell him goodbye.

Chapter 33

The drive home was long and uneventful. Marc couldn't believe the entire trip took as long as it did as it was now evening. He was relieved to see that no weird people remained gathered around his house as they returned from the disturbing meeting with Tim. *This has been a strange day.* Jack swung the car around into the driveway and brought it to a stop in front of the garage. He reached into his pocket, revealing a bottle of pills.

"Marc, Tim thought these should help with your headaches and let you get some sleep. I know you haven't been sleeping well, so why don't you take one and call it a day. I know it's been a bit stressful." He gave Marc the bottle as he strained to get out of the car.

Marc ran ahead and unlocked the door for Jack. He knew the damaged leg was causing his friend a lot of pain today. Jack had left his cane at home, and all the extra weight on his leg seemed to have become too much. Jack was panting and dragging his leg as he walked, his face tight. Marc held him steady as he led him through the doorway. Adrianna was standing in the hallway waiting for them. She had a worried look on her face, but when she saw Marc helping Jack inside, she ran over to support his other side and helped him to a chair.

"Why didn't you take your cane, you silly old man?" She looked over to Marc. "Thanks for helping him in, Marc."

Marc smiled. "Sure. I'm going to go get some rest. I haven't been feeling too well. Thank you for everything, Jack." He didn't wait for a reply and was headed to his room, but he hesitated a moment to hear anything Jack may have not been open with him about.

He could hear Jack talking in a hushed tone. "We went to the hospital today. Marc's been having really bad headaches and he passed out last night."

Sirens were blaring in the background.

"Is he OK?" Adrianna asked.

"I don't know. He has some sort of tumor. Tim gave him some medicine, but it's just so he can get some sleep."

"Poor boy. I didn't trust him at first, but he really is a good kid, and he looks up to you."

Marc quietly opened the door and slipped into his bedroom. A shiver crept up his spine when he closed the door. He could feel something was about to happen—something bad. He was scared.

He knew he shouldn't let the dog in, but he didn't want to be alone. He walked to the window, his heart beating faster as he got closer, and peeked outside. The night sky had an eerie, pinkish glow. It appeared that there were no people around.

He released the latch on the window and quietly lifted it up. There was a screen, but he easily popped it out. The night air breezed past him as he squeezed through the open window. He had purposely left the back door to the garage unlocked so that he could sneak out and visit Cerberus when he was lonely. His heart was beating even faster now. The night itself was creepy, adding to his sense that something sinister was impending. Wind blew through the trees at the edge of the property, and he could hear a decorative windmill squeaking from the neighbor's yard. He felt like he was being watched.

His eye caught some movement across the yard. *Probably just a skunk.* He picked up his pace nonetheless. He moved quickly to the door. "Just me, boy," he announced before he opened the door. He felt the hair on the nape of his neck stand as though something were behind him. A shiver ran through his body, and he could feel his arms and legs tingle. He quickly entered the garage and closed the door behind him.

Cerberus wagged his tail when he saw his friend and master enter. Marc ran over to scratch the dog's ear.

"You OK, boy? Come in and stay with me. But no barking!" He knelt down and patted the dog as it lapped his cheeks. Together they made their way back to the door.

SMACK! SMACK! SMACK!

Marc jumped when he saw a face in one of the square garage door windows. Someone was on the other side of the door, peering in and mindlessly slapping at it with both hands. Thankful that Jack always locked the main doors to the garage, Marc still felt his heart in his throat. The person peered in at him for a moment longer and then walked away.

Cerberus barked and then growled. They had to move quickly. It would take whoever was out there only a minute to get around to the side of the garage and block their escape back to house. It didn't give him much time. Cerberus's tail was standing straight as he stood and sniffed the air. He let out a slight, low growl.

Marc cringed at the noise. "No, no noise. Come."

He dragged the dog to the open bedroom window and climbed in, beckoning the dog to follow. Cerberus hesitated a minute but was able to jump through. His collar jingled as he shook his neck, excited to be with Marc.

"Shhh! You have to be quiet, boy. Lay down." Marc commanded.

Cerberus obeyed and lay down. Marc turned and closed the window, latching it tight. He could see a shadow at the edge of the garage. He turned off the light to his room and peered around through the edge of the window. The figured made its way along the back of the garage to the door, opened it, and slipped inside. *What the hell is going on?* Cerberus heard the door shut and got to his feet, letting out a loud bark.

Oh God. What am I going to say? There was a knock at the door.

"Marc, it's Jack. I'm coming in." The knob on the door turned, and Jack stepped into the room. Adrianna was standing behind him, her arms folded. Cerberus wagged his tail when he saw Jack. "We talked about this. We trusted you not to bring him into the house."

Marc looked at Jack apologetically. "I'm sorry, Jack. I was scared and I wanted him with me."

Adrianna stormed in. "I don't trust that dog! He's a violent breed and I don't want him in my house!" She frowned and she shook her head. "We've done so much for you, and you do the one thing we asked you not to." She looked to Jack, who was obviously trying to think of what to do or say next. "If I see that dog in here again, both *he* and the *dog* will stay in the garage!" she threatened, first pointing at Marc and then Cerberus. She stormed out of the room.

Jack turned to face Marc after she left. "Marc, you need to put the dog back in the garage. I can only do so much damage control." He held out his hands pleadingly.

"Please just let me just keep him here tonight and I'll never do it again." Marc reached over to pet Cerberus on the head.

Jack let out a sigh. "OK. Just tonight. But no more. Understood?" Jack glanced in the direction Adrianna had stormed off and then back at Marc and Cerberus before throwing his hands up and limping away.

Marc thought of mentioning the person he saw, but didn't want Jack to get hurt. "We'll guard the house tonight, boy." He patted Cerberus as he glanced out the window, and he was happy to see no more movement in the night.

Chapter 34

THE PRESIDENT OF THE United States! Of all times to lead a country, why me and why now? The resident let out a deep sigh. Sitting around the table were all his closest aides, as well as the war council. His vice president had the same stressed and worried look he figured he also wore. He shook his head and directed his attention to the secretary of defense.

"So, what you're telling me is that some sort of vessel is up there," he pointed up to the ceiling, "in space, and you don't have the slightest clue what it is?" He gave the older man sitting across the table a chilling look.

The man shifted in his seat uncomfortably as he spoke. "Yes, Mr. President." He looked down at his paper. "It appears that it is a UFO. There is no other way to classify it." He cleared his throat as the president frowned. The man shrugged. "It simply appeared out of nowhere. Almost as if it had been sitting there for some time. Waiting."

The president leaned back in his chair and closed his eyes. *This must be a joke. No, they would never joke about something like that. Why not the dumbass Republican before me? Why now?* He thought he had been doing a good job at the normal stuff involved with governing the country, managing the economy, and dealing with foreign affairs.

He counted his lucky stars he had not needed to deal with war issues or terrorist attacks. *Now aliens? What could possibly be worse? OK, just calm down. It's likely some weird hoax. Or maybe it's the damned Russians?* He smiled. One could always blame the Russians. *No, that can't be. That only happened in the movies.*

He would often get into this self-ranting when stressed. *OK, back to reality. Turn the negative to positive. What other sane president could say they were the first to communicate with extraterrestrial life forms?* His gaze turned to his vice president, who was quite a few years older than him. He was a consummate politician, but one who thought of the country before all else. The president had always counted on him for good advice.

"Here's my plan," the president said. "Tell me what you think." He took a sip of water from the glass sitting on the table in front of him before continuing. "I do not want to show any signs of aggression. Other countries will do what they will, but we will not show any aggressive behavior." He cleared his throat. "We need to find a way to communicate, so we'll do whatever we can to open all channels of communication."

The vice president nodded before adding his thoughts. "I agree. You know me, though. I think we must maintain an open channel with the people. They have a right to know what is going on."

The president smiled and nodded in agreement. "I was waiting for you to say that. Yes, all information is to be shared." A few around the table, mostly those in the Security Council, grunted their disapproval. The president stood up, both hands in fists on the table.

"Past administrations ran things differently than this one. It's time to remember that." He stood straight, pulling himself up to his full six feet of height, and continued. "Need I remind all those at this table that we are here because the American people put us here? We work for them."

Right before the customary uproar the president's impassioned speeches usually brought from the elite sitting around the table, a young man rushed in carrying a paper and handed it to the president.

The president stood quietly for a few moments after reading the few sentences written on the paper. His eyes moved from the paper to those around the table.

"They have reached out to us." He paused a moment and continued. "They wish to meet with us to discuss their intentions for populating the planet."

Everyone started talking at once. He heard a variety of strategies including "nuking their asses until they shit glowing turds"—that must have come from one of the old generals, most of whom were relics of the "best defense is a *good offense*" era of American foreign policy.

He raised his hands up to quiet the room. He looked at the young officer who had just delivered the paper.

"Young man, I want you to take this back to send over to them." The man pulled out a notepad and pen, eager to write what he was told. "We will meet with you. It will be at a public gathering. We will discuss, in front of the citizens of the United States, how our races will interact peacefully." He nodded at the vice president and the other man quietly clapped. He could hear a few in the room express their disapproval. He continued above their sighs and grunts. "Tell them that we need forty-eight hours to prepare. The gathering will be held at the National Mall." He walked away from the table to the door. *I have to get away from all these snakes. I need some peace before all this goes down.*

He stopped before exiting the room. The soldier watched him, eagerly waiting to write down anything else he was told.

"Notify the press as well. Explain all of this to them." Now the generals were furious. He shook his head.

"Enough!" The room fell silent. He lowered his voice again. "Answer any questions they may have. We are hiding nothing."

The president's wife was waiting for him in the living quarters with a man he did not know. When she saw him she smiled. "Hi dear. You look so stressed. It must be a difficult day."

Her demeanor didn't seem right to him, but he brushed it off, thinking it was likely that he was just tired and worried.

She doesn't know about any of this yet. She's fine; it's just my imagination. He smiled back at her and then looked over at the man she was with. He was an older man with glasses and a balding head. He was wearing casual but expensive slacks with a suit jacket and tie.

"And who might you be?" he asked the old stranger in the room.

The man cleared his throat. "Pardon me, Mr. President. I am your wife's doctor. I am honored to meet you." The First Lady responded to his questioning glance with a smile.

The doctor continued, "Your lovely wife has asked me to administer your flu shot. She says you've been avoiding it. I know your doctor usually does this for you, but I am here and I have just given the First Lady her shot. It is no bother if you are ready." He beckoned for the president to sit down. He glanced to his wife, who smiled at him and nodded to the chair. She rubbed his shoulder and guided him to sit down.

"I'm fin—" he resisted slightly, but his wife cut him off.

"No, I'm worried about you, dear. You can't get sick now with so many people depending on you to lead the nation."

Something nagged at him. Something in the air didn't feel right. *Stop it. I'm being stupid now. I need to get this done, might as well be now.* The doctor walked over and to him and began rolling up his sleeve. His wife was watching, still with that odd smile. He put his head back and closed his eyes. *She is acting strangely; something is weird.* His thoughts were a jumbled mess from everything he was dealing with. *She's being weird? Why, because she's smiling at her husband? Idiot.* He shook his head. Then he felt the pinch. At that moment, to his horror, remembered that his wife had a female doctor, not a man. His stomach cramped, and he crumpled over onto the floor, curling into a ball.

Cold! I'm cold! Did he poison me? His body shook and his head spun, and then there were voices. Many voices all at once. Then just one. One powerful and clear voice.

"Welcome," is all that it said.

His wife—or was it? he couldn't tell anymore—stared down at him, her face still stretched in that fake smile. He could sense her thoughts and feelings. It hurt to feel so much, but it also felt so powerful. His vision wavered and became black.

Chapter 35

JACK LIMPED BACK TO the living room. Adrianna was waiting for him, a volcano about to erupt. He made it to his chair before she unleashed her fury on him. "I cannot believe he did that!" She paced back and forth in front of him. "We went out of our way to treat him as family, protect him and provide him a home. The one thing we told him not to do and he went and did it!"

Jack sat and listened patiently. The air felt like it was filled with electricity. Jack watched his wife pace around. Her blonde hair trailed behind her as she moved around the room in anger. Even angry, she was beautiful. She couldn't see it, but he was smiling. It wasn't her anger that made him smile. It was how emotional she would get and how fierce she could be. This was a woman you did not want to cross without good reason.

"I was beginning to like him, Jack, and then he purposely does this!" She fell back onto the couch across from him.

When she was through, Jack smiled at Adrianna. "I know you're upset. What Marc did was wrong, and he knows it was wrong. He—"

She jumped up and started pacing again. "Damn right he was wrong! Why do you defend him? He defiantly did what we told him not to." A tear streamed down her cheek. "I wanted to trust him. But

I can't! Not ever now. I don't want to deal with it anymore. He has brought so many memories of pain here." Her eyes looked first at his cane and then traveled to his leg propped up on his chair.

"He promised he will not do it again. He's had a bad day and he's scared. I told him it's just for tonight and then the dog is back in the garage." He got to his feet and reached to hug her, but she backed away. "Why do you support him all the time? You don't owe him anything!" She looked questioningly at her husband.

"Wait, wait, maybe I do owe him something. Just before the incident, I was thinking how much I hated my job. I didn't even realize how lucky I was to have the family I had. With the insurance settlement, we have been able to have a home near a wonderful school for Ashley, you love the river and the boat, and I love working from home. We both know how lucky we are to be alive and together. How many people have that?" He tried one more time to reach out to her. "Please honey. He's a good kid. He really is. I love having him here. He's just confused. It's been a hard day." But it was no use. *I think I have the couch tonight.* She shook her head and stomped off to the bedroom, slamming the door behind her.

Jack sat back down and reached for the remote. When he clicked on the TV, to his surprise, an emergency broadcast was being shown. Headlines ran across the bottom of the screen highlighted in a red bar.

UFO sighted orbiting Earth...President holds emergency conference ...Aliens in contact with world leaders...

The news anchor was on the air. "The president is expected to address the nation once the administration has a clear understanding of whoever is operating the craft and what their motives are. What life forms are inside the ship and what they might look like is still a mystery."

Is this shit for real? He took a deep breath. *It can't be. This has to be a hoax.* The TV broadcast went white, and static came through the TV. A second later, the picture was restored, but instead of the news, a different show was running, broadcasting images including the pyramids being built, Jesus Christ carrying the cross, and events from modern history. Captions beneath the images explained that the beings in the vessel had been helping humanity to move forward since its early history and that the beings in the ship have returned to once again improve the fate of the human race. Jack changed the station to see the same broadcast. Sirens wailed in the background and tires screeched. The thought of eating that leftover pie crossed his mind. Gaining weight now probably wouldn't matter much.

Chapter 36

MAGGIE FUMBLED IN THE dark for the phone. *Christ! It must be midnight!* In the process, she knocked her book off the nightstand, and it made a loud thunk as it hit the floor.

"Who the hell is calling so late?" Max reached over and wrapped his arm around her waist. She pushed his arm aside and rolled so that she could reach the annoying phone.

"Hello?" her voice sounded groggy, even to herself. She cleared her throat.

"Maggie. It's Dwight."

Surprised that the esteemed professor would be calling her, she immediately sat up. "Yes. What's going on?" *Why on earth would he be calling me?*

"Have you seen the news, Maggie?"

She shook her head in confusion. "No, not lately. Did something happen?"

The voice on the other end sounded a bit annoyed now. "Yes. I suggest you turn it on. You'll find it interesting." He paused a moment. "There is an event taking place tomorrow afternoon. Meet me at the National Mall at noon tomorrow."

"Why are you calling me, sir?" she asked.

There was silence for a moment. "I heard from a few colleagues of mine that you show great promise in our field of science and yet you still hold strong religious beliefs. I need another good research scientist but have not approached you because I was concerned you wouldn't be able to accept our premise that science can provide answers that religious belief cannot. I think it's important for you to be there to see how wrong you have been regarding your faith. Then we can talk about the research I need help with."

She was stunned. "Excuse me? You call me at midnight to criticize my beliefs? You—"

He cut her off. "Noon at the National Mall."

She heard him hang up the phone on the other end and sat there for a moment. *What a pompous bastard!*

Too mad to go back to sleep, and knowing she'd never fall asleep with her husband's nasally snore going at full throttle, she stood up, putting her robe on to fight the chilly night air. She started to leave and then heard a loud snort from where her husband lay. She turned to see his mouth wide open, drool running down his cheek to puddle up on his pillow. She loved him dearly, but he could be a major pain in the ass sometimes. She reached over and pinched his nose, holding it shut for a moment. His body jumped and she let go. He snorted three times and was asleep again like nothing had happened. She shook her head and turned to leave. She almost made it to the doorway without hearing any more of his snores, and she had to roll her eyes when he started in again. *God! It feels like the house is shaking!*

The house, aside from the snores, was eerily quiet, but she could hear sirens in the distance. She walked over to one of the shades and moved it aside to peer out the window. The sky had a strange pinkish glow to it. She shivered. She felt anxious, almost like she had consumed too much coffee and her muscles felt jittery. *What am I? Six years old?* Thinking that way helped to ward off the creepy thoughts that she knew would send her straight back to the snoring log in the other room.

Sitting down on the couch, she reached over for the remote and turned on the TV. Expecting to see the typical late-night talk shows, she was surprised to see some sort of historical documentary. The text below what was being shown brought her heart up into her throat. *This must be a hoax of some sort.* She changed the channel. Same thing. Again. Same thing. She shook her head. "No, this is stupid." She was talking to herself out loud now. She really didn't care if anyone woke up. She got to her feet, went over to the radio, and turned it on.

We are your friends and are here to help you. Accept us and together we will aspire to great heights. We helped build the pyramids. We were there to see Jesus carry the cross. God was not and is not, but we were and are. Accept life greater than any imagination here on Earth could create. Accept us.

She changed the station to find the same messaging.

"Ok, I'm losing it." She slumped to the floor, her back resting against the wall. She glanced back at the TV and saw Jesus carrying the cross. *It can't be true. I refuse to believe it. God is with me. He always has been and always will be. He is with me now.* Unthinking, she clasped the cross hanging from her neck. *But why? Where is he now?* Tears ran down her cheeks. The TV now showed Hitler and the massacre of the Jews. She shook her head in disgust. She watched the text at the bottom of the screen.

We were there to witness the atrocities your kind inflicted upon itself. We helped by delivering you Albert Einstein.

She frowned. *How many people will believe this? Too many. God save us.* She was crying freely now. The light of the room turned on, and she looked up to see her husband standing in the doorway. Soon after, Meagan and Sam joined them. They all looked confused and worried.

"Honey? Are you OK?" Max walked forward and knelt down in front of her. He hadn't paid any attention to the TV or radio yet. She nodded to the TV, and he watched for a minute in silence before looking back to her. "What is going on?" He didn't believe it yet.

Meagan stood next to Sam. They both looked scared. The radio was still repeating the same message, and she felt rage boil inside her. She grabbed her hair and screamed.

"Turn it off! Turn it all off!" Maggie jumped to her feet and slammed the power button on the radio. Meagan had already turned off the TV. They all stood in silence for a moment before she explained her telephone conversation with Dwight.

"No, Maggie. You're not going. I don't want you anywhere near whatever is going on there." Max frowned. In all the years they had been together, for the first time looked scared.

"I have to see what is going on," she replied.

"Mom! Please don't." This time the request was from Sam.

"Someone needs to go to support our beliefs. If they wanted to kill us, they would have done so by now." She smiled.

"Mom, I don—OUCH!"

Meagan punched Sam in the shoulder to quiet him. "She doesn't care about us. She won't listen, so why bother?" Meagan turned her back to her family and stormed off.

"Maggie, don't do this. Let's go to the country and get away from all the wackos here in the city." Max reached out to hug her.

"No. I feel this is something I need to do. It will all be fine." She hugged him back tightly. Sam walked over and hugged them both as well. She could hear her daughter crying, alone, in her room. *I love you, too, Meg.*

Chapter 37

Rubbing her eyes as she stood up, Maggie felt like she had gotten only about an hour of sleep the night before. It was still very early in the morning. She wanted to get up and out of the house before her husband and kids could stop her from leaving. She and Max had fallen asleep on the couch, and their son, Sam, slept on the floor. She was scared but also excited. *History is in the making. Life from another world. Amazing!* She quietly walked to the bedroom and slipped out of her nightgown and into her suit, which consisted of navy striped pants, a white silk blouse, and a solid navy jacket.

She tiptoed past the sleeping boys—she often liked to categorize Max as a boy along with Sam. She loved him dearly even if, at times, he was as childlike as a boy. Grabbing a couple of slices of bread, she ran out of the kitchen and left in the family Caravan.

Jets flew overhead, and the sky was full of noise. The rumble of helicopters circling above was starting to give her a headache. Several of the neighbors were out in their front lawns looking up to the sky, confusion about what was happening registering on their faces.

Military convoys passed her on the highway and became more frequent as she approached DC. They were screaming down the breakdown lane on the right, passing the cars lined up in traffic. Rocks flew as they passed by, sending debris and dust into the air, hitting against the van's windshield. *Seriously! They seriously believe our guns would be of any use against beings who have developed the technology to travel here from who knows where?*

Sick of being stuck in traffic, she reached down to turn on the radio. The president was speaking and pleading for calm, asking people to show strength, not weakness, by continuing in their normal, daily routines. Maggie rolled her eyes. *Sure, go about your daily routines. Aliens are here, you idiot!* In her aggravation, she barely noticed the car in front of hers had come to a stop. "Shit!" She slammed the brake pedal to the floor, and her van skidded to a stop inches from ramming into the car ahead of her.

The man in front of her got out of his car. "Fucking idiot! Learn how to drive!" She heard the man swearing as he walked over to the small sedan in front of him. He reached into his pocket and pulled out what appeared to be a gun. *Oh my God!* she thought to herself as she watched the scene unfold.

BANG!

Through the car sitting vacant in front of her, she could make out a red splash against the back of the sedan's rear glass. Stunned by what she saw, she put her car in reverse and crashed into the car behind her. The man with the gun turned to see what the noise at his back was. She heard the horn blaring from the car she had just rammed. She had barely enough room to swerve around another car before she lay on the gas. A Humvee that was leading another approaching convoy swerved off to the side of the road to avoid hitting her and drove into the ditch. She heard another shot and the sound of metal. *He's shooting at me!* She sped off, the man still firing at her, and she saw her driver's side mirror shatter.

Other panicked drivers joined her in a row as she sped past idling cars. Glancing in her rearview mirror, cars were now moving into any open spot they could get into. *I was the domino that fell.* The highway was becoming a hazard zone, but at least she was at the head of it. She was able to make relatively good progress. It was slow, but at least she was moving. Motorists must have been parked for a long time because she passed several people who were relieving themselves just outside their vehicles.

There had been a massive pileup at this end of the procession. A man in a green pickup truck swore at her as she swerved back into the slow-moving line, practically forcing a driver to swerve into the car on his left. *If you only knew what's behind you, you'd do the same.* Military personnel were out now, helping to keep traffic moving past the accident that had been causing so much delay. Maggie let out a deep breath of relief to be back in a more normal flow of traffic. She wondered to herself what became of the people trapped with the shooter.

Once she made it past the traffic holdup, she began moving at a good clip again. When she was close to DC, the traffic became more congested, and she exited the highway to take public transportation the rest of the way. People riding the trains, buses, and subways all had the same look of panic on their faces. She tried her best to not focus on anyone for too long, afraid they might snap and blow everyone away with a gun hidden in their jacket. *I'm in the middle of a powder keg ready to go off. I should have stayed home.* The thought of her family brought a tear to her eye.

Thankful it was her stop, she exited the bus she was riding to join the crowd gathering near the Mall. Having no children with her to worry about, she was able to squeeze through the crowd to get close to the front, where she hoped to find Dwight. A security detail was preparing for the president to make his speech.

Kids were screaming and the parents were doing their best to keep them occupied. *Why on earth would you bring your kids?* She could feel her bladder filling, and it wouldn't be long before she'd have to pee. She really didn't want to have to battle the crowd, fearful she'd never get back her spot, which felt fairly safe considering the amount of armed guards so close to her. She continued to scan the crowd but caught no hint of Dwight.

As the time for the president to speak drew closer, more guards arrived and the place was now under complete lockdown. The crowd roared as the president walked to the podium. His wife was not far behind and stood behind him to the right. Her smile seemed pasted onto her face as she waved to the crowd. Maggie turned to look behind her, noting that the gathering had grown to a massive size. Her heart was racing. She didn't know how she could expect to handle herself when she saw the other being. Was she excited or scared? *Stop being such a baby!* Maggie reminded herself that if they wanted the humans dead, they'd be dead already. End of story.

The crowd quieted as the president raised his arms up and beckoned for silence. He smiled and thanked the people for coming.

"As all are gathered here are aware, we have made contact with life beyond our earthly boundaries. We are not alone after all."

A few people cheered from the crowd, and someone yelled out "Bring him out already!" The president waited for the ruckus to die back down before continuing.

"I have spoken with the commander of these beings. I am assured their intentions are peaceful." Applause broke out again and lasted for a few minutes. From out of the shadows a slender figured emerged, security guards completely surrounding it.

The figure wore dark clothing of an unknown material that shimmered with unearthly light as it reflected the sun's rays. The alien's skin resembled that of a shark, pale and gray. Its eyes, between two narrow slits, were as dark as coal. Whenever Maggie thought of aliens, she'd always thought they wouldn't have any nose, but it did have a nose. It was very small, but it was there. It also had a mouth, which looked quite funny in comparison to the size of its head. The forehead, in particular, was incredibly large in proportion to the rest of its face. She heard some in the crowd laughing. *Ignorant fools. Welcome to America.* She shook her head.

The creature climbed several steps up the podium, but not to the top, so that it would appear slightly smaller than the president. God forbid he would be allowed to be depicted as being taller than the leader of the free world! It was then that she heard its voice, which was eerie since its mouth did not move and there was no microphone, yet the voice was loud and clear. She looked around and saw others in the crowd were confused as well.

"Hello." It raised its hand into the air to greet the audience.

Some in the crowd responded with a "hello" back. Some wore smiles, excited at the moment, and others looked scared. A child cried in the distance. Sirens sounded in the background, attending to some distant emergency. News helicopters circled overhead, as did military and police choppers.

"We are your friends and only seek your acceptance. Embrace us and our ways, and we will deliver technologies you have never imagined. Your lives will be full, and no one will want."

"You are Satan's servants!" a woman shouted from a religious group to the left of where Maggie stood. The alien shifted its gaze to where the woman shouted.

"There is no Satan, and there is no God. Only you," it gestured at the crowd, "and us."

The woman shouted back, "Blasphemy!" Maggie saw the woman spit on the ground. The rest of her group clapped and egged the woman on.

The alien showed no emotion as it continued. "It's time to let go of your old ways. Religion helped carry you to the point where you are now, but it is encumbering you with hate and distrust of those who differ from you. It is preventing you from living to the potential you can achieve. Those who are wise enough to accept this are welcome to reap the benefits of our friendship and will live to untold ages and do great things your race has not even envisioned."

Some in the crowd booed at the insult to their beliefs. Maggie's face was flushed red. *God does exist, you bastard!* She thought, but she kept her mouth shut.

The president stepped in to quiet the crowd again. "Please. Hear what our new friend has to say."

The rowdy woman yelled back, "The Devil has arrived in a spacecraft! Do not listen to that creature! It is the Devil's servant!"

Security guards rushed over to withdraw her from the crowd, but the rest of the followers circled her. A breeze blew through the gathering, and Maggie hid away the nagging thought that she shouldn't be here. *Something isn't right.* Images of her family raced through her mind, and her heart felt hollow when she realized how much she wanted to be with them.

"As your president, I am committed to attending to the best interests of American citizens. I have accepted this being as my sister. It will be advisable for all of you to do the same." He nodded to the alien figure. "Nefertiry is wise beyond our imaginations. She has seen more than we could ever believe. It's my honor to step down as leader to America and to hold the honorable rank of adviser to our Supreme Leader." He smiled and looked back at his wife, who still wore her fake smile.

The vice president rushed forward. "NO! This is not what we agreed on." He stood inches away from the president, who looked down at him from the podium.

He reached his hand down toward the vice president. "Accept us and achieve new heights."

"NO! I cannot go along with this. You *owe* it to the American people to defend and represent their interests. What are you doing?"

Maggie started backing away from the stage but could not go far before she bumped into people standing behind her. People were getting rowdy now and yelling. Some were in support of the president and his alien ally, and others were shouting their disapproval. The alien stood silently watching, waiting.

The president shook his head, reached into his pocket to reveal a pistol, and held it up to his vice president's head. No hesitation. He pulled the trigger.

Blood spattered across the podium and covered the First Lady's face. Fragments of brain dripped off her cheek, but she remained unmoving, still wearing that fake smile. The dead man fell to his knees and then face-first to the floor of the platform. The crowd was screaming in disbelief. Maggie felt a jab in her ribs, leaving her on her knees and gasping for breath as someone behind her panicked and tried to flee. She looked up to the podium to see the alien standing still, only moving its eyes from person to person. It would pause on each for a moment, and it appeared to Maggie that it was analyzing them in some way. *Now is the time to get out, before it's too late!* She recovered and stood back up.

The sun shone down from a break in the clouds, and she saw a bead of light reflecting off the alien's eyes. It held up an arm to block it and then followed the track of the light over to where Maggie stood. She realized, then, that the cross she wore around her neck was the source of the light. Some strange unknown energy coursed through her at that moment. She grabbed her arm. It felt like it was on fire, burning from the inside out. It spread through her entire body. The pain was excruciating. She opened her mouth to scream, yet no sound escaped. She could not move. Ash was sprinkling down on her from above. Bright light shot from her eyes and her gaping mouth. *God help me! Please!* Her vision was the first of her senses to go, as she continued to feel the pain from the rest of her body. Her head felt as though it would explode. Then nothing.

Chapter 38

THE NOISE OF THE helicopters flying overhead was giving Dwight a headache. He rubbed his forehead. He was tired. His mind, normally working at warp speed, was too exhausted to maintain focus. His third cup of coffee sat in front of him, half empty. Dwight hated taking pain relievers for minor things such as a headache and had hoped the caffeine would help.

The idea of getting any sleep at all, considering the momentous events occurring, was a joke. The research he was performing on the corpses with the strange tumors was unnerving, but that paled in comparison to the news of another life form visiting Earth. He had always believed other beings existed, but he never thought their presence would be revealed during his lifetime. Already he had developed insomnia from the relentless hours he spent each night on his research. Now the news about the aliens was robbing him of any possibility of getting the rest he so badly needed.

He looked down to a report he had written on his findings from his work on the corpses and sighed. *It doesn't add up. Who would have the ability to create these tumors? And how did they get away with human test subjects?* Glancing up at the clock, he reminded himself he needed to get ready for the event taking place at the National Mall. Grimacing as he stood, his head throbbed with the added exertion, and he jumped at the sound of his cell phone ringing. *Probably Maggie. I forgot to tell her where we should meet at the Mall.* Reaching into his pocket, he pulled out his BlackBerry and was surprised to see his friend Tim Eddins was the caller.

"Hello," he answered.

"Dwight! Thank God!" Tim's strained voice replied.

"Tim, are you OK? Is something wrong?" he asked his friend.

"Dwight, I don't know what the hell is going on. You didn't get a flu shot, did you?" Tim asked.

Dwight laughed. "What are you talking about?"

"Just answer the question, Dwight! Did you or didn't you?" Dwight could hear noise coming through the phone as if someone were pounding on a door.

"Tim, no. I always seem to forget. What is going on over there? What's that noise?" Dwight could feel his heartbeat pick up. Form the tone in Tim's voice, he could tell something was very wrong.

"I don't know. Something with the flu shots. Everyone here at the hospital that has gotten it becomes...*different*."

Dwight sat back down in his chair at the table. "Different? How so?"

The pounding sounds coming through the phone seemed to stop, and Tim replied, "Almost as if they are no longer in control of themselves. I know, it sounds crazy." Tim explained to Dwight the situation first with the babies and then the vaccinations.

Dwight sat in silence for a moment. *The tumors, the aliens, the flu shots and vaccinations. It can't all be a coincidence.*

"Dwight? You there?"

"Yes. Sorry. Did you get the images I sent you?"

"Damnit, Dwight! Is that all you can think about? I'm trapped in the fucking morgue!"

"Sorry, it's just that I think the flu shots and the tumors might be related." The last part of Tim's reply sunk in. "Wait. You're what?"

"I'm stuck in the morgue. People are after me. They tried forcing me to get the shot, but I locked myself in the morgue." Tim's voice was shaky.

"I'll try to get you some help."

"No, I'm not sure how much longer the door will hold. I don't know who you could trust at this point anyway. I just wanted to warn you. You've always been a good friend."

"Tim, hang in there. Is there nowhere else you can go?" Dwight swallowed a knot in his throat.

"Dwight, listen. Get somewhere safe. I don't know what the hell is going on, but I read on my phone about the shit that's going on in DC. Don't go." The pounding picked up again.

"Thanks. I didn't think the aliens would be invading, but it seems like this invasion had been planned for some time and has already begun." Dwight's heart was racing. This was not good.

"A boy came to see me in my office today. Remember the mall shooting? Remember the baby?" he asked his friend.

"Oh I remember the mall shooting alright. How could I forget?"

"Well, the man I saved, remember, the one who rescued that baby? His name is Jack." Tim paused and continued without waiting for an answer. The sound of other voices yelling came through the phone. "Well, the boy who was here was the baby Jack saved. He sought him out after all these years. The kid has been having visions. Jack wanted me to help him deal with them."

"OPEN THE DOOR!" An unknown voice came through the phone, followed by the scraping of metal.

Tim continued, "Anyway, the boy has a tumor like the ones in the pictures you sent me, except much, much bigger. I'm surprised he can even function."

Dwight was surprised by the news. "Did he seem *OK*?"

"Yes. Dwight, I think this boy is special. I was worried about my friend Jack's safety, but something was unique about this boy—Marcus, I think his name was. Something different in a good way, but I don't know what."

"YOU NEED TO JOIN US!" the other voice called out.

"Dwight, take care, my friend. I'm afraid it's the end of the line for me."

"Tim, I'm going to get you help, somehow." Dwight raised his voice and could hear the pounding escalating.

"No, stay safe. I know we have disagreed in the past, but you need to have faith. Miracles happen every day, and God is watching us."

"Tim!"

The phone cut out. Dwight looked at the screen, and it displayed "no signal." He tried calling his friend back, knowing it was useless and his call would not go through. Dropping the phone on the table, he began to pace back and forth in his kitchen, his head between his hands. *I have to think! For once in my life, I have no solutions or ideas!* He ran to the window and looked outside. The sun was out, and it would have normally been a beautiful day to enjoy, but instead he was scared and sick to his stomach. The immediate urge to vomit hit him and he doubled over, spilling his half-digested breakfast on the floor before falling back to sit against the wall, his body shaking. He closed his eyes and began to cry. *Tim. Shit! This can't be happening!*

A few minutes passed before Dwight could control his emotions. Slowly, he took a deep breath and held it for a few seconds before releasing it.

I have to get it together. I'm not dead yet, and I'm still human, he told himself. *Or am I?* He laughed out loud. *I can't do anything for Tim right now. He's a smart guy; he might be OK. What do I need to do for myself in order to survive?* He looked across the room to where his golf gear leaned against the wall. He had researched what the best clubs were and spent his savings on the best gear he could buy. *All fucking useless.* He got to his feet, his head pounding. He needed sleep. *If the aliens are in fact infecting people, it's likely the military will be infected as well, not to mention government officials.* The thought scared him.

"This is bad...bad...bad," he shook his head as he talked out loud to himself. "Where can I go?" He pursed his lips in thought. *Nowhere. But, somehow, those tumors are related. Evidently, they are not working as intended, considering all three subjects died.* Staring off at nothing in particular he kept on the same line of thought. *And I might be the only person who knows about it, which makes me responsible for not yet having found a solution. I need to get my ass to the lab and lock myself away in my studies.*

He ran to the cabinet where he stored his bottled water. He never drank the tap water. It wasn't for any health reasons; he simply didn't trust other people messing with the water he drank. He pulled out two large packs of bottled water from the cabinet and set them on the counter. *This won't last long, but it will have to do.* He also grabbed whatever canned foods he had on hand and bagged them all up.

I can't imagine anyone will be at the university with everything going on. Not wanting to risk being noticed by staying any longer than he had to, he loaded up the car and was sitting in the driver's seat when he remembered Maggie. He checked the time. It was now shortly before ten o'clock, and she'd be well on her way. *Fuck! I killed her.* He slammed his hands down on the steering wheel in frustration. *Nothing I can do now. I'll make it up to her by figuring out a solution!* He nodded to himself and started the car. He was determined to figure out how he could fight back. *These aliens don't know who they're messing with! They hadn't counted on me.* The tires squealed as he backed out of the driveway. *This old four-eyed human is going to kick some ass!*

Chapter 39

A SPITBALL FLEW PAST Meagan's face and landed firmly in the shaggy hair of the boy who sat in front of her. It was Ted, the guy everyone liked to pick on. He didn't seem to notice, and the thing was oozing saliva. It made her stomach queasy just looking at it.

Her mind drifted to the argument she and her mother had the night before. She didn't know why she kept acting the way she did around her mother. She simply couldn't help it. It wasn't like she wanted to behave like a childish brat; it was more that she felt her mom did not understand what she was going through.

After all, she had lost her boyfriend—well, sort of boyfriend—to a tragic accident. In a way, deep down, she felt a little relief that he wasn't able to hurt her anymore. She was still sad though. Never in her worst nightmares would she dream of his dying. The truth of the matter was, she was sad and afraid. Sad because he was her first and she would always remember him in that way—as much of an egotistical asshole as he was, she couldn't avoid that fact. *Why on earth with him? I'm so stupid!* And afraid because she had never experienced the death of someone close to her, and it made her think of her own mortality.

She wanted to cry. She knew she had hurt her mom. She reached into her bag and picked up the cell phone to call her mother and apologize. She let it ring until the voicemail picked up, which she immediately hung up on.

Maggie had left first thing in the morning, well before anyone else had gotten out of bed. She knew everyone would have tried to stop her from going. Meagan still felt the whole ordeal was some sort of elaborate hoax and none of it was real. Still, she was worried for her mom.

The squeak of the wheels on the AV cart holding the ancient TV snapped her away from her thoughts. Mrs. Mullins, the US government teacher, had insisted all her students watch the broadcast of the event taking place at the Mall. None of the other kids had any interest in quieting down yet. Everyone was hyper about the idea that aliens were invading and from hearing the reverberations of the military craft flying overhead.

"I friggin' hope they try attacking us! We'll fry their asses!" Ryan, the class bully, was again spouting his never-ending bullshit.

"Class! Settle down." Mrs. Mullins was doing her best to gain control of the classroom. She quickly gave up, like she usually did. Classroom discipline was not one of Mrs. Mullins's strong points, and this class was never obedient. Meagan hated that the teacher was way too soft and always gave in to the troublemakers. It made for a long, useless class.

The teacher turned her back to the class to turn on the TV and Ryan made some joke about her "fat old butt" at which a few other of his jerk friends laughed. Of course the jerks were the only ones who found anything he said funny, but that was all Ryan needed to keep going.

After a few unsuccessful attempts and then one final try, the TV turned on. There wasn't a problem finding a station airing coverage of the event, since they all were showing the same footage. Meagan took a deep breath and held it when she saw the mass of people gathered around the Mall. There was no open space, and the crowd went on forever. The thought that her mom was there in the middle of it all sent chills down her spine. *This is for real!*

"Where's the damned alien already!" Ryan yelled out.

The reporter explained the situation. "There are no visuals on the alien being yet, but as you can see, the military is here in force. If they try anything against us or try to hurt our president, you can be sure they will be stopped. The largest and most powerful military force in the world is watching. Let that be a warning to them."

"Hell, yeah! Just try messin' with us!" Ryan bellowed. His band hooted and pumped their fists. Meagan turned around to see Ryan sitting on his desk, grinning.

"Shut up, you boneheads!" Meagan gave them the worst look she could manage.

"Whatever. Go back to primping your hair." He snorted.

She rolled her eyes and turned back to watch the TV. *Please mom, please. Just go home.*

"And here is the president. You may not hear it well from up here in the helicopter, but the crowd below is throwing their support behind our leader. You can see he is there at the podium, his wife behind him—not the least bit shaken by corresponding with an alien race. The vice president has taken his place near the president as well. We now cut to the president and his address to the crowd."

"Just bring out the stupid alien already!" Ryan wouldn't stop with his comments.

Mrs. Mullins skirted around the side of the room to come up behind Ryan, hoping her presence would convince him to stop. Meagan could hear his apologies.

"I'm really sorry, Mrs. Mullins. I can't help it. I'm just so scared about all of this." His voice was full of sarcasm. One of his pack snickered, but Mrs. Mullins didn't hear it—or she pretended that she didn't.

"It is a confusing and frightening time, Ryan, but I'm sure everything will be fine." She patted him on his shoulder and stepped back. Meagan turned to see him hiding a smile.

When she turned back to see what was being aired, she realized she had missed most of the president's address to the crowd.

The reporter's voice came through the TV. "And here is the moment we've all been waiting for. The alien being is climbing to the stage. You can see he is escorted by a phalanx of security officials."

Meagan's heart was pounding faster now. *This is real. Oh my God! This is real! Mom! Please don't be there!* She glanced down at her phone to see if Maggie might have called, but there was nothing. She tried dialing again, but all the circuits were busy. A tear streamed down her cheek. *Why? Why did you have to go?* The room seemed to be closing in on her. The speech, the alien, dumbass Ryan. None of it seemed to matter now. She was scared for her mother. Somehow, she knew something bad was about to happen.

A voice echoed through her mind as if someone were talking to her directly and only her. "Hello," it said.

She turned her head to see where the voice came from and saw other students doing the same, confusion and fear in their expressions. Even Ryan looked spooked. She turned back to the TV to see the alien figure with its arm raised to the air in a form of greeting.

"We are your friends and only seek your acceptance. Embrace us and our ways, and we will deliver technologies you have never imagined. Your lives will be full, and no one will want."

The voice, clear as any voice she had heard, echoed in her mind.

The reporter's voice came through on the television, "I don't know what to make of this. The alien's mouth is not moving, yet I can hear perfectly what it is saying. For those at home, it's a—"

Another voice interrupted the reporter's voice. "Others have heard as well. Even at home."

Silence, only interrupted by the sound of the helicopter, echoed through the TV, and then the reporter spoke again. "This is amazing. I am at a loss for words. It seems as though it is in communication with us through our minds."

Meagan felt her stomach shaking. It was more than she could take. She put her hand on her stomach to try and soothe the uneasiness she felt. The voice came through again.

"There is no Satan and there is no God. Only you—and us. It's time to let go of your old ways. Religion helped carry you to the point where you are now, but it is encumbering you with hate and distrust of those who differ from you. It is preventing you from living to the potential you can achieve. Those who are wise enough to accept this are welcome to reap the benefits of our friendship and will live to untold ages and do great things your race has not even envisioned."

Meagan's stomach began to revolt with fear, and her pulse was speeding like she'd been running beyond her capability. She felt her limbs trembling. Whatever else was being said on the television she did not hear, at least until she heard the burst of a gun being fired.

The reporter's excited voice shot through her shock. "Oh my God! The president of the United States has shot the vice president! I repeat, the president has shot the vice president. The second in command is down, a gunshot wound to his head."

She heard Ryan let out a gasp behind her. Her eyes were glued to the situation unfolding on the TV screen. *MOM!* The camera focused on the blood-soaked podium. The president stood as if he was only joking around, and his wife remained in the background, smiling.

The reporter began speaking again. "I am not sure what happened below. The crowd is now uncontrollable. I fear for the lives that will be lost with the panic that is unfolding. Oh my God!"

The camera focused on the crowd. Beams of light shot out in all directions from the bodies of the people below. One after the other, people seemed to be burning from the inside out. Plumes of ash where people once stood shot up into the sky. Some people were skipped over, and others disintegrated where they stood. The water in the pool turned from a crystal blue to a murky ash color.

The camera zoomed back to where the alien stood. It appeared to be intently focused on the crowd. The camera began to shake and then fall to the floor of the aircraft. Ash particles drifted down and covered the lens. Meagan fell out of her seat to the floor, vomiting. She didn't care what others thought about it. It didn't matter anyway, since she couldn't control it. She was in shock and her body was on autopilot. The noises she heard around her were of students crying and screaming.

"Shit! Oh shit!" she heard Ryan repeating over and over.

Meagan slowly got to her feet, her head spinning. *How can this be possible?* She stumbled to the door, fumbled at the handle, and fell once more to the floor in a fit of sobbing. Mrs. Mullins sat in a chair at the rear of the room, unable to process what she had seen. She stared at the television, which had gone white, showing no signal.

Meagan felt a hand on her shoulder. She looked up to see the class nerd, Ted, looking down at her. Of all the people in the class, he seemed to be the one in the most control. He helped her to her feet.

"Let's get some air." He smiled, and she nodded that she would like to.

The halls were filled with students leaving the building. Some were in a frantic rush, and others were mindlessly walking wherever the flow was taking them. She had her arm wrapped around Ted's shoulders. She had never realized how nice he really was. *I've been such a bitch.* The thought brought more tears, but Ted kept her moving to the exit. She kept feeling others bump into her in their rush to get to where they were going. The buzz that meant someone would speak over the intercom sounded.

All students must stay in the classrooms. No student is allowed to leave the building.

A student yelled back, "Fuck that! I'm going home!"

Apparently all the other students felt the same because no one turned back. Once they got outside, the warm breeze felt nice, and it offered Meagan some comfort to breath in fresh air. However, the peeling of tires as students escaped the parking lot, the piercing cry of sirens, and the constant noise from aircraft above quickly reminded her of the horrendous event that had, in all likelihood, taken her mother's life. Ted stood next to her for moment while she gathered herself together.

"Do you have a ride?" he asked.

"No, I don't."

"I would normally, but my car is broken. I had to take the bus this morning." He shrugged. "I guess we could walk."

She looked at him apologetically. "Ted, I'm sorry for not being nice to you."

He shook his head. "It's fine. I've grown used to it through the years. School's a joke; all I care about is college." He smiled at her.

"You have a spitball in your hair." She pulled it out. At least it was dry now. They both laughed. A black corvette skidded to a stop in the circle ahead of them.

Joe waved to her and hollered out the window, "Need a ride?"

She looked at Ted, and he seemed annoyed. "I can walk with you. Or we could just let him take us back. He's nice."

Ted shook his head. "No, you go ahead. I'm going to walk and think."

She felt bad about leaving him, but she really didn't want to have to walk all the way home. She wanted to find her brother and her dad as quickly as possible. She gave Ted a small peck on the cheek, and she could have sworn he blushed.

"Thank you." She ran to the car and got into the passenger seat. Joe glanced over at Ted with a scowl and then sped off.

Chapter 40

Max had learned of the happenings in DC while he was at work. He had been fretting all morning about Maggie. He couldn't understand why it was so important to her to go; after all, she had always been able to reconcile her faith in God with her scientific research. Why had she let this professor get to her?

Max and his coworkers had been reading the news delivered through the internet. Gruesome pictures of people basically being incinerated at the National Mall, followed by reports of the president assassinating the vice president sent him into a state of worry about Maggie's safety. *Knowing her, she would have been right there in the front!*

The cell phone was no use, since all he was getting was the damned recording that the network is busy. The corporate response to the disaster was to keep all employees on site. News reports on the travel conditions stated that panic was sending people to the highway looking for ways out of the city. The major arteries were completely jammed. Rioters were filling the streets, and looting was rampant. All civilians were being advised to remain inside and wait for an announcement from the authorities about how to get to a shelter. *Damnit, Maggie!*

Call me! He feared the worst. Judging from the pictures and news, not many people had walked away from the National Mall area.

Max's friend, Derek, walked by his cube. Max jumped up and grabbed his sleeve. The other man turned to face him.

"Derek. I haven't heard from Maggie yet. I need to get home to my kids." His voice was shaking.

Derek shook his head. He was a bit younger than Max and had kids of his own. "Have you looked out the window? It's crazy out there!" He pointed to the window facing the highway in front of them. Cars were piled up, and smoke spewed from some. People were standing beside their cars. Some were yelling at each other and, periodically, gunfire could be heard.

"Derek, we need to get out of the city. This is not a safe place to be." Max's grip on the other man's arm tightened, "I need to get to my kids. I think Maggie may be dead." He did the best he could to hold back the tears that flooded his eyes. "We'll do better together. Maybe we can get some others as well. You have a van, and we can part ways once we get out of the city. Please."

Derek tilted his head up to look at the ceiling and let out a sigh. "The highway won't do. We'll need to stick to the side streets to get out of the city. We can't count on GPS. See if you can pull up a map of the local streets."

Max smiled at his friend and released his grip on the other man's arm. "Thank you! I'm not sure about the computers. I think I saw a map in the break room. I'll get a note out to our friends to see if anyone else will join us." A window shattered across the room from a stray bullet.

Derek looked stunned. "Make it quick. We need to leave. Now!"

Max typed up a quick email to the people in the office and sent it off, hoping the network was still up. He informed anyone who wanted to leave to meet them at the entrance to the building. Before meeting up with Derek, Max walked over to the cafeteria. His boss, Roy, an older man with no hair and gold-rimmed glasses was fidgeting with the snack machine. When he heard Max enter the room he turned and frowned.

"This damned machine ate my dollar again! Any luck on negotiating a lower price on that fabric?"

Max shook his head in dismay. *The stupid man knows I have a family and it's likely my wife is dead.* The thought made him angry. He clenched his hand into a fist so tight his knuckles popped.

"No, and I don't give a rat's ass about the fabric. I'm going home," he said, although he would much rather have punched that corporate scum in his mealy mouth. Years of putting up with his shit were over, and he was not going to take it anymore.

Roy stood looking at him and crossed his arms. "You can't talk to me that way! You're not going anywhere. Get back to your desk and do your job, or you will have no job."

Max walked over to the break room table. "Let me help you with that snack." He grabbed one of the chairs, brushed past the older man, and then swung the chair, crashing it into the glass of the vending machine. It didn't quite break the glass, so he repeated the motion. Glass shattered, and packs of trail mix fell to the floor.

Max smiled at his boss who was standing still, afraid to move, his mouth open wide. Max moved to the side and crashed through the glass of the soda machine. When the task was done he threw the chair to the ground, making a loud scraping noise as the metal legs of the chair skidded across the floor.

"You're fired." The man's voice shook as he mustered the nerve to speak.

Max walked over to him and stood for a moment staring into the other man's eyes. Then he laid him out with one strong swing, sending him falling backward to the floor. An amazing feeling of satisfaction flowed through him. *No more from you, not now, not ever. I've wanted to do that for so long, you arrogant prick!* Roy rolled over to his hands and knees. Max pushed him back over with a well-placed swing of his foot.

"Like I give a fuck. My wife may very well be dead, my kids are alone, and you have the nerve to torment me even more." He spat on the floor next to the older man's face. "Go to hell!"

Before leaving, he grabbed several bottles of water and the packages of trail mix that had fallen from the machine. A few other people had gathered around the entrance to the cafeteria to see what the noise was about. They moved to the side to let him pass. No one wanted to get in the way of a madman worried about his family. Sweat trickled down his forehead, and it still amazed him how good it felt to let go of his inhibitions for once. *That bastard had it coming for a long time.*

Gathered at the entrance of the building were several of his coworkers. Derek was there with Michelle, an older woman who had been the office secretary for years; Ron, an accountant; and Frank, the IT guy for the department. They all looked worried and stressed. Max passed out the water and trail mix, knowing they would need something to keep them going, since no one had been able to eat after the news of the massacre at the National Mall had reached them. It might be a long time before they had access to food or water again.

Derek nodded at Max and ran out to get the van. Everyone stood waiting in silence while Derek brought the van, a beautifully refurbished Volkswagen minibus, to a stop in front of the door. Derek had been bragging a week ago about the restoration of the vehicle, and Max now understood why. The van sparkled, such a strange contrast to the dark day they were caught up in. They all piled into the vehicle, praying that they would make it out of the city in one piece.

Chapter 41

THE CITY STREETS, USUALLY bustling with traffic, were now occupied with roving gangs of looters. Not many people were driving inside the city since most employers had been told to keep their employees locked down. Max and Sam drove past several shops that were being ransacked. It appeared most of the looting was taking place at food stores. People were panicking about whether or not they'd have food next week. A police car was parked in front of a store, its driver not to be seen, when a crowd surrounded it and set it on fire. A man who was being chased by a mob ran up to the door of their cautiously moving van and tried to open it, but Derek had made sure to lock the doors before they left the company lot. The man pounded on the window, pleading to be let in. Max could see the fear in his eyes.

"We should let him in. They're going to hurt him!" Michelle cried out. She reached for the lock on the door, but Derek reached over to hold her hand down. The van jerked a little.

"NO! We're not picking up anyone! Understand?" Derek's voice was steady. "If we stopped, we could have been overrun."

The man fell down. The crowd surrounded him, and he was lost from view. Derek loosened his grip on the woman's wrist. She ripped it away when he let go.

Max watched in horror as the crowd piled on top of the man as he struggled on the ground. It reminded him of ants swarming an intruder of their nest.

"How could you do that? He needed help!" She was crying now.

"We can't trust anyone, Michelle. He could have deserved what he got. How do you know he didn't?" Derek replied.

Max wasn't sure which side he was on in this argument. He agreed on both accounts, so he kept quiet. Michelle screamed for Derek to stop the van and let her out. He shook his head and refused. She began hitting his arm and screaming at him to stop. Derek tried to block her hits and swerved the van into an alley. A pile of debris blocked the road farther ahead. *I don't like this*, Max thought. He started to say so but was shut out from the yelling and screaming.

"Derek! Stop the van!" Max finally blurted out, and Derek slammed the breaks, stopping the van inches from the debris blocking the road.

Max peered out the windshield. The debris seemed to be placed in a deliberate way as if to purposely block any oncoming traffic. Nothing felt right about the situation.

"Derek! We should go. Now!" Max pointed at a man coming from behind the rubble and climbing up the side of the pile.

"SHIT! He's got a gun!" Derek yelled.

He shifted the car to reverse, but it was too late. A loud pop followed by the sound of glass breaking sent Max ducking and covering his head. Blood spattered all over the interior of the windshield. Derek slumped forward onto the steering wheel. Max fell to the floor of the van as glass, foam from the seat filling, and his friend's blood rained down around him. Something heavy fell on top of him, but he didn't have the nerve to look and see what it was. The smell of familiar, cheap cologne next to his face gave him a hint that Ron's body was weighing him down. Blood dripped down onto Max's face and trickled to the floor.

The echo of gunfire stopped and he heard voices, then the sound of a garage door opening.

A gruff voice called out, "Go! Move it in before someone else comes along."

"You didn't have to kill them!" another voice replied, sounding much closer than the first.

"Shut up and move the damned van before someone sees it! We need whatever supplies we can find, and we can't trust anyone!" the first voice yelled back.

Footsteps echoed in the alley and stopped near the van.

"FUCK! They're all dead. It's a mess in there." The other voice called back.

Holding his breath and trying not to make any sound, Max risked a peek to the window and saw a young man, wearing a cap, looking in the driver's side window.

The original voice, once only gruff, was now filled with fury. "Move the goddamn van into the garage or you'll be joining them!"

He heard the front door to the van open and a body fall to the ground. *Derek!* Someone got into the idling van, and he felt it begin to move and turn a corner. Darkness surrounded him and the van stopped. He could feel bile rise from his stomach as he faced the very real chance of being caught. Whoever was in the driver's seat turned off the engine and stepped out of the vehicle, slamming the door closed. Footsteps echoed across the floor and then a door opened and closed.

They're all dead! Everyone is dead! His heart was beating frantically. *Meagan! Sam! I have to get home. I have to get it together.* With a heave, he tried to push the body of the accountant off him, but the weight of the dead body along with his being stuck between the seats meant he had to try again. *God, he's heavy!* With another heave, the body was off and he sat back in his seat. Taking a moment to examine himself, scared that he'd find some gaping bullet wound, he let out a breath of relief to find nothing wrong.

He looked out the windows to get an idea of where he was. It was as he expected. He was in some sort of garage. Max could see a four-panel door next to the larger garage door, but thought that was likely where the other men had exited. He didn't want to go the same route, but he didn't see any other option. He quietly slid open the van door and closed it after he stepped out. A "click" sounded and he gritted his teeth, half expecting some Rambo maniac to come bursting through the door firing in all directions. Thank God, no one came.

He took another glance around the room now that his eyes were well adjusted to the darkness and smiled when he saw a large window covered with thick fabric. He snuck over to the window and moved aside the curtain. Light spilled in from outside. It looked like he could easily slip out the window and run alongside the building away from the killers. *Shit!* he thought when the window did not give as he pushed upward with as much strength as he could muster. Not fully thinking it through, Max walked around the perimeter of the garage and found a bat lying nearby. Before picking it up and returning to the window, he noticed a mountain bike hanging from hooks in the wall. *There's my ticket out of this city.* With a little effort, he freed the bike from the wall, wheeled it over to the window, and set the kickstand down. Standing in front of the window, he raised the bat high into the air. *I'll need to run like a race horse pisses once I break that window!* It occurred to him, just before he brought the bat down in what would have been a full swing, that he hadn't checked the lock yet. He shook his head and carefully sat the bat down so that he could examine the window more closely. *Moron!* The latch clicked and the window easily opened. A breeze met him as he peered outside. *No one. Time to get the hell out of here.*

Cautiously, he slipped through the window and then reached in to pull the bike behind him. He cringed as it hit against the side of the window. *Fuck!* Now with more haste, he pulled the bike through. Movement caught his eye at the corner of the building leading to the alley. The man with the cap stood watching him, and from what Max could make out, seemed to be pondering what to do.

The two men made eye contact, and the man with the cap whispered, "Go," making hand gestures to leave the other way.

Max nodded his appreciation and got on the bike. With no plan in mind, he rode around the back of the building. He was only thinking about his survival and getting home to his family.

Chapter 42

THE ROAR OF THE Corvette engine hummed in Meagan's ears as the landscape passed by. Waves of emotions flooded through her, and she could not get her mind off her mother. No new information was playing on the radio. It was stuck in an endless loop talking about how the aliens had arrived to help humanity. She pressed the power button to turn the radio off and fought another urge to cry. Joe handed her a tissue from a pack he had stored away in one of the car's compartments. She smiled as he handed it to her. *He's so sweet.* She wiped dry her tears and running mascara and laughed to herself. *I must look like a monster!* Images of her mom's smiling face haunted her. She couldn't understand why Maggie had to go. What if her mom were hurt, or worse, dead? What would she do then? How could she live with herself for letting her mom leave like that, not being able to say goodbye or that she loved her? *Please, God. Let her be OK.* She sobbed again.

Meagan looked out the window to see where they were, and she realized they were not headed to her house but instead were on a back road she didn't know.

"Joe? Where are we going?"

"I have to swing by my house really quick. I'd rather go this way to avoid the major roads." He smiled at her, "I'll be quick. I promise."

She smiled back, feeling a bit uneasy about not being taken straight home like he said he would, but she didn't give it any more thought. *I'm being paranoid,* she told herself and tried to calm her nerves.

After a few minutes of driving through a wooded area, they began to pass more and more houses along the road. Some homes had military vehicles parked in the driveways or alongside the yard. At one, an elderly man was being dragged out unwillingly. *Why are they doing that? He's no threat to anyone.* She looked over at Joe, who looked back and shook his head that he didn't know either. It occurred to her that life had irrevocably changed in a matter of a day. Joe slowed down to get a better look at the soldiers carrying out the man. None of the servicemen seemed the least bit upset about dragging the struggling old man from his home. Instead, they all had a gaunt and expressionless demeanor. A young private ran out into the road and put his hand up for their car to stop.

"No way!" Joe muttered, and Meagan could feel the car accelerate as he pressed down on the gas pedal.

The soldier didn't move, and it seemed that he didn't care if he was hit. Joe swerved around the man at the last minute and sped off. Meagan turned to get another look at the figure standing in the middle of the road and saw him turn and pull out a pistol. He fired a couple of shots, aimlessly. They were on a straight stretch of road and the car was flying away from the scene so quickly that they would have been out of range even if the bullets had been well placed.

The houses were a blur as they sped past. Joe had to slam on the brakes as he approached a sharp curve in the road. Meagan gripped her seat, and she could feel the blood rush from her face in fear that the car would tumble into the ditch as most less expensive cars would have done. The sports car gripped the road and sped around the curve effortlessly.

Joe looked over and laughed at Meagan's pale countenance. "OK, relax. I'll slow down." He winked at her, and she felt the car slow down to a more comfortable pace.

***

Joe's family lived in a nice neighborhood, some distance away from the heavier populated areas. Instead of driving up to the front of the house, he took a small path that wrapped around the back and parked in front of a door leading to the basement. Turning off the engine, he looked over at her.

"Since my father di—" his voice choked a little bit, and he paused before trying again, "Since my father died, I set up a small apartment in the basement. I've tried to erase all traces of what went on down here by turning it into something new. I wanted to show it's possible to move on, even when really terrible things happen."

He dabbed the corner of his eye. Meagan put her hand on his shoulder. He took a deep breath. "I'd like you to come see it. I've put a lot of work into making it nice. Would you tell me what you think?"

She unbuckled her seatbelt. "Sure, Joe. I'd like to see what you've done. I'm really worried about my mom though—I'll just take a look and then we head out?" she replied as she opened the car door. An odd feeling crept through her. Something seemed off, but he seemed to really need some support. *Five minutes. That's it,* she told herself.

He smiled back. Meagan could see some of the tension release from him. "Absolutely. Thank you, Meg."

Fumbling with the keys, he found the right one and unlocked the door, swinging it open and motioning for her to enter. She stepped in but couldn't see anything. She heard Joe follow her in and then close and lock the door behind him.

Meagan tensed. Why would he lock the door?

"Joe? I can't see anything." She heard a drawer open and could make out Joe's shadow as he was getting something out of the dresser next to the door. "Joe? Where's the light? You're making me nervous. I really ought to go."

He stepped behind her and she could feel his breath on her neck. She stepped forward away from him, but he wrapped his arm around her chest just below her neck and pulled her back.

"Where do you think you're going, bitch?" he whispered into her ear.

"Joe! Please! Let me go." She tried to wrench herself free, but his hold on her was too strong.

"You are mine now. I've wanted you for so long, and now I have you." She stomped on his foot, but it didn't do much. He held her tight. "With all this crap about aliens going on, no one's going to look for a prissy little bitch." He laughed and brought his left hand up, covering her nose with a sweet-smelling cloth.

She felt like her head was a weight. *Oh my God! What is he doing to me?* She had lost control of her body. Her eyelids closed, and darkness surrounded her.

Chapter 43

Rick hadn't bothered setting foot inside school today. He figured it would be a short day. In his mind, if aliens were in fact here, they'd be here for reasons other than peace. Instead, he found a shady spot outside on a picnic table and waited. It was a nice day, so he didn't mind sitting outside.

He had taken his time getting to school and arrived a few minutes before noon. He had been right to believe that the day would be short, and he enjoyed seeing people running around in panic. Aside from the annoying noise of the helicopters and planes, it was peaceful to sit and relax.

Killing the reverend had been magical. He had looked forward to carrying that out for years, and finally he had done it. And now, with all this invasion stuff going on, he didn't have to worry about getting caught. The murder was old news at this point. It made him sad in a way that the news had faded so quickly, but there would always be others to keep the game going. It occurred to him now, though, that the fun of his hobby could be severely hindered if the alien invasion were true. *What if police didn't exist?* He pulled the knife out and set it on the table, staring at it. That would mean he could theoretically kill someone and no one would give a rat's ass about it. Wouldn't that spoil the whole thing? The knife glimmered in the sunlight. Who would he leave little clues for? Cutting people and slicing off body parts had its own excitement, but without the thought of being chased or caught, there really wasn't much to it. It would get old and boring. He could kill cheating old men, whores strutting their wares, and plain mean people all he wanted. But to what effect? Where would be the fun? *Holy shit! What else do I have?* A strange feeling of depression settled into him. He laid his head on the table and drifted off, wallowing in his misery.

***

The mixed sounds of students screaming and crying woke him up. He lifted his head off the table in time to see a horde of students exiting the building. Tears were running down many of their faces, and shock was plainly visible on others. Meagan walked out, supported by Ted on her right. She was crying hysterically, and if Ted hadn't been supporting her, Rick thought she might collapse in a crying heap. Rick stood up from the table. He loved to watch her. She was pretty even when she cried. Her blonde hair shimmered in the sunlight, and she wore the skirt he loved—short but not so short that it looked like something the sluts would wear—and a light top that clung just right. If he could talk to her, he would. It was a strange thing. He wasn't afraid of much, but for some reason he was afraid to talk to her. He didn't know how he'd react if she rejected or ignored him. His heart raced, and he hesitated a moment before beginning his walk over. *What the hell am I waiting for?* He shook away his fear and took a step toward her, but then heard a horn beep. Turning to see what idiot was honking the horn, he saw Joe waving to Meagan.

"Asshole!" He spat.

Meagan kissed Ted on the cheek and walked to the car. Rick found himself thinking, *After what I did for you, you bastard. You know I like her.* Rick ground his teeth in order to keep from saying anything. Watching the scene unfold, Rick saw Joe scowl at Ted before the car sped off.

"You snooze, you lose." He said under his breath and walked, head down, to the parking lot. He got into his car, a beat-up Chevy Cavalier.

Well, I know where he'll be taking her. He didn't care about most people, but he didn't want Joe to hurt Meagan. He knew that was exactly what Joe was going to do. Not many people knew Joe's dark side, but he did. Rick liked to think he killed with purpose—though mistakes were sometimes made. Joe, however, liked to cause pain. The longer the suffering he could inflict, the better. He hadn't done too much to people yet, mostly animals, but it was only a matter of time. The time was now, and Meagan was to be his first victim. Deciding he had to act, Rick peeled out of the parking lot, pushing the old car as fast as it could go.

Chapter 44

PAIN ASSAULTED MEAGAN'S SENSES as she regained consciousness. She was experiencing the worst headache she had ever had, and she let out a moan in agony. Slowly opening her eyes, fighting the pain of the light assaulting her vision, she could make out that she was in a dark room with a lone light hanging directly in front of her. She tried raising her hands above her eyes to block the light. From the sound of metal scraping against something and the feeling of metal scraping against the skin on her wrists, she realized she was bound to a pole pushing against her back.

God, please, help! Her heart raced, and she could feel her pulse in her neck. She screamed. Her throat burned from the effort. The sound came out muffled, and tears ran down her face as she realized the walls were covered with a thick material to block any noise. No one would hear her. Closing her eyes for a moment, warding off another terrible wave of pain in her head, she spat in an attempt to rid herself of the metallic taste in her mouth. *What did he do to me? What is he* going *to do to me?* She began sobbing now.

Everything she knew and loved seemed so distant and somehow long ago. Joe had seemed so nice. *How could he do something like this?* The pain in her head faded a fraction. She opened her eyes wider, peering through the blur of her tears. She caught sight of some objects hanging from the wall on the far side of the room. The outline of what appeared to be a whip dangled form a hook. Other objects that looked sharp and wicked hung from other hooks. A huge LED TV hung from another wall, and a disc player was mounted underneath. *This is not good. Not good at all.* Her legs were shaking and she tried to sit, but the way she was bound made it impossible.

The sound of the door opening from the floor above startled her. It was followed by a woman's slurred voice. "Joey, wherrr ya goin?"

"Downstairs, Mom. I put another bottle next to you. Drink yourself to hell." The door slammed, and then there were quick steps coming down the stairs. The shadowy outline of Joe's figure moved into the light. He smiled a wicked smile at her and winked.

"I was wondering when you'd wake up—if you would at all." He laughed. "I wasn't sure how much of that chloroform to use. Evidently, it can kill if you use too much."

Meagan cried out. "Please, Joe. Don't do this. Let me go." She thrashed with her arms enough to break the skin where she was bound and chained. She felt a warm trickle of blood flow down her hands. Her arms ached from being held in the same position for so long.

"Shut up! God, why do you have to be such a goddamn priss!" He walked back into the shadows to return with a chair and sat down in front of her. "I want you to watch something while we play. I like to have background noise while I work."

He held up a remote toward the TV. Blue light filled the room, and Meagan had to squint for her eyes to adjust to this new sensory overload. Her head still hurt. An image appeared of a little boy around five years old, standing still, looking into the camera. He wore nothing but underwear, and then some text appeared.

"Tony. Age Five."

The next scene was terrible, and Meagan had to turn her head to look away. Joe let out a loud laugh.

"What's wrong, Meg? You don't like my dear departed dad's work?" he turned off the video. "You wouldn't believe what I had to do to keep that away from the authorities." He stood up and walked over to the TV, which was back to showing the blue screen. His back turned to her and began talking again, ignoring her pleas to be allowed to go.

"I thought it best to keep some form of my dad's work. But I do my own projects now, and you'll be my first star." He pressed a button, and the image of the room appeared on the screen. Meagan, chained to a post, was the focal point.

She cried out and her heart raced. "Please! I thought you were a good person! You go to church, you practically *are* the church. People believe in you. Don't do this!" Her voice shook.

"Good person? Yeah, I get that a lot. Let's look at it this way: evidently the Lord feels that you deserve to be punished, since He delivered you to me." He turned to face her and smiled. "Some people need to be punished. I can't wait to see you bleed." He walked back to the chair and sat down again before looking up at the ceiling and laughing at something only he knew. "You know why I'm laughing, Meg?" he asked.

She shook her head that she didn't know.

"Because you're standing in the exact spot where they found my dad's body," he replied.

Meagan looked down to see the floor was still stained. She felt the urge to vomit, but somehow she kept it down. *God! Why? Why are you doing this to me?* She thought about how she had treated her mom and all the times she mistreated people in school. *I'm such a bitch. I'm so sorry for what I've done. Please, God. I'm so sorry!*

Joe walked over to the whip hanging on the wall and then walked back to where she stood, dragging the whip behind him on the floor. He stood in front of her and spat on her face.

"Time to pay for your sins, whore!" Running a finger down her cheek, he stopped at the neck of her shirt and gripped it in his fist, then grabbed another piece of her shirt with his other hand. With a quick and hard jerk, he ripped the shirt apart. The air was cool against her bared belly. He looked down at her cleavage and shook his head.

"Filth!" He stepped back and paused for a moment before swinging the whip around to his side.

She gritted her teeth at the thought of being struck with the whip. In a snap, he swung the whip back and then forward, striking across her midsection. She shrieked as a sharp jab of pain ran through her belly to her back, and her jaw clenched in response. A terrible burning feeling radiated through her, and her vision went dark for a moment. Tears ran down her cheek, and she could feel warm fluid rushing down where he had hit her with the whip. She looked down to see blood dripping from an open gash. She looked up to see Joe smiling. He had the whip behind him again, readying it for the next blow. It ripped the flesh across her breasts as it landed. Her vision went dark as the fresh burst of pain flowed through her. This time, though, it did not come back.

Chapter 45

Why didn't I exercise more? Max brought the bike to a stop beside a secluded building well screened by overgrown bushes. He pulled the bicycle into a small space between two of the forgotten shrubs, where he was hoping to catch his breath and look at the map of the city he had brought with him when he left the office. He'd been dodging in and out of side streets and alleys for well over an hour, and he was very close to getting outside of the city.

The smell of burning cars drifted through the air. The sounds of people screaming, yelling, or talking faded in and out from all directions. Sweat dripped down his forehead and stung his eyes. *Damn, does my ass hurt! Who designed these seats anyway?* He rubbed his butt, trying to work out the soreness. He had found riding a bike in business attire to be very uncomfortable. His shirt was drenched. He took off his tie, wiped his brow with it, and threw it to the ground.

The sound of footsteps caught his attention. He looked up to see a man roughly the same age as himself wandering around the corner of the building. He tried not to make eye contact with the newcomer, trying hard not to be provoking in any way. The other, smaller man didn't say anything but continued walking towards Max, his head down. Max could see he had been hit on the head by something. Dried blood covered the side of the man's face, having dripped from his ear some time back, and it remained there. Relieved, Max let his worry go; the man didn't seem to be any threat. For whatever reason, the injured man seemed to not be fully aware at the moment. A few feet away from Max, he stopped and looked up, but he didn't show any emotion.

"Hey," the man said.

"Hi," Max replied, a bit surprised at the calmness of the other man.

"Nice day, isn't it?" The man looked up to the clear sky.

"Uh-huh."

The other man looked at the bike. "Nice bike. You ride a lot?"

"Not a lot. Are you OK?" Max wondered if the other man had any idea what was going on. But how could he not? There were riots everywhere. *He's lost. Rest is over, time to get moving.* Max moved the bike a little forward, getting ready to leave.

The man realized Max didn't want to talk and turned to continue down the alley. Max yelled to him.

"I wouldn't go that way. Quite a lot of bad stuff going on there." He pointed in the direction the man was headed.

"Huh? What trouble?" The other man appeared to be very confused.

"What happened to your ear?" Max asked.

"Fuck off. Get some help." The other man flipped him the bird and turned to walk off.

Max shook his head and continued his trek toward home. Not very far away he heard a gunshot and wondered if it was meant for the strange man he had met a few minutes prior.

He had ridden for close to half an hour and was finally closing in on the outskirts of the city. He had passed more looting, but he didn't witness any more violence. Mostly, he saw people who were scared about the situation they had been thrown into and had focused their thinking on survival. He was on the last stretch of road before entering the residential section where he lived.

Not too far ahead Max saw what appeared to be military vehicles. The only thing he could think of was some sort of official checkpoint. *But why? Military? Shouldn't they be in the city helping people get out?* With a heightened sense of caution, he pulled the bike over to the side of the road, out of view. A car filled with people trying to leave the densely populated and volatile city pulled up to the checkpoint. A soldier approached the driver and motioned for him to get out of the van. Another soldier walked up beside the van, opened the door, and started pulling people out, throwing them to the ground. *They can't do that! Something is very wrong.* Max couldn't believe what he was seeing. The van started to move, and the soldier who was standing next to the driver's door began shooting into the vehicle. The van rolled forward and then off the road and into a tree. The people who were still in the vehicle were dragged out and hauled off to a large tent.

This is not good. I'll have to find another way home. The good news was, being on a mountain bike rather than driving a car would make it much easier to find—and then sneak through—an alternate route.

Backtracking wasn't exactly what he wanted to do, but reluctantly, he turned around and rode back toward the chaos of the city. His map showed a street that would eventually intersect with his road home, just a few blocks over from where he had witnessed the violent episode with the occupants of the van. Wearily, he convinced his legs and aching ass to keep the bike moving. By the time he got there, even this avenue was swarming with official vehicles and armed men. *I'll need to find a way without roads,* he thought and, once again, turned back toward the city.

It was obvious the military had quarantined the city, ensnaring those who tried to leave. *But why?* Max couldn't figure it out. Eventually he found a strip of deserted railroad tracks that skirted the checkpoints. It hadn't occurred to him how thirsty he had become, sweating and exerting himself without any replenishment. He was becoming lightheaded and a bit dizzy, but he needed to get home. Riding alongside the rails, he took a deep breath when he realized he had finally left the city behind. He came to a stretch where the old railbed intersected with a road. It was a familiar sight, and he knew he was not far from home. It was surprisingly quiet for the moment. No cars or military vehicles were in sight, so he decided to risk taking the road for the final stretch home.

The neighborhood was quiet. All the buildings appeared to be vacant, and some of the homes had their doors wide open as if everyone left—or were forced to go—in a hurry. All hope that Maggie or his family might be home sank after seeing the abandoned houses. Riding over the lawn, he skidded to a stop and jumped off the bike, letting it fall with a crash to the concrete walkway. He ran up the steps and tried the door. He figured it would be locked, but instead he heard the latch click and he swung the door open. His heart fluttered. *Someone must be here. Maggie?* He ran inside.

"Hello?" he hollered out.

"Dad?" Sam came around the corner, his face pale. "Dad! Where is everyone?" He ran up to Max and gave him a hug. Max stood there, holding his son tight. A tear ran down his face.

"What about your sister, Sam? Do you know where she is?" He prayed she was okay.

Sam let go and backed away. "I don't know, Dad. A boy, Ted, came by earlier to tell us that she's with that Reverend's son. He gave me the boy's address. I haven't heard from her." His eyes were red and swollen from crying. "What about Mom?"

Max shook his head. "I was hoping she'd be here. I've tried calling her but I can't get through."

He backed against the door and slid down to sit on the floor. He hadn't had any time to stop and reflect on anything until now. Emotions hit him, and he couldn't hold back the tears any longer. *What will I do without Maggie? She's the glue that holds us all together.* He started to cry. Sam walked over and sat down next to him. Max put his hand on his son's knee.

"We'll be OK, Sam. She may be OK, but we need to be prepared in case she isn't."

Sam shook his head. "How can this be happening? She has to be alright." He went into the kitchen, and Max heard him sit down at the table.

Max sat on the floor, alone, staring at a family photo. Maggie was as beautiful as ever. Images of when they first met raced through his mind. They had gone through so much together.

"Maggie. How can I go on without you?" He slammed his fist into the floor. "Why did you have to go, God damn it!" He held his head between his hands for a moment.

The kids still need me. Get a grip. Meagan. I need to get to Meagan. He breathed in deeply and stood up. His stomach was growling for something to eat. He opened the door to the kitchen. Sam was sitting at the table, his head resting on his folded arms. There was a note on the refrigerator from Maggie, left that morning, explaining where she had gone, that she'd be home as soon as she could, and that she loved them all. Max shook his head and opened the refrigerator door. Although he was sick at heart and exhausted, he knew he had to get something to eat in order to cope with whatever crisis came next. He grabbed some lunch meat, cheese, and a bottle of water. Turning to his son, he walked over and put his hand on the boy's back.

"Sam, I'm going to get your sister. Stay here, but keep the lights off."

Sam lifted his head, his eyes filled with tears. "I'm coming too, Dad."

Max shook his head in disapproval, "No, Sam. I need to know someone is still safe. You have to stay here, stay hidden, and keep safe." He ate a bite of the cold cuts.

"I don't want anyone knowing we're still here. Understand?"

"No. I'm coming with you. She's my sister." He stood up.

Max sighed and looked up to the ceiling. *How can I argue with that?* Reluctantly, he nodded to his son. "OK, we'll go together."

Sam smiled in triumph. Max walked over to the key rack and picked up the last set of keys left on the rungs, and together they walked to the garage.

The bike sat in the far back of the garage. A sleek black Harley Davidson Softail Classic with an attached sidecar. He and Maggie both loved the bike and took it out on special occasions as a way to escape the humdrum world of their stressful careers. It was the one big splurge purchase of their lives together. Who knew it would be used as an actual escape vehicle? Finishing his makeshift meal, he walked over to the bike and kicked the kickstand back. He then wheeled it to the garage door and set the kickstand down again. Guzzling down the contents of the bottle of water in a matter of a few seconds, he opened the door. *Well, here goes nothing.*

He didn't think he'd have much trouble with the authorities now. It seemed like everyone had either left some time ago or had been taken to wherever the military was holding people. For whatever the reason, that particular storm had moved on. Still, he wasn't looking forward to being on the road again. He was an emotional wreck, his body hurt all over, and he was so tired he could barely focus. He paused to look around before moving the bike out and closing the door. The gas tank was full, and for a split second the thought occurred to him he could leave everything behind and ride out to the country and just keep going. *Stop it!*

Sam walked over and nudged him with his shoulder.

"How about I drive?" He held out his hand for the keys, a sly smile spreading from ear to ear.

Max nudged him back. "Your seat is there, Bub." He pointed to the sidecar. "I think your mom's sun hat is in there if you'd like to wear it."

He lifted his leg over the seat of the bike and grimaced as he sat down. The bike riding, along with being pinned between the seats of a van and buried under a couple hundred pounds of dead accountant, had made him sore. Sam reluctantly sat in the sidecar next to him, muttering under his breath. The bike roared to life when he turned the key. He'd need to move quickly, considering how loud the bike was. Normally, he liked the rumble the beautifully crafted machine made, but not now.

Roaring past the houses in the neighborhood, he was determined to find his daughter and locate a safe haven for what was left of his family. He wasn't about to lose another loved one. *Maggie, if you're out there ... help me bring our daughter home.*

Chapter 46

THE SOUND OF THE motorcycle blared as he drove past vacant houses and empty streets. Max could feel his heart pounding as he sped down the roads. If Meagan was still OK, he was going to find her and protect her. Sam and Meagan were all he had left. In his heart, he knew his wife was not coming home, though he continued to hold out hope that he could be wrong.

There was a military checkpoint ahead of him, but he didn't slow down, instead putting more pressure on the throttle. The engine rumbled, and the cool air blew through his hair, sending a chill down his spine. *No way I'm going to stop! You bastards!*

Sam hollered out, "Gun it, Dad!"

Exhilarated by the speed, the power of the bike, and the feeling of the road flying by beneath them, Max hunched down over the handlebars and threw all caution away as he drove through a wooden sawhorse meant to alert drivers to stop. Wood cracked as the speeding bike crashed into it, throwing half of it into the ditch. Sam ducked down to hide his head as debris flew over them. The bike shifted, and the fear of losing control flashed in Max's mind. His knuckles turned white from the tight grip on the handles. The texture on the grips pressed into his skin. The bike shifted to the left, lifting the sidecar off the ground, and he countered to the right. Sam's excited hooting and hollering was no longer in excitement but now in fear. Max could see the ditch as he tried to counter his fall. He swerved to get back on the road, facing in the right direction. Out of the corner of his eye, he could see soldiers running to take aim at the crazed driver who had just run through their barricade. *Meagan, we're coming!* He couldn't have it end here. She needed him.

THUMP!

The Harley ran over another section of the roadblock, but he was back upright with the sidecar on the road, and he had regained his balance. Not giving a moment's hesitation, he opened the throttle again and began furthering the distance between him and the soldiers. Gunfire echoed from behind, and a whizzing noise flew by him.

He maintained his speed for a few minutes before slowing down to a stop on the side of the road. *That was too damned close!* His arms trembled and he laid his head down on the handlebars as the bike idled. He took a deep breath, holding it for a moment before letting it out. He turned to see Sam sitting still, color slowly returning to his face. Sam looked at his father and they locked eyes.

"Holy shit! That was intense!" Sam began laughing hysterically and let out a shout of approval with the way his dad had had handled the situation. Max let out a slight laugh.

Regaining his composure as much as possible, he lifted his head and started moving the Harley forward. There were no more checkpoints along the road, and he even came across neighborhoods where people were still in evidence, still moving around, still unaware of the dangers heading their way. The military must not have made it this far yet. He wanted to warn them, but no one would believe him. *No, Meagan is my priority. If I can do anything later, I will.*

Sam motioned for his father to stop, and Max pulled the bike over to the side of the road. "Dad, those people don't know what's going on, do they?" He was pointing at the one of the houses in the neighborhood. Strangely, considering what was going on in the world around them, kids were out playing in the yard.

Max shrugged. "I don't think they do. But we can't stop. We need to get to Meagan."

"Joe's neighborhood is the next one up from here. I can try to warn these people about the stuff we've seen and try to get them to hide or leave." Sam's voice was filled with excitement.

"It's a good idea, Sam, but I'm worried they won't believe you." He put his hand on his son's shoulder, proud that he could still be worried about other people when he, himself, had so much to be anxious about.

"If there's any trouble, I can run. I'll meet you here. I can hide behind that rock over there while I wait." He pointed to a large decorative boulder positioned slightly off from the side of the road.

There is no arguing when he gets this way. He's so much like his mother. I forget that he's a young man now. "OK, Sam. Just be careful. You can't trust anyone."

Sam nodded that he understood as he got out of the sidecar and ran to the neighborhood, never looking back. Max felt like he had no control of anything anymore and continued down the road to the address Sam had mentioned.

The sign for the road Joe's home came into view and he turned, searching for the oversized ranch-style house that belonged to Joe's family. A short distance from the corner of the road, he saw a house matching the description he was looking for. As he was turning into the drive, he could see from an angle that a sleek black corvette was parked behind the home. He slowed to a stop not far away from the house. Max didn't want to take any chances after what he had been through in the course of this day, so he decided to walk the rest of the way.

Considering all the crap that was going on, Max couldn't help but think about what a beautiful early evening it was. Birds still chirped in the trees, and the sound of insects humming from the shrubs nearby made him think of family picnics and gatherings from the past. A tear streamed down his cheek. *Just yesterday, life was so normal. We were still just a regular family.* He stopped for moment, looking down at the road, and realized he was still wearing his work clothes, smeared with blood, and his black shoes were permanently scuffed. *God! I must stink!* The image of his friend's ruined body flashed through his mind, and he pushed it aside. *Cry later.* He shook his head and walked up the driveway.

Voices echoed through an open window in front of the house. Quietly he walked over to hear what was being said and peered into the room. The sound of the president's voice echoed through the open window.

"My fellow Americans. I urge you to accept our new friends into our way of life. Despite rumors that have been spreading, they are here to help us. There are those who will try and sway us from our resolve, but we need to stand firm. Our friends are here to help us advance and attain things we never dreamed of before. Military convoys have been dispatched to visit your homes and to welcome you to our new family. A painless vaccine is being administered to all. This is only to prevent us from infection by diseases that we have the potential to be exposed to. Please do not resist. It is in your best interest and that of our great nation that you allow them to help you. Those who refuse will be considered enemies who endanger us all by allowing the spread of disease. God bless us all."

Not far off in the room he could make out a big woman wearing a nightgown, sprawled out in a recliner. Her robe was open and it spilled over the arms of the chair; the nightgown stretched tightly. One arm dangled off the chair and a bottle of vodka lay sideways on the floor, leaving a wet circle where it had spilled. Other bottles littered the floor, and the room was full of trash. A side table held various bottles of pills.

Now that's a depressing sight. Not at all what I would have expected. This house has seen more than its share of dirty secrets. Why is my daughter here? The smell of dirty clothes and decaying food wafted through the window and hit him. Voices from the back of the house caught his ear, and he quietly snuck around the side of the house, creeping up the dirt path that led to the parked Corvette.

As he approached the back corner of the house, the voices grew louder. He moved so his back was against the siding of the house and carefully looked around the corner. He saw a young man whom Max recognized as Joseph. He'd seen him during his few visits to the church Joe's father led and from the recent news in which Joe's family played a prominent role.

He was talking to another young man who looked very familiar. Max couldn't remember where he'd seen him before. His appearance was unsettling.

With long, jet-black hair, a black leather jacket, chains, and jeans, this young man had a definite Goth look. Although handsome, he also had something sinister about him, and it wasn't the way he was dressed. Something more, something that came from the way he moved, put Max's apprehension into overdrive. It seemed odd to him that with Joe's reputation as a God-fearing young man, he would be associating with someone like the boy in black, whose character Max judged to be questionable. On the other hand, he'd also never trusted those with extreme religious attitudes. The two young men seemed to be having some sort of argument.

"Joe, I know she's down there. You need to let her go." The Goth kid poked the other boy hard in the chest.

Joe shoved his hand aside and smiled. "Rick, are you getting mad? I don't know what you're talking about anyway."

Now Max remembered. *Rick. He's the older guy Meagan talked about. Sounds like I might be wrong about him. Looks like it's the religious one I have to deal with. Should have known.*

"Bullshit. I know what you are about, Joe. She doesn't deserve it." He reached into his pocket and withdrew a shiny blade, holding it to his side. Joe looked down and shook his head side to side, backing up a step.

"Seriously, Rick? You can't hurt me. First, if you killed me, it would point the cops right in your direction for my father's death—and how many others? Second, if you just hurt me and I live to tell about it, who will they believe? Me or you? There are so many people who look up to me. You couldn't get away with it."

"You're wrong. I don't need to worry now, Joe. All this shit going on, no one will notice or care." The blade twirled between his fingers.

Joe didn't appear too shaken by the threat or the knife. He was quite a bit taller and bigger than Rick. If a fight went down, Max wasn't sure who he'd bet on. The sound of a woman's cry escaped through the open door of the building behind where Joe stood. *Meagan!* Max's heart leaped into his throat.

"Well, get on with it then, Rick. You'll make good fertilizer for my lawn." Joe spat at Rick's feet. Rick backed off and put the blade in his pocket.

"No, not now, Joe. That's not how I operate. I'll slit your throat when you least expect it and let you bleed out, praying for help."

"You think so? You know the Mighty Lord is on my side, don't you?" Joe raised his hands up to the sky. "I pray every night, you know."

"You'll need more than God when I get to you." Rick smiled and backed away a few more steps before turning and walking away into the woods.

"Wuss!" Joe hollered out as Rick walked off, sticking his middle finger out at Rick, but the other boy didn't turn back to see. Joe wheeled around to go back inside, and Max ducked his head back, hoping he wasn't seen. "Don't worry, honey! Mr. Love is coming back." Joe's voice rang out and then came the sound of a door closing. Max clenched his hands and his nails dug into his palms, but he didn't notice the pain.

Rick wouldn't do it, but I will, you little son of a bitch! Cautiously, Max moved to the doghouse basement door. It was a solid steel door with no windows. Crossing his fingers, he tried the handle and, to his amazement, it wasn't locked. He pushed the door open slowly. It gave a slight squeak, but it wasn't loud enough to cause much concern. Stairs led down to the basement with just enough light spilling in from the outside to show him the way. Max moved inside quickly and closed the door behind him, hoping Joe didn't noticed the light. Silently, he crept down the stairs.

Joe's voice filled the room. "Women need to be punished! You're all nothing but leeches, draining men of money and life."

The sound of someone being slapped echoed through the dark basement. Max moved forward just a bit. The room was lit by a single bright light bulb dangling from the ceiling. Joe was standing in front of a young woman wearing only her underwear; there was blood oozing from cuts on both her torso and her thighs. Hands bound, she was hanging from a cement post in the center of the room. His heart pounded as he could make out his daughter's shape. *Meagan.*

"You're all the same. Using the Devil's power to seduce and use men." Joe backhanded her, and blood splattered to the floor. Her face was barely recognizable from the abuse she had taken. A television on the wall showed Meagan in the light, her eyes swollen and black. New blood and dried blood coated her face and breasts. Shame and anger filled Max as he looked at his daughter, his little girl, whom he had loved since the minute Maggie had told him she was going to have a girl. The physical pain she was in fueled the emotional pain he was trying his best to deal with.

God, what has he done? It was too much for Max to handle any longer, he could feel his blood boiling in rage. Joe reached down to pick up a whip lying at his feet. Max screamed out and charged him. Max felt the younger man's weight fall back as his shoulder landed directly into the torturer's chest. Ramming into him, he lifted Joe off his feet. Carrying him on his shoulder, he slammed Meagan's assailant into the concrete wall. The sound of Joe's ribs cracking brought a feeling of vindication. He backed off to see the younger man slump to the ground, holding his middle, gasping for the breath that Max had knocked from him. He slumped forward, coughing. Max didn't wait for him to recover. He picked him up from the floor, holding him upright.

"No, no, no," he said, shaking his head. "We're not done yet." He brought his fist down, pounding it into Joe's face, and the boy fell to the floor once more.

"You mess with my family, you mess with me." Max planted a kick square into Joe's stomach as he tried to crawl into a fetal position on the floor. Joe fell onto his back, blood running from his mouth, a tooth lying beside him.

"Please." He raised his hand in the air for Max to stop.

"Did you stop hurting my daughter when she asked you to stop? Fuck you."

Max, who had never intentionally hurt anyone in his life, could not stop the demon of anger that this boy had released in him. He kicked Joe again in his side once, twice, and a third time. "I lost my wife, you shit. And you almost took my daughter! My precious daughter, who is worth a hundred of you. I should kill you right now." As he said it, the thought struck him. *Enough. I'm better than this.* Joe lay sprawled on the floor, holding his side and coughing.

"If I see you again, I will kill you." He walked over to where Meagan was tied. She looked at him and smiled.

"Daddy. Thank God." She looked weak, but still strong enough to walk.

"Let's get you out of here." He found the keys to the handcuffs and released the lock. Meagan started to fall to the ground, but he caught her. He struggled to lift her upright, but she was able to support herself after a moment.

She looked back to see Joe, moaning, curled in a ball on the floor, and she scowled. "I thought he was a good person, Dad. He tricked me and a lot of other people. He really is evil; you should have killed him."

"No, we're not like that." He walked over to her pile of clothes and helped her get into her shirt and skirt. She cried as he dressed her, pain hitting her from all sides as the fabric covered her wounds. Max helped her climb the steps, standing behind her in case she fell back. Meagan opened the outer door and the cool night air rushed into the basement. Max took a deep breath—his baby girl was alive and she was free.

"I have my bike not too far away. Let's get the hell out of here." Max patted her gently on the back to keep her moving. She stepped outside, relieved to have actually gotten out of the cellar. Max stepped out right behind her, when a sound from behind him caused him to stop.

THUNK!

White light flashed in his eyes. The sound accompanying the blow was familiar. It reminded him of his younger days on the farm, when he helped out by chopping wood. It was the sound of the blade of an ax being planted squarely in a block of wood. Funny how he thought of that and how much he missed those days. He could feel his limbs tingle. It was as if he were floating. Something tugged from the back of his head, and he knew what it was as he was about to fall backward. His vision returned for just a moment, and he saw his daughter's confused and frightened expression. The memories of his past vanished, replaced by the feeling that something was drastically wrong. He wanted to move, but he couldn't, and his sight was fading. Warmth trickled down his neck. He wanted to cry out to Meagan, but he couldn't. He fell back to the ground staring up, black circles closing in around him.

Standing above him he could see Joe's bloodied face looking down at him and smiling. He heard him say, "Godspeed, motherfucker."

His last thoughts were of Meagan and Sam. They'd have to manage on their own now, but with unshakable faith, he knew that Maggie would be happy to see him.

Chapter 47

Rick, always aware of his surroundings, had positioned himself far enough into the cover of the woods that he was confident he wouldn't be seen. During his argument with Joe, he had seen the shadow of a man's body and had figured someone else was hiding nearby. It was the main reason he gave in to Joe so easily. He didn't need any witnesses to what his blade had come to do.

He waited a few minutes before he saw an older man, probably in his midforties, move to the door leading down to Joe's basement. *This should be interesting. Maybe I won't have to deal with Joe at all.* It made him a bit sad thinking about losing the opportunity to remove that scourge from the world himself, but there were plenty of other assholes to deal with. The door closed behind the older man as he entered the building. Time passed, and Rick began thinking about what he'd do if the man didn't come out again. He wasn't sure if he'd go in and deal with the whole situation now or find a more creative way to dispatch the God-fearing hypocrite. *I could go in the front door, slice open that bitch mother of his, wait for him to come up, and then kill him. Two in one night.* That made him smile. The sound of a door opening brought his attention back to the house.

Meagan, looking badly bruised and bleeding, ran out dressed in her shirt and skirt. She covered her front of her chest the best she could with the ripped fabric. He couldn't see much detail from as far away as he was, but other than the cuts and bruises she looked to be alright. *I wonder what the hell happened to Joe?* Her head was up like she was breathing in fresh air for the first time in her life. More noise followed, and the older man—who he figured must be her father—emerged. *Well, I guess I won't have to deal with Joe after all.*

Just then, a dark form approached from behind Meg's father. Rick could make out what appeared to be a hatchet crash down on the back of the man's head. *Ouch! Got to hand it to you Joe, you do enjoy a little blood!* The man stood there for a second only. Meagan, from several feet away, turned to see her father fall backward as Joe emerged from the shadows. A loud scream erupted from her, and she fell to her knees.

"Dad!" she cried out. Joe looked up to see her sitting on the ground, shocked at what she had witnessed.

Rick jumped out from his hiding spot in the woods and ran to the girl. Joe saw him approaching her and stood still next to the man's lifeless body.

"Thought you went home to cry, Rick," he yelled out as Rick caught up to the sobbing girl.

He put his hand on her shoulder. "Joe, she's coming with me. You've done enough. She's not one of your kittens, and she's suffered enough." Rick could feel her trembling as she cried.

"Whatever. She's nothing but a whore anyway. Take her."

Rick reached down and lifted Meagan to her feet. She seemed to be somewhere else, some world no one else could see. "Remember the promise I made to you. I'll make a visit soon."

Rick supported Meagan, not daring to carry her in case Joe decided to attack. Together they walked away from Joe's house to the woods and cut across a small section of trees to where his car was parked on the side of the road. Meagan was staring blankly, still shaking. Rick was afraid she was going into shock. That was the last thing he needed right now. Rick walked her to the passenger side of the car and opened the door for her. It let out a loud creak as it opened. He helped her into the seat. He found himself highly aroused at the sight of her bloodied breasts, barely covered by her ripped and blood-soaked blouse. Fighting the urge not to cut her more, he walked to the driver's side of the car. *Her skin would be so beautiful to carve.* He shivered at the thought. *Stop it! Try to control it. I'm saving my blade for those who deserve it. It's a different world now.* Shame replaced the erotic thoughts.

He remembered the blanket in his bag of special items. He opened the trunk to get the blanket and a bottle of water for the girl. He tucked the blanket in around her. She was in no shape to do anything for herself at the moment. Covering her made his desires a little easier to control. He got her to take a few sips of water from the bottle. He had never taken care of anyone before and found he actually liked the feeling.

He tried the engine, but it stalled after chugging for a couple seconds. "Goddamn car!" He tried once more, and as the car started chugging out, he applied some gas. A big cloud of smoke shot from the back of the car. This time, though, it continued to run. He had no idea where to go. He only knew he couldn't stay there. He had seen the military convoy moving in, and that could not be a good sign no matter what the news was reporting.

The car chugged down the road a ways before it started to run a little smoother. He decided to stick to the little-traveled back roads as much as he could. He knew them well. He had been scouting them out for years. The first plan was to get further away from the city and try to get to a less-populated area. Rick looked over at Meagan, her hair stringy and in need of a shower, the matted blonde strands clinging to her face where blood had dried. She seemed to be pulling herself together some now, and he pulled the car over to the side of the road to try and talk to her.

"Meagan," he said. No response.

"Meagan." This time he shook her shoulder slightly. She jolted and looked at him, a dazed expression on her usually vibrant face.

"Meagan, we need to get somewhere where we can rest. Do you know anywhere we can go?" he asked. She shook her head that she didn't know.

"OK. I'm thinking we can head north, skirting major cities and try to get away from DC and Philly." He paused and looked around to make sure no military vehicles had shown up while he was stopped. "We can try to find a place to crash once we're more in the country." He looked over at Meagan again, and she was back to staring straight ahead in a daze.

"Why? Why would he do that?" she asked.

"Some people are that way." He replied. *Including me. Stop kidding yourself. I'm just like him.* He started moving the car again. "We need to get moving."

"I have an uncle in Maine." Meagan turned to look at Rick.

"Maine would be better than here, I think, but it would be a long haul, especially on the back roads."

She looked out the window as the houses flew by. "We were going to go out as a family this weekend. I yelled at my mom. That was the last time I talked with her."

Shit! I got myself a girl with a ton of baggage. I should kill her and ditch her. He pressed the gas pedal further, and the car struggled to speed up. *NO! That's not me anymore! I have to at least try. I can start over.* He pictured himself with Meagan. He felt lighter knowing his past didn't matter anymore. He could actually be *good.*

"We have all done things we're not proud of, but it doesn't mean you can't change," he said.

"No, I'm an awful person. I know I am. An awful person can't change to being a good person." She wiped a tear away. "I sent my mom off to die, and my dad died because of me."

He took a deep breath. "Let's go find this uncle of yours. If nothing else, it will be a good road trip and it will get us out of here." He decided he'd do his best to see if he could cope with all the ranting. If he could, it would prove he was on his way to being a better person, regardless what she said about changing. She obviously knew nothing about good and bad if she thought the stuff she'd done was evil. Hell, she was probably the best person he'd ever met. She actually had a conscience. Then again, if worse came to worse and he couldn't take it anymore, it would mean one less hormonal girl in the world.

Chapter 48

THE AIR WAS BEGINNING to get cooler, and Sam shivered as he sat on the ground behind the rock where he'd promised to wait for his father. He had visited all the houses in the neighborhood. Of the few families home, everyone he spoke to ignored him and told him to move on. Some people even threatened to report him for spreading false stories. Very few of the people had shown any signs of concern. He didn't really care what the people thought. At least he'd made the attempt to warn them.

Come on, Dad! Where are you? His butt was cold from sitting on the cool earth, so he stood up and moved around a little bit. No cars had passed through for some time. A helicopter hovered overhead, and he looked up to see that it was a military chopper. The rumble of vehicles from a short distance down the road meant the military was on its way.

"Shit!" He could feel himself becoming more anxious. Not wanting to stick around, he began running up the road leading to the next neighborhood where he had told his dad to go. Sam would see him if he were heading back on the motorcycle anyway.

As Sam turned down the street to Joe's home, he spotted his dad's motorcycle. Stopping next to the Harley, he reached down to touch the side and felt that it was cool. The bike had not been running for some time. *Dad, what are you doing?* He looked over to Joe's house. It seemed quiet. *Why aren't you out yet?* Throwing caution away, he ran to the driveway. The sound of someone swearing from the back of the house caught his attention before he rang the doorbell. He moved around the side to listen closer. It sounded like Joe's voice, and he was muttering under his breath. Sam knew Joe from school. Although they were not friends, they were never on bad terms, so he walked around the corner.

The sight that he took in was unimaginable. He fell to his knees, unable to comprehend the situation. His stomach betrayed him, and he began vomiting onto the grass. Joe was hunched over Sam's father's body, dragging it by the armpits to a shallow grave dug in the soft dirt. The back of his father's head had a huge gash and was covered in blood. A trail of blood led from the door of the basement to the limp body, from where it had been dragged across the ground. Joe had heard Sam's approach and looked up to see him retching on the lawn.

"Sam! I'm so sorry!" Joe set the body down and hurried over to the younger boy.

Sam sprung up, wiping his mouth on his sleeve and backing away from Joe. "What the hell did you do?" His heart was pounding. *Dad! Meagan?* He swallowed hard, hoping he would be able to keep from puking again. His mouth tasted foul. His limbs wouldn't stop shaking.

"Sam! It was Rick! I didn't do this." Joe held out his hands to emphasize that he had no part in it. "Please, Sam. I love Meagan. I've loved her for a long time. You have to believe me." He took another step, and Sam backed as far back as he could, until he felt the fence behind him stopping him from going any further.

Sam shook his head. *This can't be happening. It was only a few hours ago that I was with Dad on our way to rescue Meagan. We were going to be the heroes. It was going to be fine.*

"Sam. Please. I'm so sorry." This time Joe stood still, unmoving.

"How do I know it wasn't you?" Sam said, his jaw shaking.

"Meg was here with me, and we were leaving when Rick showed up. He was in a rage that I was with Meg. He really liked her, and he thought she'd be his after Rob died. I don't know where he got that idea. As if a girl like Meagan would date a Goth freak. We fought." He pointed at his face, covered in bruises. "He knocked me down and kicked me, hard." He lifted his shirt to show the bruising underneath.

"If it weren't for your dad, he'd have killed me." Joe put his head between his hands to cover his eyes for a moment. "He hurt Rick pretty good and figured he'd taught him a lesson. Unfortunately, he didn't finish the job. He turned his back and Rick found that hatchet against the wall over there. He killed your dad with it. I'm so sorry, Sam." Tears rushed to Sam's eyes, and he stared at Joe in horror.

"Why did he leave you?" Sam asked.

Joe shook his head and shrugged. "I think he was scared about what he'd done."

"Why not call the cops? Why are you burying him?"

"You know the cops won't do shit right now. The world's too fucked up with all this stuff about the invasion. You can't even trust the authorities. I thought your dad should at least be buried. I didn't know when any real help would show up to take care of him."

Sam fell to his knees, grief overtaking him. Joe rushed over to him and sat down, putting his arm around his shoulder, holding him close while he cried.

"Your father was a good man, Sam. I'm sure the Lord has accepted him with open arms."

Sam pulled away from Joe's embrace, realizing he had no idea what had happened to his sister. He slowly got to his feet, wiping his face with his sleeve. "Where's Meagan? What happened to her? Why isn't she here helping you with my dad?"

Joe looked sympathetic. "Rick took her with him Sam. I'll help you find her. It's the least I can do."

Sam felt drained. But where there had been only sadness and grief, those feelings had been temporarily replaced with hatred and the need for revenge. "Let's find this bastard and rip his balls off!" Sam helped Joe off the ground.

"Ha! Now that sounds like a plan!"

"First, let's finish the job you started and bury my Dad. Can you give him a good prayer, please, Joe?"

"I would be honored." He smiled.

Together they walked over to the figure lying on the ground and pulled it to the cavity in the freshly dug earth. The body looked strange to Sam. None of what had happened today really seemed real or, at least, it hadn't officially set in yet. He let out a deep breath and fought back a fresh round of tears. With spade in hand, he threw a scoop of dirt on his father's body. He tried not to focus on the gaping wound that had so disfigured the remains of the man he had loved and respected. A fresh surge of vomit ripped through his throat, and he had to turn away to puke. *I can't take much more of this.* The feeling of Joe's hand on his back helped him get back to his feet.

"I'll do the rest." He reached to take the shovel away from him, and Sam didn't refuse.

"Thank you. You're a good person." Sam turned away and looked off into the sky. The sun had set and night was arriving, hopefully bringing this awful day to a close. Then the realization that the military was on its way finally sank in. With all that he had now witnessed, nothing more seemed to matter. He was living in the moment, not thinking about the future or the past, only the present. A group of birds flew off into the sky, startled by a horde of green army trucks driving through the small residential streets. Sam turned to see Joe looking back at him, smiling.

"Don't worry, we'll be fine. They aren't after us. They won't harm a man of God, right?" He set the shovel down.

***

Max's remains were covered with dirt now. Joe came forward and put his hand on Sam's shoulder, leading him around to the front of the house. Armed soldiers were pouring out of a large truck. *God! I hope Joe's right!* Separated into groups of four, they dispersed to the houses along the street. The soldiers running to Joe's home split up. Two ran to stand in front of Joe and Sam. The two armed men, similar in height and wearing the same blank expression, motioned for the two teenagers to lie on the ground. Sam saw Joe get to his knees. He looked up at Sam.

"Do what he says, Sam. We'll be fine."

Sam hesitated. Every nerve in his body told him something about this was very wrong. *No, run!* He turned to run, but then felt a shock flow through his back. He fell to the ground, breathless. The soldier had hit him with the butt of his rifle. He rolled to his back and saw the other soldier standing over Joe.

"What are you doing? Don't you know who I am?" Joe yelled out, but the soldier did not seem to hear or simply didn't care.

He grabbed Joe's arm, and Joe let out a yelp, squirming to release his arm. It was no use. The soldier had his knee on Joe's back. He injected him with some fluid before letting him go. Joe rolled to his side, rubbing his arm.

"God have mer—" he stopped short, appearing to be in pain. His face twisted and he curled into a ball, holding onto his stomach.

Sam crawled away and tried to get up to run. It was no use. The soldier watching over him kicked him back to the ground. The second soldier, who had been looking off to something in the distance, nodded to his partner. The man closer to Sam reached down and yanked him to his feet, cuffing his hands behind his back. He tried to struggle. The cuffs cut into his skin, and they wouldn't budge. He felt a push from behind, forcing him to move forward. *What do they want with me? Why didn't they give me a shot like they did to Joe?* He looked down to see Joe convulsing on the ground, sticky foam dripping from his mouth.

The sound of gunfire rang in his ears. It seemed to have come from inside the house. Sam kept moving, being prodded along by the man behind him. Other houses were now in view. He could hear people screaming. A man ran out from the house across the street and fell to the ground shaking, just like Joe had done after receiving the injection.

Sam looked over to see where his dad's bike was parked. It had been knocked over by the trucks passing by, the sidecar vertical in the air. *They were so proud of that bike. Mom, Dad, what am I going to do?* He wanted to cry, but now wasn't the time. The man behind him walked him up to the truck and motioned for him to climb into the back. He started to, but he couldn't get far with his hands behind his back, so the man helped by lifting him up.

The truck had metal benches attached to either side. He sat down on one. The thought of getting up and jumping out entered his mind, but a guard had been posted outside the truck. He figured he'd make it about three steps before he was either shot or captured again. This time, he might get one of those injections. It wasn't worth the risk yet. He let out a deep breath and waited. Time passed.

Soldiers began entering the truck. A tall older man, who appeared to be in command, stepped forward and looked down at Sam. His face was pale like the other soldiers. As he looked at Sam, it was almost like someone else—not the man in front of him—was looking at him.

"We have need of you. If you don't obey, you will be forced to join us. Understood?" the commander asked.

Sam nodded his head yes. He really didn't understand, but had no interest in finding out what the alternative was. The commander moved to sit down on the other side of the truck, across from him. No one in the vehicle spoke. They all stared straight ahead, all with the same mindless expressions frozen on their faces.

The truck engine rumbled as the driver started it, and they began to move. Sam turned his head to see Joe, on his feet now, left behind, staring at the truck. He watched as the truck drove away. Sam hadn't any time to think about all that had transpired. This was the only free moment he'd had since waiting for his dad behind the rock in the neighborhood he so foolishly tried to warn of the impending danger. The truck bounced as it drove over the crumbling roads, and he could feel every crack and pothole. He still didn't have time to grieve. He couldn't focus on the loss of his parents. He just tried to stay alert and think about what his next move should be. If Meagan was still alive, he had to think of a way to get to her. He could be her only hope. But first he had to get away. *I'm in a pile of shit now. How the hell am I going to get out this?* His arms hurt from being tied behind his back. Exhausted, he hung his head down and closed his eyes. At least he could get some rest. Given the way things were going, he'd need every bit of rest he could get.

Chapter 49

Marc closed the shades on the windows in his room, hoping whoever was outside would leave him and Jack's family alone and move on. He looked down at Cerberus, whose hackles were up as he paced the floor. Cerberus sensed something wicked was impending. It had cost Marcus dearly to bring the dog inside, but he needed the comfort the animal gave him, especially when both he and the dog were aware evil was on its way.

He knew he had crossed a line with Adrianna. He had worked hard to forge a relationship with her and had made good progress getting on her good side. He knew she was very protective of those she loved and had hoped she would feel that way about him as time passed. Unfortunately, finding out he had the dog in his room seemed to erase all of the goodwill he had achieved. The sound of wind against the window distracted him for a moment. It wasn't exactly the wind, it was more like a white noise mixed with the muffled and faint sounds of people talking. *What do they want? Why don't they go away?* He looked down to see Cerberus's head up, alert, his ears held back. The dog heard it too.

Marc felt his heart beating faster with the realization that people were still out there. Still waiting and watching. Deep down, he knew he should tell someone. Jack was no longer young and not in the best of shape. Marc couldn't bear it if Jack got hurt because of him. Adrianna had already gone to bed. She was so upset with him at the moment; she certainly would not listen to him about this. Ashley was off doing homework at a friend's house. Jack, as always, was someone he could trust, and he the only one who would believe him. Quietly, he opened the door. He could hear the TV playing.

"Holy shit!" he heard Jack mutter.

Well, must be something interesting on TV. Jack doesn't get excited that often. He moved out of his room and closed the door, leaving it open a crack to avoid any additional noise and motioning to Cerberus to stay. He didn't want to cause any more issues with Adrianna tonight. Stepping in the spots in the hallway he knew would not creak, he made his way to the living room where Jack was leaning forward in his chair, trying to get closer to the TV, intently listening to the broadcast.

He went to stand next to Jack, who hadn't noticed him yet, or if he had, was more interested in the news. The news broadcast was about an alien presence arriving on Earth. Marc shook his head. *This can't be true.* Pressure began to build in his head. He held a hand up to his forehead. *The visions? Could they have been real?* The beginning symptoms of an impending brutal headache attacked him.

"Jack, something isn't right. I think someo—" Jack cut him off.

"Marc. Those visions you have. Tell me about them." Jack's face was a mask made of a combination of fear, concern, and worry.

The pressure became intense, and Marc's vision darkened. A tear ran down Marc's face; the pain was more than he could handle. He fell to his knees from the excruciating pain and held his head with both hands. Jack got to his feet and put his hand on the boy's shoulder.

"Marc! Are you OK? Ma—" another voice shot through, interrupting Jack's question.

"Give in. Accept us or die. The choice is yours, and time is shor—" A surge of anger bursting from deep within Marc's subconscious cut the voice off, and he shouted back.

"No! Get out of my head!" The pain faded, and the black circle in his vision receded.

"Marc! Please, Marc. Hang in there." Jack was now on the floor, his arms wrapped around Marc and holding tight.

"Jack. I think we're in trouble." Marc could see blood dripping from his nose, running onto the man's shoulder. "Please, Jack. I need to go."

"Bullshit. No one is going to hurt you. I fought to save you once, and I'll be damned if I will let anyone hurt you now."

A crashing noise echoed through the hall. Jack turned to look in the direction of the entryway. Another crash sounded, and the door shimmied from the force behind it.

"Shit! Who's there?" Jack hollered and struggled to his feet.

"Jack! Please, just leave me here. They want me."

Another crash and the top two hinges of the door snapped from the wall. The door swung open at an odd angle. It was left hanging from a single hinge. Cool air blew in from the outside. Jack, unable to comprehend what was happening, stood looking at the three figures coming through the opening. A tall and burly police officer came in first, followed by a large, bearded man, and then John, the next door neighbor. All three had the same vacant gaze as the people they had seen outside the car when Jack and Marc had gone to the hospital to meet with Tim.

"Just who the hell do you think you are?" Jack reached for his cane.

The policeman rushed past Jack, pushing him aside. Jack tried to swing the cane at him but fell to the floor in a crumpled heap. Thick, meaty hands grabbed Marc and lifted him clear off the floor. Eyes devoid of emotion stared into his.

Accept us or die, a voice in his mind told him.

Not sure how he was able to, he replied. *Accept you? Why would I accept you?*

Vivid visions flooded his thoughts, almost as if he had been an actual witness to the events. He saw a young girl with strangely familiar features playing alone in a playground on a sunny day. Light began to surround her, growing brighter. The girl, afraid of the light, began to scream. No sound escaped the glowing ring enveloping her. Her back arched as the bright ring wrapped around her until she was no longer visible. Her body was completely covered in impenetrable light.

The next scene he observed occurred inside an operating room filled with machines and equipment Marc had never seen before. A strange being stood over the young girl. A long needle was inserted into the child's abdomen, and something was withdrawn as the vial attached to the needle filled with fluid. The girl cried out in pain. The poor child was screaming for her mother, but no one listened and no one came. Another needle was inserted, and this time instead of withdrawing, something was being injected.

Finally, a flash of white light filled his senses. When it cleared, the young girl was back in the playground, lying unconscious on the ground. She opened her eyes and yawned as she sat upright. She looked confused, but she got to her feet and went calling out to her mother.

The vision faded and was replaced by a young, beautiful woman holding a newborn baby. With the scenes completed, the vision faded back to black, and Marc was returned to the present situation unfolding in the living room.

Mom! he shouted in his mind. His heart raced as he recognized the woman in the vision.

Yes, that was your mother. She delivered you into this world for us. You are part of us, Marc. We are family.

Regaining a sense of his current predicament, Marc kicked out as hard as he could, trying to break free from the giant man holding him off the ground. His legs, dangling in the air, were able to get a good swing going. His foot hit the man square in the chest. The big man's cringed only slightly, and he did not budge.

Die, then!

With a violent heave, the man threw Marc like a bag of trash. Marc felt the wind rush from his chest as his back smashed against the wall, leaving an indentation in the drywall. He slumped to the floor, dazed. Jack was pinned to the floor by the second assailant, the bearded man, who was fishing in his pocket for something.

God, please! Marc thought as he tried to get to his feet, but he was hit with a bolt of pain in his head.

This is your last chance. Accept us or die!

The policeman was walking toward him.

What about them? he thought.

The voice came through again. *They are nothing. Just pawns,* it replied.

No! They are good people. Leave them alone!

The policeman was standing above him now. He reached down with both hands and clasped Marc's neck in a vice-like grip. Marc found himself struggling to get a breath. He thrashed out with both hands, clawing and kicking, but it was no use. The man was too big for him to do anything. Already in a panic, his fears intensified as he saw Jack's assailant holding a hypodermic needle filled with fluid. Jack was helpless.

Why? Why hurt them?

In addition to the panic, he was bewildered at why these beings would hurt people who had done them no harm. Summoning all of his inner strength and willpower to fight the panic and stay alive, his thoughts turned to the friend who had protected and comforted him during the last few years. At that moment, he could feel the presence of another, not only in his mind, but actually nearby. A known entity, a friend, in fear for its loved one. Rage boiled within it, and it took action.

A feeling of hope filled him. It was the reassurance of a friend letting him know, "It's OK. I'm here!" A loud and deep growl erupted from the hallway, followed by the rapid clicking of nails on wood.

Around the corner, the hulking shape of the big, angry dog came into view. It aimed straight for the huge policeman choking Marc. As he neared, Marc could feel the fury growing inside the dog. It was such a powerful force that Marc felt like they might both explode. The dog moved with amazing speed. With his jaws open wide, he leaped from the floor to Jack's chair and sprang onto Marc's attacker. Loss of air was causing Marc's vision to fade. Just before passing out, he felt the man's grip let go and heard the sounds of ripping and tearing flesh and a body hitting the floor.

Chapter 50

Jack struggled against the man who was holding him down. No matter what he did, he was unable to break the hold that the much larger and heavier aggressor had on him. Jack looked to where John, his neighbor, stood, watching apathetically.

"John! Please help me!" Jack called to him.

John stared at the two men scuffling on the floor in front of him. Jack was in horrific pain from the weight of the bearded man on his crippled leg. Jack could see Marc was in no position to help him. He was being strangled by the man in the police uniform. Desperate to do something to get free and help Marc, he felt around for anything he could use as a weapon and found his cane. With a strong swing, he struck his foe on the forehead. It raised a welt immediately but did little to change Jack's plight. He tried again, but this time the man saw it coming. Pinning Jack's arm to the floor with one hand, the attacker he used his free hand to punch Jack in the nose. The taste of blood filled his mouth. He could see that the man now brandished a needle and was getting ready to inject him with some sort of fluid.

"Let me go, you bastard!" he yelled, but it was no use.

A loud growl echoed through the room, and Jack could see the large shape of Cerberus attacking the man hurting Marc. The policeman fell back and landed on the floor away from Marcus. Jack could hear a sickening ripping noise followed by a disgusting gurgling sound as the dog tore flesh away from the man's throat.

John was moving toward where Marc lay unconscious on the floor.

Jack's efforts to break free were taking a toll on him. So far he had been able to keep his attacker off balance just enough to forestall receiving the injection. The large man continued to try to stab Jack with the needle. It was just a matter of time before he would succeed.

"Get off my husband!" Adrianna's determined voice broke through the noise of the fighting. It was followed by a click and then a loud bang.

Blood spattered in the air above Jack. Where the man's head had been was now a dripping mass of mush. The body fell lifeless to the floor. Jack turned to see Adrianna standing in the hallway, holding one of the shotguns they had bought a few years back. *Not bad considering we hardly ever fired the damned thing!* She had never looked more beautiful to him. Her hair was hanging loosely around her shoulders. She wore her nightgown and robe. Her face was tight with anger and resolve.

She saw John about to continue attacking Marc where the policeman had left off. She didn't give any warning before pulling the trigger the second time.

The sound of gunfire echoed through the room, and another splash of blood coated the wall. The large man fell forward in a heap next to Marc, who was still unconscious. Cerberus had not so neatly dispatched the police officer. His body had been ripped apart, leaving a gaping hole where his neck had been. The dog walked over to where Marc lay against the wall and licked his face. Adrianna rushed to Jack and helped him up. He winced as she supported him, his leg wracked with pain. He hugged her tightly.

"Bastards didn't count on you," he whispered.

"Who the hell were they? My God, I killed them!" Her body shook in his arms.

"I don't know, but they weren't themselves. They didn't seem to know what they were doing. We've known John for years. He's been a good neighbor. I don't know what happened to him. I do know that man was trying to inject something into me."

"I killed them!" She was crying now.

"They would have killed us. You did the right thing."

"Is he OK?" She nodded to Marc before continuing, "I didn't mean those things I said to him. Do you think he's OK?"

Jack limped to where the boy lay still on the floor, watched over by Cerberus. The dog did not growl or show any sign of aggression as Jack reached down to feel if the boy was breathing. Jack let out a sigh of relief. "Yes, he's breathing."

Adrianna wiped a tear away. "Thank God. They were after him, weren't they?"

"Yes, I think so."

"I've been so hard on him, but I know he's special. I've know it for a long time. We need to help him. I was wrong about the dog." She looked at all the blood and then noticed the police uniform.

"God! We killed a cop! They're going to lock us up, then fry us!" She fell into the chair.

Jack shook his head. "No. No one is going to get us. You need to see what's on the television."

She looked confused. "You want me to watch TV? We've got three dead bodies in here, and you want me to watch TV?"

"Just watch it, honey."

Adrianna watched for a few minutes and then grabbed the remote from Jack to turn it off. "I can't watch it anymore." She took a deep breath. "So these people," she pointed to the bodies on the floor, "were aliens? That one was our neighbor!" She paused. "Plus, they looked human to me!" Her voice was filled with skepticism.

"Honey, that one was trying to inject me with something. The needle is still there on the floor." He pointed to the syringe. "Maybe it does something to you when you get injected?"

She walked to one of the bodies and kicked it, testing to make sure it was dead. She looked back at Jack. "You never know. They are *aliens*. Maybe they have other brains up their asses." She reached down and picked up the needle, examining it in the light. There was nothing to be discovered from it, but there was some sort of clear fluid in it.

"We need to call Ashley and make sure she's OK," she said.

"I tried, but there isn't any dial tone on the phone."

Lights reflected off the wall. The sound of a car pulling into the driveway and parking alerted both of them. Adrianna rushed to where she had set the gun down and picked it up. Footsteps approached the ruined door.

"Mom? Dad?" Ashley's voice brought relief to both Jack and Adrianna.

Adrianna rushed out to hug her daughter. Jack slowly walked to the door, his leg burning from the aftermath of the attack.

Ashley looked fine but frightened and confused. "What is going on?" She had been crying. "The police are everywhere, and people are going crazy." She tried to catch her breath. "The radio keeps tal—" She noticed the broken door. "What happened to the door?"

"What you are hearing on the radio is true, Ash," Jack said.

"No. It can't be." She didn't want to believe any of it.

"It is. For some reason they want Marc. They are after him. They were here.

"They almost got us all." Adrianna chimed in.

Ashley started to walk inside, and Jack grabbed her shoulders.

"Ash, its rough inside. We had to kill or be killed. It's not pretty in there." Jack looked into her eyes to make sure she understood.

She pushed past her father and stopped short, her mouth open wide.

"Oh no!" was all she said before fainting and falling back into Jack's arms.

Chapter 51

MARC AWOKE TO A terrible headache. He rubbed his neck to soothe the soreness. *Was it a dream?* Cerberus was lying next to him on his bed. He could hear Jack and Adrianna talking and moving something heavy.

"Damn! He weighs a ton!" Adrianna's voice came through the hallway, followed by the sound of gagging. "How are we going to clean this up?" she said through a coughing fit.

"I don't know. I've never had to do anything like this before. Why don't you go get some air?" Jack's voice replied.

Shit! Maybe it wasn't a dream. Marc moved his legs off the bed. resting them on the floor. His head was pounding. Cerberus jumped down, his feet clicking on the hardwood floor. Light shined through the curtains, and Marc realized he must have slept quite a while. Slowly, he stood up, his hand across his forehead. He moved to the window and peered through the curtains. It was a beautiful day with no clouds in the sky. It was hard to believe that the night before there had been so much chaos. He still hoped it was a dream, but deep down knew that it was not.

He made his way down the hallway and into the living room. Furniture had been moved to the side, and the body of the policeman still lay against the back of the room. The other two bodies had been wrapped in black plastic bags and moved close to the doorway. Red blotches stained the carpet, and a splatter of blood coated the wall. Jack and Adrianna stood over one of the plastic-wrapped bodies and were both coated with sweat.

"Glad to see you're up, Marc. How are you feeling?" Jack asked.

"My head hurts, but I'm OK," he replied, looking around at the mess.

"You should go back to your room. We'll take care of this," Adrianna said as she walked over to put her hand on his shoulder.

"No, this is my fault. Let me help," he replied as he looked at the body of the big man who had almost killed him lying lifeless on the floor.

Adrianna looked at Marc with an air of confusion. "How on earth could this be your fault?" she asked.

Marc explained about the visions he had experienced in the past. Adrianna smiled when he finished.

"Jack and I both know that these men—or *aliens*—were after you." She reached over and held her husband's hand. "But this," she pointed to the mess and the bodies with her free hand, "is not your fault. I'll be damned if some assholes think they're going to bust down *my* door and hurt the ones I love without a fight."

"That's the woman I married!" Jack blurted out and gave her waist a squeeze.

"Jack, there's still brain gunk over there in the carpet." She wearily smiled back as he let out a slight gagging noise.

"Marc, I'm really sorry. Even as angry as I was the other night, I do consider you part of our family. I wouldn't let anyone hurt you if I could help it."

Marc was speechless. He had never known anyone, other than Jack, who was willing to risk anything for him. "Thank you, Adrianna" was all he could manage as he bent to help wrap the big man's body in the remaining plastic bags.

The rest of the day was spent scrubbing the floors and walls to rid them of blood and other remnants of the intruders. Marc's body ached from the bruises he had sustained during the attack and from the exertion of cleaning and tearing up old carpeting. There was no way the blood could be removed from it, and no one wanted to have to look at stains and be reminded of what had taken place there. Jack took a break from cleaning and asked Marc to help him fix the door. It felt good to be needed.

Adrianna kept fretting about the policeman and was sure the rest of the department would haul her and her family away. Sirens blared in the distance. Each time she heard one, she ran to the window expecting to see the SWAT team standing in her yard. Fortunately, each time she looked, no one was there. Ashley made an entrance later in the day to see what was going on, but when she saw all the blood and the dead bodies, she fainted again and was hauled back to her bedroom. This time, though, Jack put a bell on her door so that the next time she woke he'd hear her and keep her away while they continued to clean up.

It amazed Marc how hard it was to clean up blood. It felt like he spent the whole day scrubbing the wall. When the sky darkened, they hauled the bodies out to the backyard. Even Ashley helped. Everything had been cleaned up, aside from the most stubborn stains, but she had been able to cope without fainting again.

Once all the bodies were piled on top of each other, Jack pulled up in the four-wheeler, hauling a cart behind it. Together they heaved the bodies onto the cart. The plan was to drive the bodies to the river behind the house. Marc sat behind Jack as he drove the ATV through an opening into the woods that led to a trail. It was fun to be riding in the dark, but the task took away the enjoyment.

Night sounds mixed with the rushing of the river and the noise of the four-wheeler. Soon the rapidly moving water was in view below from the side of the trail. The current was swift, and whitecaps from the water cresting over rocks sent a shiver up his spine. The water looked cold. Jack pulled the ATV to the side of the trail near the edge, showing a clear drop to the water.

"This river goes straight to the ocean," Jack hollered to him over the noise. "The water should carry them away, I hope." Jack lifted his bad leg over the seat to stand up. He moved to the back of the trailer and started to pull one of the bodies off, letting it fall to the cold ground.

Marc saw what he was doing and jumped to help pull the other bodies from the trailer. *God, they're heavy!* It amazed him how Jack made it look easy, even with a bad leg. Together they pushed the bodies, one by one, down the drop-off, watching the bodies hit the water with a splash. It was hard to imagine that these people had been doing their everyday activities a short time ago.

Jack pointed to a small cove a little further down the riverbank where a nice boat was docked next to a pier. "If things get really bad, that's our ticket out of here." Jack said.

Satisfied with seeing the bodies safely deposited in the river, the two rode back home. Both were anxious to be back inside for the night.

Jack pulled the ATV up behind the house and turned off the engine. Cerberus let out a bark as the sound of a vehicle entered the driveway. *What now?* Marc's heart began to race faster at the thought. Jack must have realized what Marc was thinking because he put his hand on the boy's shoulder in reassurance.

Marc walked to the front of the house to see a rusted car with Pennsylvania plates parked in the driveway. A young man dressed in dark clothing was helping a young woman out of the passenger seat. She looked exhausted, and her clothes were coated in blood. Whatever she had been through had not been good.

When Jack saw her, he rushed forward to help her. "Meagan! Are you OK?" Jack hugged her.

"Uncle Jack!" She hugged him back.

Marc couldn't help but notice how beautiful she was. Even with the dirty clothing, her blonde hair disheveled, her face bruised, and her state of distress, he still thought she was gorgeous. The man with her saw him looking at her and shot him an evil glance. *OK, guess that must be her boyfriend.*

"Uncle Jack, I don't know what to do." The girl began to cry.

"Let's get you inside, Meg." Jack helped her to the house, leaving her friend behind. He was still staring at Marc. Marc turned to follow them in when he felt the newcomer's hand on his shoulder, spinning him around. Cerberus let out a growl and the man simply ignored it, not appearing to worry a bit about what the dog might be capable of.

"I saw how you looked at her." He nodded to the open door where Meagan had entered. "Back off, little boy. She's mine. Don't mess with me."

Marc glanced down at the man's other hand and saw a shiny blade. It reminded Marc of his days with Henry and getting by on the streets. *Just another punk like Henry. That's all he is.* Marc looked into his eyes and saw empty space, devoid of warmth or feeling. He was not all that different from the attackers of the night before. "Try it, and that knife of yours will be sticking out of your throat." He brushed the man's hand away from his shoulder.

The sound of footsteps came from inside the house. The man with the knife put it away in a flash. Marc turned to see Jack standing in the doorway.

"Marc, come on in. You need to hear what Meagan has to say."

Marc nodded. As he moved past Jack, he heard him talking to the other man.

"Your name is Rick?" he asked.

"Yes, sir." Rick replied.

"Meagan told me how you helped her get here. Thank you. It must have been scary driving on the roads."

"It's fine. I only wanted Meagan to be safe." Jack put his arm around Rick's shoulders, and they walked in behind Marc.

Meagan sat in the living room, wrapped in a blanket. Ashley and Adrianna came in from outside, surprised to see Meagan and the stranger in the room.

"Meagan has come from home without stopping." Jack had a sad expression. "My brother was killed, and Maggie is likely dead as well."

Meagan explained all that had taken place, starting with her mother attending the event at the DC Mall, to being taken by Joe, and then to her father's death.

Marc sat nearby listening. *How could this be happening?* He felt a surge of anger thinking about all the people who had died. He thought about Libby and wondered if she was OK. Not wanting to make a scene, he walked outside to get some air and tend to Cerberus. The night breeze was crisp, and it felt good to be away from people. All the sirens had stopped, and it had become eerily quiet. There was a bench was on the porch, and he sat down. The big dog put his head on Marc's leg.

He couldn't remember when he noticed that all the noises had disappeared. *Maybe all the nutjobs predicting the end of the world were right!* He blew some air out and watched the steam escape into the night. A tear streamed down his cheek. He had finally found a place where people accepted him, and now it was all being torn away. The sound of someone approaching from inside startled him, and he wiped away tears. *Idiot! That's all I need—people to think I'm a wimp.* He did his best to clean up before turning to see who was there. Meagan came over and sat next to him. *My luck gets better and better. She probably thinks I'm a moron!*

"Nice night," she said.

Marc nodded. He didn't know what to say. He was never good around girls, especially pretty ones.

"Jack told me about some of the visions you've been having." She looked up to the sky as she continued. "My mom knew a scientist who had been researching brain stuff."

Marc shook his head. "So now everyone thinks I'm nuts?"

"Sorry. No, Jack mentioned the tumor. He knows you know about it as well. He said he heard you by the door when the doctor was explaining it to him." She looked over and smiled at him. "You need to be better at sneaking around if you expect to get anything by him. He's like my dad that way. Like my dad was, I mean. I just can't believe he is gone." She looked down and took a deep breath.

"This scientist I was telling you about has been studying tumors and the field of mind control. Maybe, if he's still around, and he's still one of us, he could help you."

"Well, I can't say I have any other options. I don't want anyone here to get hurt. I think, for some reason, these beings are after me. Maybe if I go, Jack and his family will stand a chance." He rubbed his head. It still hurt him from the night before. "But I don't have any way to get there, and I don't know where to go."

Meagan began to cry, but did her best to remain in control of her emotions. "I lost everyone, Marc. And I left my brother. I don't know where he is." As hard as she tried to keep herself together, the tears were flowing steadily down her cheeks, and she put her head down into her hands.

Marc didn't know what to do; he hadn't had much experience comforting others. But he reached over and held her as she cried. It felt nice to hold her. He was ashamed that he was happy to be hugging her when she was crying. He had never been close to a girl before. She cried for a few minutes before she could get past this round of grief, and then she wiped away the tears once again.

"I need to find Sam. He's the only one left in my family. If he's OK, I need to find him! I owe it to my parents."

If Marc needed any motivation, a pretty girl in distress did it for him. "Well, let's go find him then. And if we have any luck, we can try and find this scientist. Maybe he has some answers for me."

She nodded, and they sat in silence looking out into the night sky. Marc's arm was still wrapped around her shoulders, and he was hoping she wouldn't move away.

Chapter 52

Rick watched as Meagan left the room. All this talk about Marc was grating on him. *Marc this. Marc that. Blah blah blah.* He squeezed his hands and could feel the blood escape. *I'm the one that fucking brought her here. I'm the one who saved her goddamned life! She should be sitting with me!* He looked around the room and felt no one was paying any attention to him. It was like he was a ghost. Just like always, no one ever wanted to talk to him. Yet some asshole like Marc comes in the picture and everyone wants to be his friend. Having had enough, he stood up and went to stand by a window near where Marc and Meagan were sitting. He opened the window a crack so that he could hear what was being said.

Meagan was crying, and he could make out the shadow of Marc reaching over to hold her. If he had been angry before, he was pissed now. *He's making a move on her already, and we just got here. He'll pay for that. I'll get him where it will really hurt. If one thing is for sure, the kid loves that gimp, Jack.*

Meagan and Marc came into the living room together, looking for Jack. "Uncle Jack, we've been talking, and we think we need to leave. I want to find Sam, and Marc is worried that he's the reason for the attack that happened here."

"No, we need to stay together. We have a better chance if we help each other." Jack's voice was firm.

"I'm sorry, sir, but you have to get out of here with your family. I know where you said you would go, and I can find you if I can get back. I will bring Meagan and Sam, too. As long as I am with you, you'll be in worse danger. Besides, we both know I need help. Maybe this scientist Meg was talking about can give me some relief from the visions." Marc felt his eyes well up with tears but held them back. Leaving was the right thing to do, even if it felt like it would tear him apart.

Adrianna stepped forward, her arms crossed. "Let's think about this for a few minutes, and then we'll figure out what to do." Rick sensed that Adrianna was the organized one in the group.

The two young people went back outside, where Cerberus sat waiting for them. Tired and frightened, they just sat. The big dog's presence gave them the sense of security they desperately needed. In their own pain and sadness, they had forgotten about Rick.

Rick looked over to see Jack standing near Adrianna, talking about letting Marc use one of their cars. Through the open window, Rick had heard Marc and Meagan mentioning something about going to Philadelphia together to find her brother. *What about me? Who gives a shit about Rick?* He had heard enough. He had been nice for too long now, and he had once again learned that being nice didn't get him anywhere in life. He saw Jack limp to the kitchen and return with some cheese. He stopped by where Rick stood and offered him some.

"Sorry, Rick. We don't have much right now. It was our grocery day today, but as you can see by the mess, we were sidetracked."

Rick shook his head. "No, thank you. I'm all set."

"OK. You are welcome to get anything out of the fridge, if you get hungry. It's not much, but what we have is yours, too. Thank you again, Rick, for bringing Meagan to us." He limped over to where Ashley still sat, and she took some of the food.

Not able to contain himself any longer, Rick walked out front to where Marc and Meg were sitting. They both looked cozy, and they jumped when he came out to join them. Marc moved away from Meagan when he saw Rick scowling at him.

"Why don't you come in, Meg? It's getting cold out here. Jack brought out some snacks. You should eat something." Rick smiled his best smile.

Meagan looked up at Rick. "I'm not really hungry right now," she said, "but you can join us." She patted the empty spot next to her. Rick looked over to Marc and could feel his anger beginning to rise even more. Unable express how he felt without slitting the other boy's throat, he turned and stormed back inside. *That little bastard doesn't know what's coming to him!* He heard Meagan get up and follow him in.

"Rick? Are you OK?" She asked as he walked away.

He stopped and didn't turn around. "Go back to your little boy, Meg." Before she could talk more, he was out the back door, and she watched as he slipped into the shadows of the night.

Chapter 53

Don't let the door hit you on the ass on the way out! Marc thought to himself when Meagan told him that Rick had taken off in a fit. Meagan was quite upset about her friend leaving like that, but it didn't bother him in the least. He didn't think Meg really knew Rick for what he was. Rick had a dark side Marc didn't want to know any more about. So long as he was out of the house, Marc was happy.

Jack had gathered the family in the living room to talk about what to do next. He was standing next to Adrianna, their hands clasped together. Ashley sat nearby on a clean section of floor that was amazingly not stained.

"Marc, I know that you and Meagan are planning on heading down to DC to try and find this doctor and Sam." He looked concerned.

"I really would rather you didn't go that way, given what happened to Max and Maggie, but I also know it's something you both feel you need to do."

Adrianna took over. "The SUV is in the garage and has a full tank of gas, if you decide to go through with your plans. Jack, Ashley, and I are going to be leaving as soon as possible. We'll be heading north. We still have family there. They are well prepared for any kind of emergency. I am sure they can help us."

Jack stepped forward to stand closer to Marc. "You are part of our family now, Marc. If you want to stay, we'd prefer that."

Marc shook his head. "No, I need to get some answers, and Meg needs my help."

Jack sighed. "I knew you'd say that." He looked over at Adrianna and then back to Marc. "We'll try and pack you up with some supplies early tomorrow and get you out before the sun rises. You two will need to get some sleep; I'm afraid you'll both need it. We all need some rest. I think we will be fine tonight. I have the guns loaded and ready."

Meagan stayed with Ashley that night.

Adrianna didn't seem to have an issue any more about allowing Cerberus to stay in the house and in the room with Marc. He even thought she preferred to have the dog in the house now. He tried to sleep, but he was too wound up to relax. Instead, he pulled his mother's picture out of the drawer. He wondered what she would think of Jack and Adrianna as he stared at the photo. His mind drifted off, and he began thinking about Meagan. He wondered what was worse, losing your parents and never knowing them or losing them after knowing them your entire life. He set the picture down and heard some movement in the hallway. Cerberus lifted his head, a low growl rumbling from his throat.

"Quiet, boy," he told the dog as he quietly got up and turned the light off.

He heard the sound of footsteps walking past his door and moving towards Jack and Adrianna's room. *But they already went to bed.* It had been about an hour since everyone had settled down for the night. He hadn't heard anyone moving around since then. Silently, he went to the door and opened it a crack, peering through the small opening. A shadowy shape slipped into Jack's room. Marc's heart began to beat a little faster. *Maybe it was Jack or Adrianna and I just didn't hear them get up.* But he knew that was not the case. He decided to make sure they were both OK. He motioned for Cerberus to stay and slipped out into the hallway. There was no noise coming from the bedroom, and he began to think he was losing his mind and should go back to bed.

No, I'm up now. Better check it out, or I won't be able to sleep at all. Determined, he slowly walked down the rest of the hallway.

The bedroom door was open, where it had been closed before. He stopped short of standing in front of the entryway and peered around the corner. Jack and Adrianna were asleep. About ready to go back to bed, he noticed someone sitting in a chair in the corner of the room. Whoever it was wore dark clothing. *Rick! What the hell is he doing?* Rick sat in the rocking chair, rocking quietly, and he appeared to be thinking about something.

Marc could make out the knife in his hands. He was holding it up, playing with the light as it bounced off the shiny blade. Marc stood outside the room watching, wondering what Rick was thinking about. If he tried anything, Marc felt confident he could get there in time to take him out before he could hurt anyone. Rick must have finished whatever it was he was thinking about, because he stood up. Marc wasn't sure if he still had the knife out or not, but he didn't want to risk it.

Without hesitation, he ran into the bedroom and leaped at the shadowy form. Together they spun around and tumbled to the floor, shattering the chair Rick had been sitting in just a moment before. Marc could feel the impact from the chair against his ribs as shards of wood flew into the air. Rick was on top of him now, pinning his arms to the floor. He was much stronger than Marc had first calculated. Rick's head was close to Marc's, and with no other options, Marc slammed his head into Rick's forehead. Rick rolled off to the side, holding his head between his hands. Leaving no time for Rick to recover, Marc rolled over so that he was now on top of him. Pinning him to the floor, Marc grasped Rick's neck with his left hand and swung with his right, hitting Rick on the jaw. Blood spilled to the floor, dripping from Rick's mouth.

"What the hell is going on?" Jack was out of bed now and ran over to where the two young men were fighting. Marc felt Jack yank him upright and then put his hand on his chest to move him away from Rick's body before he helped Rick up. "What is going on here? Why are you both in my room?" He asked. Adrianna was out of bed now, covering her nightgown with a robe. Rick spit a stream of blood to the floor. Jack let out a disgusted sigh. He looked over to Marc. "So, what the hell is going on?"

"You can't trust him, Jack. He looked like he was going to kill you. He had a knife." Marc pointed to the floor where he thought the knife was, but it was nowhere to be found. His heart was pounding in his throat. Jack turned to face Rick.

"You have a knife?" he asked.

"No, sir. I heard a noise, and with everything going on, I wanted to make sure you both were alright." He looked back at Marc. "I guess he must have been on edge and saw something that wasn't happening. You had mentioned something about visions." He smirked as he said the last part, and Marc's blood began to boil.

"Jack, don't listen to that. He was up to something. Ask him how he got back in the house!" Marc stepped forward but felt Jack hold him back.

"Look, we're all on edge. Rick, go clean up. Marc, go back to your room to cool off. We can talk about this tomorrow."

Bastard! I can't believe he's getting away with this! Marc turned and saw Meagan standing in the doorway. She saw Marc looking at her and she shook her head in dismay before walking back to her room. He turned his head to look back at Rick, who was watching him leave. *If I ever see you do anything again, I will kill you!* Turning away, he left the room and could overhear Rick talking to Jack.

"I'm really sorry, sir. I meant no harm. I just thought something was wrong."

"It's fine, Rick. Go clean up. I think it's best if you two don't travel together, though," Jack replied.

"He needs help, sir."

"Time for you to go to bed, too, Rick. You've got the couch in the living room. I set it up for you in case you came back. How did you get back in? Never mind, I don't want to know. You get some sleep. I'll probably be up the rest of the night. Good night."

"Yes, sir."

Marc was back in his room before Rick could see him. Marc listened as Rick approached the door and felt his presence as he stopped a moment. Marc could tell from the way he blocked the light coming in under the door that he was standing directly in front of it. A moment passed before Rick moved away. Before getting back into bed he patted Cerberus on the head, who responded by licking his arm. He knew he wouldn't get much sleep, but he needed to try. He had a feeling the trip ahead would be difficult.

Chapter 54

A SENSE OF SADNESS filled Jack as he looked at the broken rocking chair in the corner of the room. It reminded him of his younger days, when he had spent many nights holding Ashley as a baby, rocking her to sleep when all she wanted to do was cry. The chair had been handed down to him from his parents, and they had in turn had received it from his grandparents. It was an antique, an heirloom that he cherished. Its age was unknown, and its value to him had been in the memories it held. *It's only material. Let it go.* Adrianna was watching him. She walked up behind him and wrapped her arms around his shoulders.

"Why would Marc attack Rick like that? I can't imagine he would have done that without a reason. He hasn't shown any kind of violent streak since he got here," he said.

Adrianna paused for a moment before replying. "Who knows why boys do the things they do when a woman is involved."

Jack rubbed her arm that was wrapped around his chest. "What do you mean?"

"Well, they both seem to like Meg. You did stupid things too when we were first dating."

He let out a small laugh and turned to hold her. "Well, look at you! What guy in his right mind wouldn't?"

She shook her head. "Being an idiot again." She stretched her neck to reach up to kiss him.

Something about the incident continued to nag at Jack. "I don't trust Rick. I have a feeling there was more to this than just two boys interested in the same girl. We have to make sure they go their separate ways tomorrow."

"I don't really trust him either, but he did help Meg." She let go of Jack and took off her robe before getting back into bed. "You're right, though, they shouldn't go together."

Jack walked over to the other side of the bed and slipped back under the covers. It felt good to be back in the warmth of the bed. The night seemed to go on forever. Jack couldn't get his mind off all the events that had transpired. He thought of his brother and all the fun times they had enjoyed together. Max was a few years younger than him, and Jack had relished his role as the big brother.

He remembered when Max had met Maggie and how his little brother was so proud of how beautiful and smart she was. He thought of how little he had been in contact with them these past few years, and he deeply regretted it. *Why them? They were good people.* The realization that he was the last of his family brought a rush of tears to his eyes. He rolled to his side and silently cried. Other than himself and Adrianna, Ashley had no one. He took a deep breath. *I have to be strong.* He tried to focus his thoughts on the good things in life, and he finally drifted off to a restless sleep.

***

The alarm rang, and it seemed like he had only slept for a few minutes. It was very early in the morning and not yet light outside. He wanted to get Marc and Meagan out on the road before dawn. With luck, they'd be most of the way to Philadelphia by early afternoon. Reluctantly, he pulled himself out of bed. Adrianna was still trying to open her eyes. The room was chilly from the morning air. Lights were on in the hallway, and Jack wondered who was up already. Marc and Meagan were sitting in the kitchen, eating cereal. They were both already dressed and ready to go. *Well, this is easier than I thought.*

"Morning, Jack." Marc smiled at him.

"Morning. You two are early risers," he said.

"We both thought we needed to get out as soon as we could. We're ready to go. We wanted to say goodbye first," Meagan said.

She stood up and walked over to give Jack a hug. "Thank you, Jack. We'll treat the car well."

He hugged her back. "I really wish you'd stay with us, Meg, but I know you need to find Sam."

Marc walked over to Jack, his head down. "Jack, I'm really sorry about last night."

"It's fine, Marc. You take care of yourself. You know you have a place with us anytime." Jack pulled him close and gave him a strong hug.

Marc hugged back. "You and Adrianna have been so good to me. I'll never forget it," he said as he brushed a small tear aside.

Jack watched as the two young people packed the car. Cerberus, quick to join his master, jumped into the car, and Jack waved as they backed out of the driveway. *The world has changed in a matter of a day.* The SUV drove out of the neighborhood into the night, and he could no longer see the car. The neighborhood was silent, and the air was crisp. Shivering, he went back inside to wake everyone up. They needed to leave as well. He didn't feel it was safe to stay any longer.

Adrianna and Ashley weren't happy with his plans, but they didn't argue.

Rick, who had somehow slept soundly and had not been awakened when Meg and Marc prepared to leave, was furious when he woke and found that Meagan had left him there to fend for himself. He rushed to his car without as much as a thank you or a goodbye. Jack let him go without argument since Marc and Meg had a head start on him.

Adrianna rushed to serve breakfast to everyone before they made their exit as well. As they were nearly finished packing, the noise from many vehicles passing by radiated through the house. They all rushed to the window to see what the newest crisis was bringing.

The sound of brakes squeaking in the driveway meant a car had parked front of the house. Jack peered through the window and saw a military Humvee sitting in the driveway. Troops were getting out. He looked over to Adrianna. Her face had lost its color. Ashley looked scared as well. Meagan had told them of the military going after the civilians.

"Change of plans. Come on." He grabbed one of Adrianna's hands in his right hand and Ashley's in his left, pulling them to the back entrance of the house. Pulling away, Adrianna grabbed the shotgun propped up against the wall and cocked it. Jack opened the slider at the back of the house as the front door flew off the makeshift hinges left from the last intrusion. A soldier wearing the same gaunt look as the men from their previous encounter stood in the opening. Dust from the outside blew in as the door crashed to the floor once again. Adrianna didn't wait to see what would happen next. She let off a shot. Shards of wood flew from the molding as the spray from the buckshot created a moment of havoc around the soldier. He was not fatally wounded, but it slowed his response down enough to give the family a chance.

The man brought up his weapon and began to open fire. Jack pulled Adrianna around the corner to hide from the bullet spray with him and Ashley. When the firing paused, Ashley and Jack ran as fast as they could to the four-wheeler waiting in the backyard. Jack's leg was sending shooting pain up his back.

Ashley positioned herself directly behind him on the four-wheeler, wrapping her arms around him as tightly as she could. Adrianna still stood off to the side by the door. She waved for him to go and fired another shot into the house. Jack moved the ATV forward. He could see pieces of wood and glass flying all around Adrianna as she hunched down. Circling around, Ashley hugging him tight, he brought the four-wheeler up next to his wife.

The firing had stopped for a moment, and Jack could see movement around the further side of the house. *God, they're coming around.* Adrianna leaped onto the empty trailer attached to the ATV. She lay on her back, holding the gun above her.

Jack didn't hesitate. He took off to the trail he and Marc had driven down the night they had disposed of the bodies. He could hear Adrianna firing off a shot at the soldiers gathering in the backyard. She wasn't hitting anyone given the bumpiness of the ride, but at least it was keeping them at bay and buying them a few precious seconds.

He was almost to the tree line when he glanced back to see the Humvee sliding around the house, plowing towards them. Jack ducked as a tree limb passed over his head and then he pulled onto the path, turning hard to avoid the trees on the other side. Adrianna rolled on the trailer bed, the gun flying off to the woods. She grabbed a tie-down at the top of the trailer and managed to stay on. The Humvee crashed through the brush and was not far enough behind them to give them any comfort.

Jack drove like a demon on the familiar trail and was able to create some distance between them as he squeaked between trees that the Humvee had to maneuver around. His heart pounded as he drove faster than he had ever driven on the trail. The water below rushed, and he kept thinking he'd soon be tumbling down to the river below. The trail narrowed more, and the gap between them and the soldiers widened. *That should give us a minute or two,* he thought. Looking up, he saw the dock with his speedboat ready to take them to safety. He turned down a path leading to the dock and checked back to see Adrianna still holding on fiercely to the trailer but giving him a nod that she was okay.

Jack pulled the four-wheeler up to the side of the boat. He helped Adrianna down from the trailer. She looked relieved to be on her feet again. Ashley was already in the boat, firing up the engine. Adrianna and Jack followed. He glanced up the hill to see the military vehicle approaching.

Too late! With well-practiced ease, he quickly untied the boat and backed it out into the river as the current moved it forward. The Humvee was nearing the dock now. Before hammering the throttle forward, Jack paused long enough to stick his middle finger out at the troops. The boat roared as the engines kicked in, and he let out a deep breath when the soldiers disappeared from view. He looked over at Adrianna. She sat on the seat next to him, rubbing her hands. She looked up and smiled at him. Ashley moved to sit next to her mother and put her head on her shoulder.

Jack returned his attention to driving the boat. The river would soon open up to the ocean. He had no idea where he was going next, other then he'd need to find a car to take them north. *If one thing is for sure, country hicks all have guns and won't want to be bothered by these alien bastards.* The spray of the water splashed into the air and cooled his face. He had lost all his belongings, but his family was safe, at least for the moment.

Continue The Journey

If you enjoyed *Conduit*, the story continues in **Conduit 2** where the consequences deepen, the world expands, and the truth becomes impossible to ignore.

Tap the link or scan the QR code to keep reading.

https://books2read.com/u/bMox9X

Stay connected for early access, exclusive chapters, and updates on future books:

https://writerjamesalexander.com/join

About the Author

James Alexander writes psychological and speculative fiction that explores the hidden edges of human consciousness, the mysteries of identity, and the forces-seen and unseen-that shape our world. Drawn to stories that blend tension, emotion, and the uncanny, he creates character driven narratives where the unknown is as internal as it is cosmic. A lifelong explorer of science fiction, technology, and the strange possibilities that lie just beyond ordinary life, James brings a grounded, human perspective to the extraordinary. When he's not writing, he enjoys diving into information technology, spending time with his kids, tinkering with home projects (with mixed results), and imagining new worlds and unsettling what-ifs. He is a lifelong resident of Maine, USA.

If you'd like to explore more of his work or follow along as new stories take shape, you can visit his website or join his newsletter for occasional updates, bonus fiction, and glimpses into the ideas that inspire his worlds.

https://writerjamesalexander.com/join

Conduit: The Surge Sample

The cool ocean air breezed past Eddy Royse's face as he whipped the fishing rod back and swung it forward with a snap, sending the lure flying into the air to finally land in the calm ocean waters with a satisfying *plop*. The night's weather was perfect, and if one could let go of thoughts about the turmoil, the world had sunk into after the alien invasion—it still sounded strange to him—then they might almost feel normal, as if life was the way everyone still remembered it being.

Eddy was tired, and the cool night air and the sound of the small waves brushing against the dock made it hard for him to keep from nodding off. The only thing keeping him at his task was the growling in his stomach. He tried to think of how long it had been since he had a good meal. *At least a few weeks, I guess.* He spat into the water with disgust. He had packed up as much as he could carry and fled his home, leaving behind his wife and two kids—or what physical resemblance they still had, anyway. That was all that was left. Like so many others, they had fallen victim to the alien infection. They had been stripped of all self-control, and he'd had to fight his way out of the house. He sighed at the memory of hitting his younger son in order to break free of his other son's grasp. He rubbed his arm where a bandage was wrapped around it; his wife had slashed at him with a knife before he got away. She had been injected with the serum moments before. A tear streamed down his craggy face. The noise of bone crushing from the hit he'd dealt his son reemerged in his mind many times a day. *I've never hit my kids. Why did I run? I should have just let them take me. They were my life, and I left them.* Guilt crept through him, but he shook it off like he'd done so many times before.

"You were scared; no one can blame you for that," he told himself out loud.

Sounds of singing helped him to pull himself out of his self-pity, and he turned to look at the church that sat at the end of the winding trail leading up from the dock.   The light from inside the building spilled through the stained-glass windows, forming shadows on the ground below. Eddy shook his head.

"Got nothin' better to do than sing? Am I the only one with half a damned brain? Let's just shine the damn light around and call the bastards to us." He reached down to pick up the almost empty bottle of whiskey sitting beside him and took a swig, not even noticing the nibble at the end of the fishing line. *Shit, that ain't right. Those people have been good to me, and that's all that is left—around here anyway,* Eddy scolded himself. *I'm drunk, that's all, and there ain't any damned fish tonight.*

Reeling the line back in and frowning at the empty hook, he set the pole beside him on the dock and gave in to dizziness. He fell back, resting his head on his backpack to stare at the stars. He thought about how fast it had all happened.

Eddy had been unloading his boat from the day's catch. Few fish-ermen were working that day because of the event taking place at the

Washington Mall. Everyone was excited to find out what the newcomers were going to say. The president had made it clear that he felt they came in peace.

Eddy didn't give a "rat's ass," as he told his family when he'd left for work that morning, about any damned alien mumbo jumbo. Either it was the end of the world or it wasn't. Nothing he could do about it. *That's when all hell broke loose*. He rubbed his forehead as if to rub away the thoughts. The radio repeating the alien message over and over, the chaos that was taking place. So many people burned to a crisp.

"My wife! My kids!" he shouted to sky now, as if someone were listening to him ramble. "God, how could you do this to us? So many people . . ." his voice trailed off, and his eyes were heavy. The church music from up the hill continued as a strange rumbling noise reverberated from in the distance. Eddy tried to keep himself steady as the dock shimmied from side to side. *I drank too much!* he thought.

Pulling himself upright the best he could, he gasped, his breath lost. The ocean water around the dock had receded. Crabs and other sea creatures under the dock scrambled for protection as their homes disappeared. Eddy, head spinning, raised himself to stand. The water continued to pull away from the shore a moment longer before a slight pause. A red glow shone far in the distance, becoming brighter and brighter. Eddy squinted, trying to see in the darkness what the light was from. The churchgoers continued their singing, unaware of what Eddy was witnessing.

A large, dark shadow rose and was approaching fast. "What the fu—" Eddy couldn't finish his favorite phrase. He realized what the shadow was. Water, lots of it, rushing straight to him. Eddy grabbed a dock post before the water crashed into the old wooden platform. Planks ripped and flew into the air like they were cardboard.

Gasping for air, Eddy shivered as the cold water splashed over him and knocked him back. He grabbed for anything he could, but he was flying backward. His shoulder hit something hard, and he could feel a pop. No pain, which was odd.

Rolling to his side, he took in his surroundings. He was some distance away from the dock. The water was back to where it should be, but the dock was gone, except for two dock pilings. Looking back to the red light he had seen a moment before, it was now steady and bright. A dark shape approached, gliding across the water.

Eddy's pulse quickened. The shape was moving silently and fast. He scurried to hide behind a nearby rock on the shore. The dark figure was now where the dock had once stood. It was tall and resembled the aliens that had invaded, but it was different; this one appeared to have an aura around it as it hovered near him. *More alien shitheads.*

The figure stopped and turned slightly toward where Eddy had hidden. He felt his knees give, and if he'd had any need to shit, he'd have done so. He held his breath steady, hoping the shape would move on.

When it did, Eddy fell to the ground. Remembering the church, he glanced up the hill to see the figure halfway to where the building stood. The figure stopped.

A flash of light blinded Eddy. It was not his eyes. It was *in* his head.

"Come. Come see who you will now worship. See my power," a voice echoed in his mind.

"What are you?" Eddy yelled to the shape that did not move.

"Your lord, who you now worship. I am Nezbollah, leader of the Netarius."

"No, my lord is Jesus Christ. You are not Jesus Christ."

"No, I'm not. I am more."

Pain spread through Eddy's body, and he fell back to the ground. He shrieked into the night. Curling into a ball, he could not pinpoint the pain. It was throughout him. Blood pooled on the ground under his head, and his vision became red.

"Please . . ." He couldn't say more. It hurt too much, and he coughed up a ball of blood. His mind felt like it was crawling. Something—or someone—was in his head. *You bastard! Get out of my head!* he thought.

"Who do you worship?"

"Christ!"

The pain became stronger. Eddy grabbed his head. The aliens had taken his family. Now they were taking him. "Kill me! I don't care anymore!" Eddy shrieked, unable to steady his voice.

Ah, family. A voice in his head—his own voice—said.

"Yes, you hate our enemies, too. They took your family from you." The shape stood still staring at him, its eyes glowing white in the night.

Eddy clenched his teeth. The pain lightened, and he took a breath of relief.

"The pain they caused you," the voice in his mind became deeper, "the pain they caused us!"

Images of another world flashed through Eddy's mind. An alien who looked much like the shape standing before him sat in front of many electrical panels. The window in front of the alien showed a dusty land, full of smog and pollution. Another alien being knelt behind the other. It wore what appeared to be a robe, embellished with elaborate patterns, much like what Nezbollah wore. It appeared to Eddy that the alien kneeling was pleading to the other. In a flash, the kneeling alien disintegrated into ash. The vision faded, and Eddy found himself staring at the figure again.

The voice, now lighter, began again. "Our race divided into believers—the Netarius—and nonbelievers—the Solaryu. The Solaryu created new technologies, thinking they could live forever. They mined our home until there was nothing left and the air became foul. The male gender became extinct, and we could not multiply. We believers found strength in our faith and challenged the scientific scum for control before it was too late for us. They killed our leaders, and only a few of us escaped. We have been lying under your sea on life support. We knew our brethren would seek out the human race to use your bodies to carry forward our race once again. We will kill them before they can do this, once and for all." A blinding white glow surrounded the shape. Eddy raised his hand to shield his eyes. "We will link with believers of your race, and together we will be strong. We can protect your race from our sick sisters."

"Why do you need me?" Eddy, now kneeling, shook his head. "What can I do? I'm a fisherman."

"You are loyal to your friends, I can tell. I need you to seek one of your own—a strong believer. His name is Joseph Baxter." Images of a young man of medium build filled Eddy's mind. He was a sharp-looking boy, but his dark-blue eyes hinted at something dark within.

"There is one you must watch for. A human and a creation of my race, Marcus Mireles. He is powerful, and he will kill you if he discovers who you are. Find Joseph at all costs. Do this and we can help your family."

Eddy's pulse quickened. "You will help me?"

"Yes, bring Joseph to me, and we can help you and yours. Submit to me."

Eddy found his head lowering until it touched the ground, as though someone was pushing him down, but he did not fight. His mind crawled and tingled as what felt like clamps were being pressed into his brain. The pain he once felt dissipated, and he sensed warmth flood his limbs. He felt good.

"Who do you worship?"

His lips moved, and the words flowed without him willing them. "You, my savior."

A pleased voice responded, "Come, witness my power. We have much to do."

Eddy rose, his eyes focused on his leader. The mere thought of anyone who might bring harm to his lord infuriated him. He could never let that happen. He'd lay down his life for this amazing being.

Eddy followed the dark shape to the church to witness the savior's arrival.

--— END OF SAMPLE —-

Continue the Journey – The Surge is available now.

Click the link or scan the code below:
https://books2read.com/b/mv9dRl